MW01181771

Third in the Series:

The Marriage of White Rabbit
Papa's Vow

A Young Adult Novel

By Dolores White Kiser

AMEBA PUBLISHING

Durant, Oklahoma, USA

i

RECONCILIATION

First Edition

Copyright © 2008 Dolores White Kiser

Photos used with permission from Ameba Publishing

Published by:
Ameba Publishing
Post Office Box 383
Durant, OK 74702
www.amebapublishing.com

This is a work of fiction. Any resemblance to real persons is unintentional.

All scripture quotations are from the King James Version of the bible.

ISBN, print edition   978-0-9744827-2-9

Printed in the United States of America

Acknowledgements

Appreciation is extended to Bobby Glenn for letting us photograph his cabin; Sabrina Jaber and Zion Payne who posed for photographs; my grown children for support given regarding this work.

I am grateful to Nancy Johnson for allowing me to use her grandmother's antique locket for photographs. Thank you, Nancy.

Thank you to my uncle, Gene Whitfield, for allowing me to use one of his early day photos in the locket. The photograph of the girl in the locket is used in memory of my mother, Johnie Mae Whitfield Portman.

A sincere expression of gratitude is offered to Kathy Carpenter of Ameba Publishing for the care she used in formatting the book, pictures and cover.

Praise the Lord for His creative handiwork.

CHAPTER ONE

Safe! Jenny Blackwell had managed to sneak away from the boarding school without being caught. Slumping before the door of a dilapidated log cabin, she gazed at a hole carved in the aged wood. A worn strip of leather protruding from the opening rippled when a slight breeze blew. Jenny felt as if her life was tied together with a raveled string that might break at any moment. Breathing a sigh mingled with relief and fear, she summoned all the courage she could muster, and then gave the weather-beaten door a hard shove. It flew open and Jenny stumbled inside.

Breathless from running across the rough pastureland, she dropped into the lopsided chair beside a table and cradled her head on her arms.

At fifteen, Jenny realized some days were almost too hard to endure. A picture of Mama, lying on her deathbed, sent a tear streaming down her cheek. Wiping it away with the back of her hand, she scolded herself for allowing tears to control her. While taking a minute to catch her breath, her fingers touched the rough wooden bucket resting on the table. Thirst for a drink of fresh water drove her to look up. Inside the dry bucket, Jenny saw a misshapen white enamel dipper. In a minute, she'd walk outside to look for the water well. She blinked hard to stop the tears, but she felt them sting as they slipped from her eyes.

She jumped from the chair, knocking it over. Grabbing the bucket, she rushed outside to see a big open well. The rope fastened to the bucket was a worn cord of raveled strands, but if Jenny drew just a cup of water, the thin rope should hold together. After pulling up enough water to satisfy her thirst, she gazed around searching for a loose board or rock to even the chair legs. Her tight-fitting patent leather slippers had pinched her feet for more than a week, so back inside, she leveled the chair legs and kicked off her shoes. Then she plunged the dented dipper into the bucket.

A swallow of cool water sent a soothing feeling all the way down to her stomach. Perhaps the refreshing drink would help her devise a good excuse for having run away from school.

Glancing around the room, she saw a faded patchwork quilt. Jenny knew the grubby ragged cover had provided warmth to lonely girls who took shelter in the cabin. She remembered Louisa Grant telling her about

this place. How she'd spent lonely hours, days, and weeks here, waiting for the birth of her baby. A girl in trouble hiding in the cabin probably didn't notice the stains and rips in the coverlet.

Jenny walked over to pick up the quilt. Snuggling under the lumpy cover, she remembered Louisa telling her story.

How had Louisa forced herself to stay alone here for the last few weeks before her baby was born? She said she wanted to protect her family's good name, especially since her papa was a preacher. But to hide out here in isolation day and night—it must have been like living through a nightmare. Louisa's sister, Katrina, had asked a girl who attended the boarding school to see about Louisa. It had taken a bit of conniving, but Hallie Grant had found Louisa and delivered the baby.

All that happened before Jenny met Hallie and her brothers, Samuel and Toby. Later Doc Coleman introduced Jenny to Samuel when the two came to take care of her mama before she died. There she went, thinking about Mama again—she must stop. She pressed her palms to her forehead, trying to push away the painful thoughts.

Was that a noise outside? Had she been found already? She dropped the quilt and ran to the door to look. She saw nothing but lonely pine trees. She listened for the crunch of pine needles snapping under the feet of the pursuers, but heard nothing except the eerie whistling of the wind. Maybe no one had even noticed she ran away from school. A chill ran through her. Did anyone care?

She grabbed the quilt and sat huddled at the table. Surely a search party would be organized when the superintendent learned about her disappearance. Why did she do stupid things? Why did she yearn for the other students to notice her? The desire for attention had caused her to commit many irresponsible acts, but she couldn't help herself. She searched continuously for a way to fill the empty spot her mama's death left.

Jenny heard a racket on the porch. Was it a whamming sound of feet hitting the boards out front? She didn't want to face the superintendent now—she hadn't decided on an excuse—so she raced to the window, hoisted it open, and stuck the prop under it. Jutting one leg out the window, she swung her body across the sill and lunged forward. A sharp pain shot through her foot when she hit the ground. Her stomach lurched when she stared down at a jagged gash. Was that a bone showing through the cut? Covering her mouth to muffle the sobs, she peeked inside the window, but saw no one. Her jittery feelings had deceived her again.

Jenny's heart almost stopped beating when she stared at the blood flowing from the cut. She must get inside the cabin and tie a rag around her foot to stop the bleeding. Digging her fingers into the crevices of logs, she hopped on one foot around the side of the cabin. Like a drunken man, she pulled herself along the wall of the porch and back inside.

Frantically she searched around the bare cabin for something to bind her wound. She had to act fast, because she saw blood streaming from the cut. Glancing at the hem of her pink cotton dress, she sucked in a deep breath. Why had she worn her best dress today? She felt as if she was ripping her flesh when she tore a long strip from the edge of the pretty skirt and bound it tightly around her foot.

That ought to do for now, she decided. She lowered her foot to the floor to test it for pain. She screamed when she put pressure on the rough boards. How could she get back to school? No one knew she had run away. No one could help her. Would she stay here a long time? Gazing around the room, she dismissed the possibility of finding any food to eat. It probably had been months since anyone lived here. Surely she wouldn't be trapped in the cabin for many hours.

What am I gonna do? Why did I run away? She'd been foolish, leaving without any thought about finding food or shelter.

Her foot throbbed. She felt weak. She tugged at the ragged quilt and spread it on the floor. She lay down to rest. *Just for a little while,* she thought. She pulled at the cover and bunched a lump to use for a pillow the way Mama did.

Mama. A familiar wave of loneliness swept through her. She had to quit thinking about Mama. She tried to make herself comfortable lying on the quilt, while she gazed at the sparsely furnished cabin. The table rested against the wall with rickety chairs at either end. She tried to picture Louisa sitting in an unbalanced chair, hunched over. The wooden bucket and an oil lamp sat on the table. The chimney was so smudged with soot it probably gave no more than a glimmer of light.

What if she had to spend the night here? Were there even any matches?

Oh—what a scary thought, enduring the night alone in this cabin. Jenny scanned the room looking for matches. She lifted herself from the quilt and hopped over to a chair. Using it as a crutch, she moved close to the walls while she poked inside the cracks between the logs. No matches yet. It would take a long time for her to feel inside every space between all the

logs. She dropped into the chair to rest. She couldn't stand up long enough to reach inside every crack. She'd just have to keep at it, however slowly.

After resting a while, Jenny pulled the chair farther along the wall. Just one match could make the difference between life and death. She glanced at the lamp. Her heart jumped with gratitude when she saw a small amount of coal oil. Now all she needed was a match to light the wick. Resolutely, she continued her search. Sometimes she yelled out when a splinter gouged her finger.

Maybe if she called and screamed at the top of her lungs, a student out on the school grounds would hear her cries. She'd save that as a last resort. For now, she'd keep searching for matches.

Jenny glanced at her foot. The cloth was blood-soaked. She needed to wrap a clean rag around her foot, and rest for a while. She untied the sashes of her dress to rip off one of them. She needed to save the other one for later. No use trying to save the dress, it would be torn to tatters before someone found her.

Carefully, she untied the soiled cloth and replaced it with the clean sash. Should she wash this nasty one and hang it out to dry? How long would she be here, anyway?

She lay back on the quilt and shifted restlessly, attempting to find a comfortable position. She looked around the cabin again trying to think positive thoughts. She gazed at the door where a large rock rested. She studied the closure made of a single layer of boards nailed onto planks at the top, middle, and bottom. Like her, it was not very sturdy. If a black panther fell against it, Jenny would provide a tasty meal. How had Louisa stayed alone in this pitiful place?

Probably Louisa fastened the door with the string and then pushed the rock against it at night. Jenny would need to shove that rock in front of the door after dark if she hadn't been rescued.

In one corner, she noticed a wood burning heater squatting on a sheet of metal to catch coals before they hit the floor. Jenny knew Louisa sacrificed a big chunk out of her life, trying to protect her Papa. And he didn't understand. He was downright mean to Louisa. Jenny shuddered at the thoughts of living alone in the cabin with such sparse furnishings. And with no food.

She squirmed on the quilt and scooted it closer to the big rock. She

4

draped part of the quilt onto the rock so she could raise her foot. As she got closer to the stone, she noticed ragged edges of paper sticking from under the rock.

Jenny slipped the papers from the rock. Unfolding the yellowed pages, she read a scribbled message composed of several misspelled words, but she deciphered the sentences as she read them aloud.

"What's Junior going to think? Does he still love me? Will he take our baby? Will Junior ever marry me?"

Junior? Another unwanted tear trickled down her face. She swiped the back of her hand across her cheek. She looked at the other page. It was a sketch of a youth. Jenny decided a girl had spent hours drawing the picture of a young Indian man. Underneath his picture was the word, "Junior."

Jenny knew a young man called by that name. Wonder which Junior this was? Couldn't be Junior Maytubby, could it? She lay back on the quilt while she considered the possibility of this Junior having been the cause of a girl living alone in the cabin.

No, it couldn't be the one she knew. She'd save the picture, though. She folded the papers and stuck them inside her pocket. Her mind wandered back to making up an excuse to use when the superintendent learned of her sudden disappearance. She might say she ran away so she could have peace and quiet while she wrote a poem. Or maybe tell Brother Solomon she didn't want to walk the bullring because she got in trouble. Yeah, that excuse worked. Maybe they'd stop making students walk it if enough of them complained.

She rested a few more moments before she arose to continue her search for matches. Loathing the task, she reached inside the cracks between the logs, pausing frequently to pull off sticky cobwebs and shake the dust from her fingers. When she touched a different texture, her heart raced with hope. Had she found a package of matches someone stashed away for future use? When she opened the small bundle to find two faded heart-shaped photographs, her hopes hit the floor. The pictures appeared to be old, but they offered no answer to her dilemma. Jenny dragged the chair to the doorway and she sat down to study the pictures. She squinted at the image of a smiling Indian girl and a handsome young man.

Probably sweethearts.

The pictures were nothing more than scraps of paper, but she decided

to save them along with the note and hand drawn picture. She should just give up the search for a while. Surely, someone would miss her, maybe at lunchtime.

Jenny decided to move the chair outside the cabin where the sun shone. Relaxing in the soothing warmth of the sun's rays, she felt her eyes beginning to droop. She had gotten up so early in order to slip away from school unnoticed, she felt the need to take a nap. Soon, she drifted off to sleep.

The sound of footsteps hitting the porch awakened Jenny. She was rescued. She didn't need to find matches. She peeked in the window to see—of all people—Louisa Grant. Why had Samuel's wife returned to the cabin? Jenny started to yell, but she saw Louisa clutch the quilt and snuggle it to her breast. When Louisa lifted her face, Jenny saw tears streaming down the young wife's cheeks.

"Louisa, what are you doing out here?" Jenny called through the open window. She watched Louisa look around frantically, searching for the voice.

"I'm out here by the window," Jenny explained.

Louisa looked toward Jenny, surprise covering her face. "The question is, what are you doing out here?" Louisa asked, walking to the window.

"Come help me back inside and I'll tell you," Jenny answered.

In a few moments, the two sat opposite each other at the table. "You go first. How did you hurt your foot?" Louisa asked, nodding toward Jenny's foot.

"I got lonesome for Mama and ran away from school. When I heard a noise, I thought the superintendent had found me, so I jumped out the window and cut my foot." Jenny glanced down. "Will you look at the cut and see how bad it is?"

Louisa leaped from the chair and knelt on the floor beside Jenny. She pulled off the blood soaked cloth. "I've got to doctor this cut," she said. "This coal oil will do for now." She pulled a handkerchief from her purse, and reached for the oil-burning lamp. Tipping it, she poured a small amount of oil on the cloth and clamped it to Jenny's foot.

"Ouch, that hurts," Jenny cried. She covered her mouth in an effort to control the screams about to burst forth, while Louisa rubbed the kerosene onto the cut.

6

"Now I need to wrap it up," Louisa said. She then pinched the wound together and bound it tightly with her handkerchief.

"Why were you going barefooted?" Louisa asked. She sat down slowly; making certain the flat rock was in the right position under the chair leg.

"My shoes were hurting my feet and I took them off."

"What are you doing out here?"

"I ran away from school," Jenny said. She began sobbing.

"But why?" Louisa asked. The look in her black eyes seemed to overflow with concern. "The last time we were at White Rabbit's and Tobias', they said you were doing real good in school. Why would you run away?"

"I-don't-want-to-to-tell," Jenny sobbed. She knew she couldn't tell Louisa that she just wanted someone to search for her—that her uncontrollable desire for attention forced her to slip away.

"You know you can tell me. I hid out in this cabin a long time ago. I know what it's like to run away," Louisa said, rubbing Jenny's back. "Come on, tell me."

Jenny decided to make up an excuse; she'd just tell a little white lie. "Some boys have been hounding me and I just-couldn't-take-it," Jenny said, between sobs.

"What?" Louisa demanded, her eyes flashing with anger. "Why didn't you tell Brother Solomon? He would have taken care of the problem."

"I just couldn't. It's who the boys are—their daddy is one of the teachers," Jenny confessed, searching for a good alibi. "I know their daddy wouldn't believe me. Besides, I just couldn't tell him. So I ran away early this morning. I'd heard White Rabbit talking about you hiding out in a cabin, and I decided to come stay here till school is out. When I heard a noise on the porch, I jumped out of the window. I landed on a piece of glass and cut my foot." Jenny glanced at the blood-soaked handkerchief.

"I need to tie something else on your foot. The handkerchief is already soaked with blood."

"You can use the other sash off my dress," Jenny said, holding it out. "I've already torn one side off."

Louisa yanked at the sash. She folded it into a bandage.

"Hand me your right shoe. You can't wear it now, so I'll take out the shoestring to tie the cloth on with it. Prop up you foot," Louisa ordered. Jenny winced when Louisa pinched the cut together, and carefully laid the bandage around the wound. She tied it in place with the shoestring. "That'll do for a while."

"Now it's your turn to tell me why you came back to the cabin."

"It's been a long time since Maria Angela was born here. I've thought about this place many times," Louisa said, looking around. "I always wanted to clean it up and have it ready for another girl who might come to stay. I hoped maybe I could get a cot and some sheets."

Jenny touched the outline of the papers she'd stuck inside her pocket. "I believe other girls have stayed here," she said. "I found some pictures somebody drew of a boy named Junior."

"I'm sure other girls have lived here. I wish there was a way for Sam and me to build a new cabin for girls who are in trouble," Louisa said quietly. "I've wanted to do this so long, but we haven't been able to. Let me see the pictures you found," Louisa said. "Brother Solomon said sometimes other girls stay here, the way I did. It was like living in a well with no rope to hang onto until Hallie came to see about me. If I could just help one girl the way Hallie helped me, I'll feel better."

Jenny watched as Louisa unfolded the picture and note the girl had written about Junior. Tears filled Louisa's eyes. "This girl probably felt the same way I did. I know what I can do. I'll leave a message for the next girl who stays here," she said softly. "Maybe I can help her. If it hadn't been for Hallie and Sam, no telling where I'd be today. Maria and I might have died."

Jenny saw Louisa dig into her purse to pull out a piece of paper and a pencil. She scribbled a message. Jenny listened to Louisa reading aloud. "How does this sound?

"'Do you need help? I stayed in this cabin one time. I'd like to help you if you'll get in touch with me. Here's my address - - '"

"If I was looking for a place to hide, finding that note would give me a flicker of hope," Jenny said.

Louisa arranged the note on the table so it was if full view, then she stepped outside and returned with a rock. She placed it against the paper.

8

"Jenny, I have so much to be thankful for because the Lord sent Hallie, Toby, and Sam to take care of me. I want to help another girl who's as hopeless as I was. It still hurts a lot because Papa never forgave me." Louisa wiped tears from her eyes. "Maybe someday he will."

Louisa straightened her shoulders and gazed at Jenny. "But now, we've got to take care of you. There's no way I can get you back to the school." She rubbed her forehead. "You'll have to stay here, while I go get help. Brother Solomon will know what to do. You sit with your foot propped up till someone comes to get you, okay?"

Jenny nodded, but looked around wildly. "What if those boys find me while you're gone? I couldn't run from them, not with my foot bleeding this way."

"I don't think that will happen," Louisa said, folding the quilt and putting it beneath Jenny's leg and foot. "Just stay real quiet and don't make any noise. I'll hurry as fast as I can."

With a limp hand, Jenny waved goodbye. She closed her eyes, hoping the pain in her foot would go away.

How long would she be alone? She certainly had not intended to injure her foot. She hoped somebody came before dark. She jammed her hands into her pockets. Her fingers touched the pieces of folded paper. She pulled out the packet containing the heart-shaped pictures. Squinting at the faded faces of a young woman and a young man, she tried to see them better. She hopped on her good foot to the door and held the pictures in the light.

Doubtless, they were sweethearts. The pictures were probably left here long ago. Jenny wondered if they were worth keeping. They must've been stuffed in the cracks back when another girl was living here. She wrapped them back in the paper, deciding to keep them. It wouldn't hurt to keep them for a while. They were old; that was for sure.

Jenny eased back to her chair. She sat staring at the door, wishing someone would step onto the porch.

When would the rescuers arrive?

* * *

Brother Solomon looked up and smiled when Louisa burst into his office. Maria stirred in his arms.

"She's played so hard, she's tuckered out," Brother Solomon said,

9

glancing down at the girl he held. He smoothed the black curls from Maria's forehead, and snuggled her close. "Want to stay—"

"Brother Solomon, I need help, right now. Jenny Blackwell is at the cabin—"

"No! She can't be, not Jenny."

"Just let me explain. She says a teacher's boys have been pestering her—"

"What teacher? I can take care of that," Brother Solomon said, rising quickly. He handed the sleeping child to Louisa.

"I don't know which teacher it is," Louisa said. She positioned Maria's head on her shoulder, trying not to awaken her. "The problem is that Jenny was so scared when she heard a noise on the porch, she jumped out the window and cut her foot pretty bad. Someone needs to go get her. She can't walk back."

"I'll send someone over on a horse to get her." Brother Solomon paced back and forth across the floor. "Whoever the boys are—I wonder if they have really been bothering her? Otherwise, she wouldn't have . . . "

Louisa doesn't know how Jenny's been acting lately, he thought. He watched Louisa breathe a sigh of relief. *Jenny's convinced Louisa the excuse is legitimate.*

"I wish I could stay till she comes back, but I've got to hurry to Piney Ridge to catch the train," Louisa said. "I know the conductor won't keep it waiting for me. I need to be home to help Sam. He has a lot of studying to do now that he's about to graduate."

"Okay, I'll drive you, but first let me send someone after Jenny," Brother Solomon said, walking toward the door. "Then I'll get the sedan and we'll leave for town. Sure wish your visit had been longer, but I'm so glad you found out about Jenny. That problem must be taken care of right now."

In a few minutes Brother Solomon had returned and peeked in the door. "Let's get to moving," he said. "I need to get back to make sure Jenny's in the dorm. She's having so many problems, I'm thinking of putting her in a school closer to her brothers."

"That sounds like a good idea."

Soon Brother Solomon, along with Louisa and Maria, stood at the depot waiting for the train.

"Would you please keep a close eye on Jenny?" Louisa asked. "I don't think a girl as tough as she is would have run away without a reason. She's had so many problems, I can't believe she'd just up and leave the dorm."

"As soon as I get back to Clear Creek I'll see what's going on," Brother Solomon promised.

"I left a note in the cabin so that another girl who needs help can write to me," Louisa said, while caressing Maria's shoulders.

"Don't be disappointed if no one responds," Brother Solomon cautioned. "These are private times in the lives of the girls staying in the cabin. You know that from personal experience."

"You're right," Louisa said. She smiled at Brother Solomon. "You really care for girls who are in trouble, don't you?"

"You know I do. They're close to my heart," Brother Solomon said, glancing down the tracks. "Tell Sammy I'm praying for him." He hugged Louisa and Maria. "I'm glad he's preparing to do the Lord's work."

"We're all glad, but it's hard on him. He has to work and study all the time. When he graduates, I need to get more education. A preacher's wife needs to be up to date on the latest ideas."

"You're right," Brother Solomon agreed. "There's the train. If I learn that a girl is staying in the cabin, I'll get in touch."

"I'd appreciate that," Louisa said, starting up the steps of the train. She held tightly to Maria's hand.

Brother Frank Solomon stood at the depot watching the train as it chugged out of sight. Louisa Grant and his granddaughter, Maria, were passengers on that train.

God works in mysterious ways, His wonders to perform, Brother Solomon thought. He lifted his hand for a final wave before he walked to his sedan. He needed to get back to school to find out what was going on with Jenny.

He hoped it was just another one of those schemes of hers for getting attention. Since she'd been living at the school, her actions kept swinging from one extreme to the other. Up one day and down the next, he never knew what to expect.

Mentally, Brother Solomon rehearsed the events of the last five years,

as he drove the rambling sedan down the road. Louisa Wade, whose father had been his close friend for many years, had hidden in the cabin not far from the boarding school. Unwilling to disgrace her family, Louisa had told her parents she was going away to boarding school. In truth, she awaited the birth of her baby, beautiful Maria.

During a visit to Tobias Grant's house Brother Wade's younger daughter, Katrina, told Hallie Grant about Louisa's problem. Hallie had birthed the baby, with the help of her brother, Sammy Grant. Sammy fell in love with Louisa and they married. Now they were away at Southeastern State Teachers' College in Durant where Sammy was getting his basics preparing to serve in some area of the Lord's work.

How long had it been, since he, Frank Solomon, was a young whippersnapper with enough self-confidence to take the world by the tail? Close to twenty-five years. He fought for composure, remembering the liberties he had taken with a young Choctaw girl several nights after church.

"She was only too willing", Frank told himself. "She practically threw herself at me. Still, I should have used more self-control. Papa would have fainted had he known of my misbehavior. I left home to go away to school. Just like Louisa, I had to keep from disgracing my family."

Soon, Brother Solomon turned the sedan onto the grounds of Clear Creek Boarding School. He walked to the chapel and stepped into his office. He knelt beside his chair to pray.

"Dear Jesus, You know how many times I have asked for forgiveness of the sins of my youth. I know You've forgiven me, but my heart is still heavy because of those sins. How can I help my son Caleb? How can I make restitution to his mother? And right now, how can I help Jenny Blackwell?"

He arose from his knees and reached for his Bible.

Searching the Scriptures, he believed God would reveal a plan for him to take so he could help those he had wounded. He didn't find the exact verses to answer his questions. After a while, he closed the Bible and started shuffling through the papers on his desk.

"Rome wasn't built in a day, and I know I won't be able to settle these questions in a matter of minutes," he told himself. "Right now, I need to clear up the problems with Jenny."

Brother Solomon stepped from his office and hurriedly walked toward the dorm for junior high girls. "I need a woman with me, so I'll get Betty to come along," he said, veering toward the dining area.

Soon, he and Betty stood at the door of the dorm. The other students were in class, except for Rachel who lay in her bed, shifting aimlessly. Jenny read while she rested. She propped her bandaged foot on a pillow.

"Rachel, would you step outside for a few minutes? We need to speak alone with Jenny," Brother Solomon requested. Rachel sighed, wrapped herself in a quilt, and stumbled out the door.

"Okay, Jenny. What's your problem now? Why did you sneak off to the cabin to hide?" Brother Solomon asked. His patience was growing thin with Jenny's unpredictable behavior.

Betty clasped her cheeks with her palms. "You didn't go hide there! Jenny do you know why girls go to the cabin?"

"Yeah, Betty, I know." She turned to Brother Solomon. "I'm supposed to walk the bullring. I don't think it's fair for me to have to walk round and round in front of all the other kids. You need another punishment," she said, defiantly.

"You're going be a sight—out there walking on crutches," Betty said. She chuckled softly.

"I thought you liked for everyone to see you walking the bullring," Brother Solomon countered. "You're always showing off and it seems like you're trying to get the students' attention. At least, that's the way it appears to me."

"No, I don't try to get attention. I think walking the bullring is a stupid way of punishing kids. That's why I ran away, so you'd know us students have feelings."

"I don't mind walking the bullring," Rachel called from the hall. "I wish I was well enough, I'd go walk it right now."

"That's because she wants to flounce around in front of her feller," Jenny whispered. "He's always watching her when she walks."

"Rachel, you aren't supposed to be listening. Go on down the hall," Brother Solomon instructed. He walked to the door and closed it. "Let's get to the real reason. Why did you hide in the cabin? What if Louisa hadn't come along?"

"Louisa?" Betty interrupted. "You mean the girl who stayed in my room a few years ago?"

"Yes. She came to visit. While she was here, she went out to the cabin. She happened to be there after Jenny cut her foot. We can discuss Louisa's visit later." He turned to Jenny. "Wasn't losing both your parents bad enough? Must you deliberately bring more problems into your life? That's what you're doing when you disobey the rules."

Jenny sat upright on the edge of the bed. "You don't think I'd hurt myself on purpose, do you?" she asked angrily. "My brothers are gone off to another school and there's no one left but me." Tears welled in her eyes.

"Louisa and I discussed your family situation before she left."

"What do you mean?" Jenny questioned. She turned down the page of the book and closed it with a thud.

"I can't tell you today because if my plans fall through you'll have more disappointments to deal with."

"If I can be closer to my brothers, I won't run off. I promise I won't."

I hope so, thought Brother Solomon, trying to free himself when Betty tugged at his jacket.

"Are you ready to go? I need to get back to the kitchen and check on the pot of beans."

"Yes, we can go," he answered. "Jenny, I'll tell you more when we get the details worked out."

Brother Solomon and Betty walked out the door. At that moment, Miss James, a matron at the school, ran toward him. "I'm sorry to disturb you, Brother Solomon, but Hallie Grant is trying to get in touch with you. She seems frantic."

"Is she on the phone now?" Brother Solomon asked, turning toward her.

"Yes. She's desperate to speak with you."

Brother Solomon hurried toward the main office of the boarding school. He noticed Miss James running to keep up with him.

Inside the office, he picked up the phone. "This is Brother Solomon. How may I—"

"Brother Solomon, this is Hallie Maytubby; used to be Grant. Something terrible is happening," Hallie said in a rush of words. "Caleb—you know—the young man who lives with Louisa's family, he and Brother Wade are locked up in the smokehouse. Caleb's threatening to kill Brother Wade and himself."

CHAPTER TWO

A chill flew through Brother Solomon's body. He clutched the receiver with a death grip. "Get a hold on yourself. Has someone tried to reason with Caleb?"

"Yes, Sister Wade has talked to him till she's blue in the face, but Caleb won't listen. Keeps threatening to kill Brother Wade. Something has to be done fast or they're both going to die."

"What about another preacher? Is there a pastor in town who can reason with Caleb? What about your papa? He said he made a vow to become a preacher."

How do I help Paul Wade's family? Frank Solomon wondered. And more importantly, my son?

Before Hallie had a chance to reply, he continued, "Ask someone to get your papa. I was visiting your church when Tobias said he'd made a vow to God to become a preacher. Maybe Doc Coleman will drive out there in his Model T, if you can catch him at his office. Will you try that?"

"Yes. We'll go get him. Maybe Mama can help Sister Wade. But could you come, Brother Solomon?" Hallie pled. "I don't know what Caleb's up to. Papa hasn't had any experience talking to people like him. At least, not that I know of."

"Yes, but he served in the war. He should be able to help till I get there. I'm leaving soon, Hallie. I'll come straight to Brother Wade's house. Bye."

Brother Solomon replaced the receiver on the hook. He turned to the matron. "Miss, James, I have to leave for a while. I don't know how long I'll be gone. Would you get help from some of the staff if you need it?"

"Yes, but what do I tell them?"

"That a preacher is being held prisoner by a-a young man who lives in his house. I'm going to try to talk some sense into the boy's head. You all can pray for Brother and Sister Wade and Caleb. Oh, pray for me, too."

He started toward his office, but paused and turned toward Miss James. "Tell Jenny Blackwell to grab some clothes and come to my office. I'm taking her with me."

Miss James' face mirrored bewilderment.

"Tobias Grant's family took Jenny in when her mother died, remember? She can visit them while I'm there. I know we'll be gone all night. I don't know if we'll get back tomorrow or not."

"A visit home may help Jenny," Miss James said. She hurried toward the junior high girls' dorm to tell Jenny to get ready for the trip.

Brother Solomon rushed to his room to grab a jacket. He dashed to his office. He scribbled a note stating his whereabouts for anyone who needed to know how to reach him. Then he walked out to stand beside the car, drumming his fingers on the hood. He gazed toward the junior high girls' dorm, scowling each time he removed his pocket watch to check the time.

After a while, Miss James came out of the dorm with Jenny. The matron held onto Jenny's arm as the girl hopped toward the car. In a few moments, Jenny was settled in the vehicle, her change of clothes in the backseat.

"It'll take a while to get there, but I'll drive as fast as I can," he said, glancing at the sun. "I'll try to get there before dark." He paused before opening the door, to whisper a prayer. "Dear Jesus, please help me get to Paul Wade's before anything bad happens."

He climbed in beside Jenny. The sedan moved along as fast as Brother Solomon dared push it. He was aggravated at how long it took for them to reach Piney Ridge. The familiar landmarks appeared and disappeared as if they had just crawled out of bed and didn't want to get moving. "And I'm tired to boot," he complained to Jenny. "If I'd just had a decent night's sleep last night it would be easier to concentrate on how to handle this problem."

"What problem, Brother Solomon?" Jenny looked into his face. "Is it me? Why are we going home? Are you taking me back to White Rabbit's house because I ran away?"

"This isn't a punishment for you, Jenny. It's somebody else."

He noticed Jenny breathing a sigh of relief. He believed she still had a sense of right and wrong.

"Well, what's the problem?" Jenny persisted. "Why are we just up and leaving out of the blue? And why did I have to come along?"

Brother Solomon expelled a long breath. "Jenny, I've never faced anything like this before and I don't want you to get upset. You'll find out soon enough."

"But when?"

"When we get there. How about that?"

"Come on," Jenny begged, tugging at his shirtsleeve. "You can trust me."

"Oh, all right. You'll learn soon enough," Brother Solomon said. "Remember Caleb?"

He watched Jenny frown, then she nodded. "Yeah, that crippled man. Sometimes, he's mean."

Brother Solomon felt a pain shoot through his heart. *My son has a reputation for acting mean? I know she's right.* "Let's don't be judgmental, Jenny," he scolded. "Just because Caleb's clubfooted, doesn't make him bad."

"Yeah, but he's got lots of room for improvement," Jenny responded.

"Regardless of how bad Caleb was, what he's doing now won't make him look any better. He's holed up in the smokehouse with Louisa's papa. Caleb's threatening to kill both of them."

"If that don't beat a goose 'a gobblin'," Jenny declared. "I guess everybody is scared."

"And I'm supposed to try to talk him out of hurting anyone."

"How are you gonna do that?"

"Only the Lord knows," Brother Solomon answered.

What do I say? He wondered. Silently, he prayed, "Dear Jesus, show me how to comfort those two men. Or maybe I need strong words that will knock Caleb for a loop, so he'll free Paul. I need wisdom and direction as much now as I've ever needed it."

Following a short pause, Jenny said, "I know what you could do. Get somebody to start making a loud noise outside, and everybody starts screaming. Make it sound like a war party is attacking."

Brother Solomon watched Jenny smile in satisfaction. "Sounds good, but where do we get a war party?"

"Oh. I don't know. I'm not the district chief," Jenny grumbled and slumped down in the seat.

"Do you know where Brother Wade lives?" Brother Solomon asked,

glancing at Jenny. "I don't even know where I'm going, once we get to town."

He watched Jenny's face light up. "Yes. I've been there with Louisa. But it was awful. Brother Wade was madder'n 'a old wet hen."

"If he's angry today, he has good cause to be," Brother Solomon said. "I'll tell you what we're going to do. You can show me where Brother Wade lives, then I'll take you to White Rabbit's to stay."

"Why?"

"You have to stay somewhere so you won't get hurt. Remember, if there's any danger you can't be running around on your crippled foot."

"Yeah. I'd hate to be running from Caleb—" Jenny covered her mouth, but a giggle slipped out. "He's crippled, too, so why would I need to run from him?"

"He might have a rifle. You couldn't get away from a bullet," Brother Solomon replied. "Now use that brain of yours and think of another way to tackle the problem."

"Okay. I'll try," Jenny said. She closed her eyes as if in deep thought. However, before long Brother Solomon noticed Jenny's head sinking lower onto her chest and her breathing grew regular.

"Asleep," Brother Solomon said. He smiled. "She needs the rest. Louisa said Jenny's cut was pretty deep."

He questioned why Jenny kept running away. It seemed as if she took dangerous risks just to get attention. He hoped she'd confide in White Rabbit about her problems.

As he drove along, Brother Solomon tried to devise schemes for freeing Paul.

Surely getting Paul away from a man who couldn't run wouldn't be too hard—unless he used the rifle. Hallie said he had one.

Jenny was still sleeping when Brother Solomon pulled into town. He touched Jenny's shoulder and shook her gently. "Jenny, wake up. You need to tell me which road to take."

Jenny opened her eyes and rubbed them. She yawned and looked out the window as if searching for the right place to turn off.

"Do you know where Doc Coleman's office is? If you can find it, then I'll tell you where to go from there," Jenny said.

"Yes, I know. When I was here one time Sammy took me by Doc's office to show me where he worked. I'll head there first."

In a few moments, Jenny pointed toward the house across from Doc's. "Go around the corner from that house."

"It wouldn't have been hard to find," Brother Solomon said a moment later. "Look at that crowd gathered around the place. Now, I'll take you to stay at White Rabbit's while I'm trying to help coax Caleb to come out peaceably."

"I'd rather go with you."

"You will not go with me. I'll take you to White Rabbit's. I am in a hurry and don't have time to quibble about this."

Soon, Brother Solomon drove into the yard at White Rabbit's. He walked to the passenger side and lifted Jenny from the car. He carried Jenny to the front porch and set her in a chair. Quickly, he knocked on the door. When White Rabbit peeked out he said, "I don't have time to talk because I'm in hurry. Hallie called to tell me about Caleb. I'm going to try to help." He waved goodbye and ran down the steps.

"It's a terrible situation," White Rabbit called to him, as she stepped out onto the porch.

* * *

"Why Jenny, what are you doing here? Aren't you supposed to be in school?" White Rabbit peered at Jenny's foot. "What happened to your foot? And why did Brother Solomon hurry off so fast?" She dropped into a chair beside Jenny.

"The main reason we're here is because Hallie called the school and told Brother Solomon about Caleb being fastened in the smokehouse with Louisa's pa," Jenny explained. She paused to take a deep breath before rushing on. "Hallie asked Brother Solomon to come down and see if he can help settle the problem without anybody getting shot."

A look of concern covered White Rabbit's plump face. "You could have knocked me over with a feather when Papa came in and told me about the way Caleb's acting. I can't imagine him getting so mad that he's holding a gun on Brother Wade. Nobody knows what to do." She turned to face

Jenny, "But why are you here and what's wrong with your foot?"

"My shoes are getting too tight and I was going barefooted. Stepped on a piece of glass. Brother Solomon said I couldn't do nothing at school so I should come with him and visit y'all while he's here."

Jenny knew better than to tell the whole story. It might get her into more trouble.

"Well, I'm glad you're here. Maybe we can get you a new pair of shoes while you're visiting."

"I can't wear no shoe on this foot for a while." Jenny held up her bandaged foot. "I need another pair, though. Don't want to cut my other foot.

"You think we'll be by ourselves tonight? Will Tobias stay up at Brother Wade's till the shootout is over?"

"Don't call it a shootout, Jenny. That sounds too much like the Wild West." White Rabbit patted Jenny's arm, then nodded her head. "Yes, I imagine Papa will be staying up there as long as both men are in the smokehouse. After all, Louisa is our daughter-in-law and it's a family problem. I don't guess Louisa knows about her pa, does she?"

"Not that I know of. Do you think that maybe Hallie called Louisa? What about Katrina? Does she know?"

"I don't know anything about this. Doc drove out to get Tobias and they hurried back to town. Doc asked if I wanted to go, but Papa didn't want me to go. Said I needed to stay here and feed the chickens and the dogs."

Jenny felt a hint of jealousy seep into her heart.

"He was protecting you. He loves you too much to see you standing out by the smokehouse wondering when all the trouble will end. You ought to be glad you have a husband who cares . . ." She felt those stinking tears bothering her again.

"Yes, Jenny, I am glad." She fiddled with the buttons at the top of her faded print dress, pushing them back and forth through the openings. After a few moments of silence, White Rabbit stood and smoothed the wrinkles from her apron.

"Have you had anything to eat lately? Papa probably won't be coming home tonight, so come on in and we'll have a bite. I have some cornbread and sweet milk."

After she finished eating, Jenny's foot still throbbed so much that she asked White Rabbit to bandage the cut and she went to bed.

Early the next morning Brother Solomon and Tobias returned for a few moments to see about White Rabbit.

Jenny insisted on returning with the men. "I want to go with y'all and see what's happening," Jenny protested. "I won't cause no trouble."

"You know what I told you when we left yesterday. You can't run on your injured foot, so you may not go to Paul Wade's house," Brother Solomon reiterated. "Is that clear?"

"It's clear," Jenny said, pushing a loose curl behind her ear. "But how can a crippled man run after me?"

When they drove into the edge of town Brother Solomon frowned at Jenny and said, "You're getting out of the car, Little Lady. Where are you staying?"

"If I have to stay away from the excitement, how about Doc's office? It's not far from the Wade's. At least I can watch through the window."

"That's a good place for you to stay," Tobias agreed. Brother Solomon stopped the car in front of Doc's.

"Okay. Let me carry you in because I'm in a hurry. Is that all right?" asked Brother Solomon.

"Kind of silly, but it's okay with me," Jenny said.

"I believe I'll leave the car here, and we can just walk down to the smokehouse. That way I won't cause a big stir like I might if I drove to the house and parked."

Soon, Jenny was alone, sitting in Doc's office. No one was there, but that would have to do during the crisis.

* * *

Tobias walked toward the smokehouse with Brother Solomon. Soon they melted in with the crowd, which was what Brother Solomon wanted to do—blend in with everyone. He didn't want to stand out, causing a stir among the people. He walked around the yard observing the action.

First, he recognized Hallie. Brother Solomon slipped over to stand beside her. When he touched her arm, Hallie jumped and looked around.

Brother Solomon put his finger to his lips. "Sh-h-h," he whispered. "Don't talk out loud. What's going on?"

"Brother Wade is still in there with Caleb," Hallie said, pointing toward the smokehouse.

"Has there been any gunfire?"

"No. Just loud yelling and cussing from Caleb," Hallie answered. Unconsciously, she played with the locket hanging on the chain around her neck.

Frank gazed at the necklace. He recognized it as the same one he had given to Caleb's mother. Were their pictures still in it? Not the perfect time to ask to look at it, but he decided to take a chance and get her permission.

"Could I see your necklace for a minute, Hallie?" Brother Solomon asked.

"Sure," Hallie answered, reaching for the fastener. "It's the one Louisa gave me when Maria was born." She handed the necklace to Brother Solomon.

He started to open the locket when a loud burst of foul language erupted from inside the smokehouse.

"See what I told you? That's Caleb cussing again," Hallie explained.

Brother Solomon felt like a knife sliced through his heart. His son was cursing the man who gave him a home.

The preacher closed the locket to look at later and dropped it inside his pocket. He bowed his head and pressed his fingers to his forehead. "Father," he whispered, "I must get Paul out, but how?"

He recalled reading about battles in the Old Testament. Create a stir in the rear and get the enemy's attention. Then while his back's turned, attack from the front. Would that work today?

Brother Solomon raised his head. "Where's Junior?" he whispered.

"He's over there by the door," Hallie said, pointing toward her husband. "And some other men are there who served in the war with Papa."

"Sneak over and get Junior. Tell him not to cause a commotion. I'm thinking about how to tackle this situation."

Brother Solomon watched Hallie weave her way through the crowd of keyed-up observers. "Please, Dear Lord, show me a way," he prayed silently.

Junior squeezed through the swarm of spectators. He smiled when his eyes met the preacher's, but he remained quiet. Brother Solomon motioned for Junior and Tobias to follow him. He kicked at clumps of grass growing beside the road while he led the way to his sedan. He motioned for the men to sit in the car. He stood at the open window while they talked. Hallie walked over to stand beside him.

"Hallie, why don't you go inside Doc's office and talk to Jenny?"

Hallie raised her eyebrows and asked, "What's she doing with you?"

"She cut her foot pretty bad yesterday. I knew she couldn't get around at school, so I brought her with me to let her visit your folks. She stayed all night with White Rabbit."

"I'd like to see how Jenny's doing. I'll run see her a few minutes."

"Is Caleb making any new threats since we left earlier?" Brother Solomon asked, leaning inside the window.

"He's got a rifle aimed at Brother Wade's back," answered Junior, playing with the steering wheel. "I think he would use it if anybody tried to go inside the smokehouse."

Tobias nodded in agreement. "I think he would pull the trigger. I don't know what caused the problem. I thought Caleb was fairly happy here. He never laughed or carried on much, but I believed that was just his way," he said. He studied his work worn hands and remained silent for a moment. "Maybe it's because of his clubfeet. He's lived with Paul most all his life. He should be grateful that the Wade's gave him a home."

"You're right, he should show gratitude," Brother Solomon said, nodding. "Do you think he'll listen to reason?"

"He hasn't listened to anybody so far, but there's always a chance he might pay attention to a new voice," Tobias said.

"He might." Junior agreed. He practiced twisting the steering wheel.

"Let's go back to see if there's been any change since we left," Brother Solomon said. "Y'all come on with me. I need moral support."

"Brother Solomon, don't try anything that'll cause you to get hurt," Junior warned. He crawled out of the vehicle and slammed the door.

"I won't."

The three men walked back into the yard. They squeezed their way through the crowd of white men and Indians. Junior led the way to the door. He put his finger to his lips and cracked the door.

"Shut that door!" Caleb yelled.

"Do what he says," Paul Wade shouted. "He's got the rifle aimed at my back."

"Shut it," Brother Solomon advised. He knew he had to take action. A lot of this was his fault. He'd run out on Caleb's mama before his birth and ignored her plight. Today, he must make up for past sins. He wanted to take a good look at the smokehouse from the outside. He couldn't see it at all last night.

Frank Solomon walked to the side of the smokehouse. He gazed at every board, looking for knotholes and cracks. He touched the rough boards, searching for weak spots in the lumber. He could feel the eyes of onlookers gazing at him. Turning around, he saw men shaking their heads, sending a silent message that there was no hole through which to stick a barrel. He went to the back of the shed. He found no flaws in the lumber. With hope diminishing of finding an opening, he walked to the other side of the smokehouse. The building had been constructed with care.

He leaned over and pointed underneath the shed. The men following him shook their heads. They had already thought of that.

Brother Solomon glanced at the roof. The onlookers indicated a ladder standing nearby and shook their heads again.

When he came back to the front of the smokehouse, he saw an Indian woman wearing a faded dress and apron wandering around. She clutched a handkerchief in her hand. Occasionally, she stopped and dabbed at her eyes. When she turned to face the smokehouse, she covered her face with her hands and sobbed for a moment. Then, taking a deep breath, she walked toward the structure. The crowd parted to let her stand at the door.

"Papa, can you hear me?" she asked, opening the door just a slit.

"Don't try anything, Wife. Caleb is on the war-path."

"What does he want? Maybe we can get whatever he's asking for."

"Mama, you can't get anything I need," Caleb yelled. "What about two new feet so I can walk out of this smokehouse? Answer that."

"We didn't cause your clubfeet," Paul Wade said. "Your feet were ruined when you came here."

"What about a wife and a home? Answer that."

"You may have a wife and a home some day," Sister Wade answered.

"Not if he keeps acting this way," Brother Wade interjected. "He's ruining his life right this minute."

"What about telling me who my parents are? Answer that."

Brother Solomon winced. A conceivable solution, if he confessed to Caleb that he was his father.

"How would we know? We found you on the steps of the church one Sunday," Sister Wade answered, interrupting Brother Solomon's thoughts. He watched her twisting her handkerchief into knots.

"What reason do I have to live? I can't walk—I can't have a family of my own—I don't know who my parents are. Why should I care? Tell me, Mama, what reason do I have to give a hoot about living?"

When Brother Solomon heard the clicking sound of the rifle in the smokehouse, the hairs on the back of his neck stood up. Caleb's demands were almost impossible to meet, but he must try another tactic.

"Sister Wade, why don't you go in the house and fix a cup of coffee for your husband?" he asked. "Caleb, do you want a cup of coffee, too?"

"Naw. Don't be trying to trick me, neither."

"Make it boiling hot," Brother Solomon whispered to Sister Wade. He raised his eyebrows to give her a signal of what he had in mind. He motioned as if dashing the coffee inside the smokehouse. Maybe Paul could throw hot coffee in Caleb's face and then grab the rifle.

* * *

Inside Doc's office, when Jenny saw Hallie walk behind the counter to pick up a large bottle of pills, she decided Hallie's frustrations were at the boiling point. Hallie opened the lid and sniffed the medication.

"You think maybe you ought to leave Doc's pills alone? I know you feel like you're setting in a bed of hot ashes, but Doc might get mad if he came in and caught you looking in the pill bottles."

Hallie sighed loudly. She tightened the lid and set the bottle back on the shelf with a thud. "Caleb is as stinking mean as a civet cat. Why won't he let Brother Wade go?"

"He's probably started thinking about his real parents, like I do sometimes. And he got all worked up because he never seen 'em," Jenny said, thoughtfully. "I think I know how he feels, because Mama and Papa both died, and ever so often I get lonesome. I did live with 'em a long time, so I have my memories to dream about."

Jenny felt tears stinging her eyes. She blinked rapidly to get rid of them. She walked toward the window and pretended to look out. She mustn't let Hallie see her crying.

"You think if we can get Caleb to talking about who his parents might be, he would come out of the smokehouse? I could tell him how I felt after Mama and Papa both died. Why don't we go down there and let me talk to him?"

"Yeah, and let you get shot in the other foot. That'd be the final straw. No, Brother Solomon would skin me alive if I let you go. Look at your foot, girl. How would you get down there, anyway?"

"I could hop on my good foot," Jenny responded. "Somebody's about to get killed. What's a cut on my foot, compared to the danger Brother Wade's in? He deserves to live, even if he is as ornery as all get out."

"He deserves to live and then get horsewhipped because of the way he treated Louisa." Hallie expelled a long breath and raked her fingers through her shiny black hair.

Jenny noticed Hallie looking her way as if trying to read her reaction. Though secretly she agreed with Hallie, she didn't let on that she understood the message.

Hallie walked toward the door. "You stay here. You could be right about your feelings. You and the boys have been through the same kind of problems and you know more about how Caleb feels than any of us do. I'll see if I can get a man to carry you down to the smokehouse. I'll be back in a few minutes."

"Okay." Jenny watched Hallie step outside. Her offer to talk with Caleb smacked her up the side of the head, causing her to tremble.

What have I got myself into now? Jenny wondered. Like Mama used to

say, I was always good at jumping out of the frying pan and into the fire. Jenny's tremors turned into shudders. She wrapped both arms around her body trying to calm herself. Why had she opened her big mouth? She knew nothing to say to Caleb. She did know how it felt to be an orphan, a stray, unwanted by most everyone. She did have three brothers, but they were enrolled in another school. Caleb didn't have any real brothers or sisters that he knew about.

She wondered if she should hide outside behind a bush, in case somebody did come to get her. She didn't know what to say to anybody, not even Brother Wade. She was always putting her big foot into her mouth. Jenny hopped toward the backdoor. She held onto the doorframe while she looked outside.

"Wonder if I can hide behind that big bush?" she asked herself. Just as she started to hop onto the step, the door to Doc's house opened and Mrs. Coleman stepped outside. She stopped and lifted both hands in the air.

"Why, hi, girl! What are you doing home in the middle of the school year?" She looked at Jenny's bandaged foot. "Oh, you've hurt your foot. Doc's not here now, but maybe I can put a clean dressing on it. Go back inside the office. I'll see what I can do."

Oh, stinking on it! She couldn't hide from the man if he decided to come get her.

Jenny hopped back inside and sat in a chair. She smiled, pretending gratitude for Mrs. Coleman's help. "That's nice of you," she mumbled.

But I wish you'd go back to your house.

"How'd you cut your foot?" Mrs. Coleman asked, after she had taken off the dressing.

"Stepped on a piece of glass." *That's not a lie, just not the full story.*

"Going barefooted?" Mrs. Coleman asked. She reached for a piece of cotton to dab monkey blood on the cut.

Jenny winced in pain. "Yeah. My shoes hurt. I guess I need a new pair."

"But what are you doing down here today, away from boarding school?"

"Brother Solomon got a call about Caleb holding Brother Wade in the

29

smokehouse. He came down to try to settle the problem and brought me with him, since I can't walk around yet. He took me to visit White Rabbit last night. Him and Tobias stayed up here all night. I came back with 'em this morning."

"That's bad about Caleb. I don't know the full story. I've just heard bits and pieces when patients come in to see Doc."

Jenny looked around, trying to find a place inside to hide in the office if Mrs. Coleman would only hurry and go back into her house.

"The bandage looks fine, Mrs. Coleman. I'll be all right. You can go back to your housework." *Please hurry. I've got to hide somewhere.*

"But what are you doing in the office, Jenny?" Mrs. Coleman asked.

"Brother Solomon said I wouldn't be able to run if Caleb started shooting the gun. He told me to stay up here to be out of danger. It's okay, ain't it?"

"Yeah. It's all right. I was just wondering how all of a sudden you showed up from boarding school. How're your grades?"

"I'm passing all my subjects."

Mrs. Coleman washed her hands and dried them on a grayish-white towel. She turned to face Jenny. "I know life has been rough for you and the boys. Doc has sure been worried about you since your ma died. Everybody around town has been concerned."

"I'm doing okay," Jenny insisted. *If she really knew how I feel sometimes, she'd understand. It's hard to lose your mama and papa.*

Tears were stinging her eyes again. She batted her eyelids to get rid of them. She must act like she wasn't feeling pain. She needed to get Mrs. Coleman talking on a different subject. Maybe some ideas about capturing Caleb.

"How can the men get Caleb to throw down the gun and come out of the smokehouse?" Jenny asked.

Mrs. Coleman shrugged her shoulders and gestured helplessly. "I wish I knew. The whole town is in a big turmoil. Some men are saying they should charge the smokehouse and take Caleb, dead or alive."

"That would be awful, if those men killed a man who don't have a chance to escape. He can't run or nothin'." That's the way she felt about her brothers. They were at the mercy of anyone who wanted to help them or hurt them.

Sometimes I want to take a big dose of sleeping powders and forget all about life. Sleeping powders, that's an idea.

"Mrs. Coleman, do you have any sleeping powders that make a person go to sleep real fast?"

"Do you need to go to sleep?"

"No, not me. I'm thinking about Caleb. If Doc has some powerful medicine that would knock a person out real fast, maybe we could get this problem solved."

"You may have something there." Mrs. Coleman walked behind the counter and started picking through packets of powder. "Doc does have some liquid and some powder that helps babies go to sleep. But it would take a big dose to knock out a man Caleb's size." She lifted a packet from a box. "This one is strong. But how can they get Caleb to drink it?"

"Maybe put some in a cup of coffee? He's probably tired after being cramped in that smokehouse all night."

"It's worth a try. Here, take this packet. You have to mix it with liquid, but you said coffee didn't you? Maybe it'll work."

The door opened and two brawny men stepped in, followed by Hallie. "Where's the girl we're supposed to tote back to Brother Wade's?" asked one man. He glanced at the bandage on Jenny's foot. "Oh, it's you. I could 'a carried you under one arm. But we're gonna make a packsaddle. Come on, Jake. Let's get goin'. Gotta let this kid try to be a hero."

"I'm not trying to be a hero," Jenny said. She glared at the man. How dare he make fun of her?

"Don't see what a kid like you can do," Jake grumbled. "There's ten good men down there who can't bring the clubfooted-man to his senses. How's a weakling like you going to make any difference?"

"I was just thinking the same thing," Jenny admitted, as she slipped the packet of powder in her blouse pocket. "But let me try. Caleb might listen to me since I'm not grown up."

Jake laughed sarcastically. "Yeah. And he'll pay attention to a owl hootin'."

Jenny frowned at Jake, but didn't say anything. *Calling me a weakling and comparing me to a hoot owl. Of all the low down men, I get one like him to carry me to the smokehouse.*

31

"Jenny has a packet of strong sleeping powder," Mrs. Coleman said. "She's going to try to put some in a cup of coffee and see if Caleb will drink it."

"That's a good idea!" Hallie exclaimed.

"Brother Wade was drinking a cup of coffee while ago," Jake said "but I doubt you'll get Caleb to drink anything. Maybe by now he'll want some. But how do we keep Paul Wade from drinking the coffee that's got sleeping powders in it?"

"We're not going to worry. We'll put it in all the coffee. It won't hurt Brother Wade, will it, Mrs. Coleman?"

"No. He'll just have to sleep it off."

Jenny sat on the packsaddle the men made by holding to each other's wrists. She trembled as she put her arms around the necks of both men. This was a fine kettle of fish. A kid like her trying to talk sense into a grown man's head was plain stupid. Too quickly, the men headed toward Brother Wade's house. Jenny noticed Hallie walking fast to keep up with them.

"This scheme may work," Jake said.

"And more 'n likely it won't," his friend added.

"I need to talk to somebody before we get to the smokehouse. We need to be sure the coffee is ready to hand inside, once I've talked to Caleb," Jenny said. "Where's Brother Solomon? Let me talk to him before we do anything."

Her better judgment pricked Jenny. *Why don't I think before I open my big mouth? Caleb will think I'm just a kid actin' stupid . . . which I am. I said I wanted to do this, so I have to stick by my word. If I ever get out of this, I'll be careful makin' reckless statements.*

Soon the men set Jenny down a short way from the smokehouse. She touched her blouse pocket to make sure the sleeping powder remained in place.

"What you got here, Jake?" the storekeeper asked. Jenny knew he worked in a store by seeing the strips of elastic tied around his sleeves. "Gonna play a trick on him?"

"Don't ask me," Jake answered, raising his hands in exasperation. "I don't know what she's doing."

"Don't let 'em bother you," Hallie said, patting Jenny on the back. "You go on with your plan. Remember, 'nothing ventured, nothing gained'."

"Yeah, a big bunch 'a nothin'," yelled a cowboy. "Let me use my lariat. I'll rope him and drag him down Main Street. I'll make him wish he never seen a smokehouse."

Brother Solomon stepped from behind the shed. He held up his hand. "Paul Wade will be rescued in an orderly way. If you have roping on your mind, I suggest you go back to your herd of cattle."

Most of the onlookers laughed and turned to gaze at the cowboy. The cowpoke's face turned pink and he stared at the ground. "It would 'a worked," he mumbled.

"Brother Solomon, I need to talk to you," Jenny said, motioning for him to come closer.

"Hey, everybody! Look at that skinny kid trying to get us to feel sorry for her 'cause she's got a big bandage on her foot," a woman said, pointing toward Jenny. "What's wrong with you, kid? Tryin' to pretend you've got a clubfoot, too?" She giggled hysterically, then she pulled out a piece of bubble gum. She stuck it in her mouth and began to chomp on it.

"Madam, I suggest you keep your opinion to yourself," Brother Solomon said, and frowned at the woman.

The lady returned the frown then lifted her hand to cover her mouth. She whispered to a man standing behind her. The man nodded and grinned.

"You don't know who my brother is. He could wrap this up in five minutes if he was here." She said, then she snapped her gum loudly. "That gal wouldn't stand a chance." She nodded toward Jenny.

"They're talking about me. They don't think my plan will work," Jenny mumbled. She stared at the smart-aleck woman wondering what kind of garb she was decked out in. Jenny gazed at her short dress, her bobbed hair and her painted cheeks. The lady looked like she was trying to be one of the women Jenny had read about called "flappers."

Jenny turned to Brother Solomon. "Come over here. I have a plan."

"It better be a good one. I told you not to come down here."

Brother Solomon held Jenny's arm while she hopped to the side of the smokehouse. She whispered to him.

"I've got a packet of real strong sleeping powders in my pocket. Mrs. Coleman gave it to me." She touched the parcel in her pocket.

"Jenny! What are you going to think of next?" Brother Solomon asked. He laughed. "You're not even dry behind the ears yet."

Wonder what that means? Jenny thought, but ignored his sarcasm. "Do you think you can get Caleb and Brother Wade to drink coffee?"

"Paul is drinking coffee now. So what does coffee have to do with your plan?"

"I want somebody to dump the sleeping powders into a cup of coffee and give it to Caleb and . . ."

"It won't work, Jenny," interrupted Brother Solomon. "We've tried to get him to eat or drink something but he refuses."

"The sleeping powders won't hurt him, just knocks him out so somebody can tie his hands behind his back or fasten him up one way or another," Jenny continued, ignoring the remark. "First, we need to get Brother Wade to take another cup of coffee. Fix one without the powders, then if Caleb will take one, we can put the sleeping powders in the coffee pot."

"I'm telling you, it won't work," Brother Solomon said. He led Jenny to the front of the smokehouse.

"What you gonna do, Miss Priss?" asked the smart-mouthed woman, touching the short hair hanging around her neck. "Why don't you hop in the smokehouse and show Caleb your crippled foot?" Her taunting remark echoed through the nervous crowd. Several folks snickered. Others frowned angrily at the woman. The storekeeper kicked at the ground, digging up a tuft of grass.

Noises came from the smokehouse, like someone was moving around.

"Need more coffee, Paul?" asked Brother Solomon.

"Yeah. It helps me stay awake. It's been a long night," Paul Wade answered through the door, followed by the sound of a loud yawn. "Here's my cup."

"Just a minute. I'll get Sister Wade to bring the coffeepot back. She was keeping it hot for you."

At the mention of coffeepot, Sister Wade hurried into the house. Soon she returned with a blue-flecked granite container.

Brother Solomon poured more coffee into Paul's cup. "Here, reach over and get it. I'm afraid Caleb might get an itchy trigger finger if I tried to step inside."

Jenny peeked inside the cracked door. "Caleb, I kind of know how you're feeling," she called.

"Stay out, kid. You don't have no idea how I feel," Caleb said. Jenny heard a crash as if Caleb had thrown a hammer or a rock across the room. She shivered, but plunged ahead with her speech.

"I don't know how it feels to be crippled, but my mama died when I was ten and Papa died before that. They left us four kids as orphans. I know how it feels to be cast aside all by yourself," Jenny yelled through the crack in the door. Her voice trembled, because she was ready to cry. "I've got three brothers who don't have no parents. It gets lonesome sometimes. I do know kind of how you feel. But you ain't never seen your mama or papa, have you?"

"It ain't gonna work, kid," yelled a cowboy. "Let me throw my rope in there and drag him out."

"Yeah, go on, Cowboy," yelled the heckler. "But if my brother was here he'd settle this right now." She blew a big bubble. It burst with a loud snap. "Too bad he's out on 'a important case right now."

Another collective chorus of snickers rippled among the onlookers.

Jenny wondered who the woman's brother was, anyway. The flapper said this wouldn't work. She may know what she was talking about, but Jenny felt she needed to try her plan before she gave up. She wanted to keep on begging Caleb and letting him know somebody else hurt besides him.

Jenny looked at the crowd, angrily. "I bet none of you know how it feels to be a' orphan before you turn 'leven," she yelled. "My mama had consumption. She coughed all the time. We didn't have hardly nothin' to eat."

Jenny felt those dreaded tears about to surface again. She rubbed at her eyes, trying to get them to stop. "Y'all have plenty of food to eat, but Mama must of starved herself to death, trying to let us eat what food we did have. Caleb, you know Doc Coleman?"

"Yeah. But he can't help me none. My feet can't be fixed."

"Doc Coleman is the one who took care of Mama. He cared about us orphans. He got me a place to live with White Rabbit and Tobias. And Brother Solomon got us into boarding schools. While I'm studying, I don't worry as much about Mama. Going to school can take your mind off your problems."

The smart-mouthed woman started laughing again. She pointed toward the smokehouse door and yelled, "Him? Go to school?"

"She's right, kid. People like me don't go to school, so shut up."

"Yeah, but Caleb, you can still learn. I bet Brother Solomon could get somebody to teach you to read and write."

Jenny looked at Brother Solomon and asked loudly, "Could you get somebody to teach him? He'd have a reason to live if he could study lessons."

"Teach him? When Red River freezes over in the middle of July." The woman clutched her waist and doubled over with laughter. Several of the observers frowned angrily at her.

"Why don't you tend to your own business, you, you, flapper?" yelled a farmer, pulling at the straps on his overalls. "Leave that orphan alone."

The woman glared in return. "Just 'cause I've got my hair bobbed don't mean I'm a flapper," she answered. She turned to the cowboy and smiled.

"What about all that face paint you're wearin'?" the farmer retorted.

"They noticed," the woman whispered to her companion. Jenny felt as if the lady's smile proved she was trying to be a flapper.

"Sure, Jenny," Brother Solomon answered, ignoring the loud remarks. "We could work that out. And I think there's another person who needs an education as well." He glanced toward the woman causing the scene.

"Did you hear that, Caleb? You can learn to read and write. Your feet don't have nothin' to do with schoolin'. Would you like to drink a cup of coffee while you think it over?"

Jenny reached into her pocket for the sleeping powder, and then she shook her head. She changed her mind. Drugging Caleb wouldn't be fair. He needed to make up his mind while he drank a good cup of hot coffee.

Sister Wade poured a fresh cup of coffee. She held it out for Jenny to

pour in the sleeping powder. Jenny shook her head and whispered, "Not yet. Give him a chance to make up his mind."

Brother Solomon pushed the cup through the crack in the door. "Paul, you'll have to hand it to Caleb. I know he won't let me come in."

Paul Wade reached out to take the cup.

Jenny froze, hoping Paul didn't pour hot coffee on Caleb. He should be free to make up his own mind. He'd been hurting all his life.

"Don't that taste good, Caleb? Sister Wade fixed it for you. And that ain't all she's done for you. Why, she's rocked you to sleep when you didn't have a mama of your own to take care of you. Probably rubbed your poor crippled feet when you was a baby. And she got up in the night to see about you when you cried and she did all kinds of nice things for you."

Jenny turned to see Sister Wade wiping tears from her eyes. She believed this hurt the preacher's wife more than Paul Wade.

"Do you have some vittles we can scoot in for Caleb to eat?" Jenny asked.

Sister Wade nodded.

"Go get something out of the kitchen safe that Caleb likes."

"I told you it wouldn't work," giggled the woman. She blew another bubble and it exploded with a loud pop.

Sister Wade left in a trot to go after a dish of food for Caleb. Soon, she returned with a piece of cherry pie on a plate. She gave the dish to Brother Solomon. He handed it in to Brother Wade.

"This is for Caleb," Brother Solomon said.

"Where's mine?" asked Brother Wade, grouchily.

"Keep it, Papa," Caleb said. "I'll go eat mine in the kitchen. I'm coming out, men. Take the rifle."

When Jenny heard the clattering of the firearm hitting the floor, she began to jump up and down till she felt warm blood oozing from the cut on her foot. "He's coming out. He's coming out," she yelled.

The spectators held their breath while they waited for the two Indian men to come out of the smokehouse. When Brother Wade opened the door,

the smell of cured hams wafted out. Caleb followed in an agonizingly slow exit from the building. Sighs of elation ran through the crowd of onlookers. Others covered their mouths while watching Caleb emerge.

Sister Wade ran to the shed and touched Caleb's arm when he sat with his wrapped feet protruding from the door.

"Thank God, it's over," she said softly. "We love you, Caleb. You're like our own son."

"You're speaking for yourself," Paul Wade scoffed.

Brother Solomon held onto Caleb as he came all the way out of the smokehouse.

Caleb looked into the crowd. "Where's that smart-aleck old woman?"

Jenny breathed a sigh of relief when she heard "old woman." She thought Caleb was about to call her a smart-aleck kid.

A few people pointed at the heckler. Her face turned as pink as her painted cheeks.

"Just wanted to get a good look at you, lady. Jenny come here," Caleb beckoned. "Go tell that old hag I'm going to learn to read and write. Then I'll mail a letter to her." He pointed toward the embarrassed lady. "Can you read, lady?"

The woman's face turned a deeper shade of red. She turned away.

* * *

Later, Brother Solomon sat in a ladder back chair to rest a few minutes before he and Jenny returned to boarding school. Caleb slouched in his corner, shuffling his rag-covered feet to find a comfortable position. He'd eat a big bite of cherry pie, followed by a loud yawn.

"Before Jenny and I leave, I want us to have a prayer thanking God for protecting everyone. Is that all right?" Brother Solomon asked, looking at Paul Wade for approval.

"Go ahead, Frank," Paul said. He sat staring into space. "And you better ask God to keep me from beating the tar out of Caleb. What he did is absolutely intolerable."

"I'll ask God to give you a forgiving spirit," Brother Solomon said. He knelt by his chair and thanked the Lord for His protection of everyone

involved in the standoff, including gratitude that Caleb had surrendered peaceably.

"Caleb, you need to go to bed. And you, too, Papa," Sister Wade suggested, after the prayer ended.

Paul Wade took a deep breath and stood before the group. "Caleb is no longer welcome here," he said, his voice filled with hatred. "He leaves today."

A gasp went up from everyone in the room. The loudest one was from Sister Wade. "But, Papa, what will he do?" she asked, and then covered her face with trembling fingers.

"That is up to him. He leaves today. Or else I turn him over to the sheriff." Paul slapped his fist and stamped his foot for emphasis. "Do you think I will tolerate him sleeping under my roof after all he's done? No, I will not."

"Please let him stay, Papa," Sister Wade pled. "You've already run Louisa off. We don't ever get to see Maria. Papa . . . " She broke into tears.

"Evil is evil regardless of who commits it," Brother Wade bellowed. "I will not allow sinful people to live in this house." He looked at Caleb. "Better decide where you're going to stay. I'll give you thirty minutes to get your things together and leave. After that I'll send for the sheriff and you can see how it feels to sleep in jail."

A tremor flew through Brother Solomon. He looked from Hallie and Junior to Tobias. Which one of them would offer to take Caleb into his home? He watched Hallie and Junior whispering. Would they take him?

And what is my part in this? What do I do?

"Help me, Lord," Brother Solomon prayed silently.

The lot is cast into the lap; but the whole disposing thereof is of the LORD.

That's the answer—from the book of Proverbs.

"Caleb, would you go to your room with Sister Wade?" he heard himself asking from a long way off. "Show her your belongings so she can pack them."

Did I say that?

"No. He can't leave," Sister Wade said, sobbing. "He can't take care of himself."

"He can learn," Paul said. "He was able to hold a rifle to my back. He'll have to make out. Go with him. Get his stuff together."

"It's all right, Sister Wade. I'll take him back to school with me," Brother Solomon said, trying to smile. His lips quivered, but turning to Caleb he added, "I said I'd get someone to teach you to read, so we'll start sooner than I had in mind. Go, help your mama."

Brother Solomon watched Caleb holding onto the wall as he tottered into a room that obviously had been added onto the main part of the house. Caleb was talking under his breath, spewing out vile language.

Brother Solomon glanced at Jenny. Her smile melted the chill around his heart.

Soon, the three travelers walked out, ready to leave. Jenny crawled into the backseat of the sedan. Junior helped as Caleb pulled himself in the front with Brother Solomon. All of Caleb's earthly belongings surrounded Jenny.

The good byes were a bittersweet mix. Brother Wade did not walk out to bid Caleb farewell. Sister Wade hugged Caleb and sobbed quietly. Junior and Tobias shook hands silently with Caleb. Hallie clung to his arm while she looked into his eyes.

"We'll see you when school is out," she said.

Caleb stared at her with a stony gaze.

I prayed for a way to help my son. Dear Lord, is this the answer to my prayer?

CHAPTER THREE

Brother Solomon started the engine. "Look, there's your friends, Jenny," he said, nodding toward a group of cowboys on horseback. Some tossed lariats roping imaginary steers. Taking center stage stood the flapper, lifting her too-short skirt and performing a parody of the Charleston. The onlookers laughed and pointed toward the sedan. Brother Solomon gave the engine a loud roar.

"Good riddance," yelled the woman.

"Wonder what they're up to?"

"No good, that's for sure," Jenny answered. "Hurry up. Let's get away from that bunch."

Brother Solomon gave the engine more gas and the car pitched forward. When he pulled onto the main gravel road, he slowed the sedan and looked over his shoulder toward Jenny. "When the sight of that woman fades from my mind, I may get sleepy," he said, then chuckled. "If I do, y'all try to keep me awake. I stayed up all night."

"What about me? I had to stay awake," Caleb complained.

"Whoa there, back up," Brother Solomon said. "You had to stay awake? Put that in different words, Caleb."

"I was mad, Preacher. I wouldn't have hurt Papa. He just pushed me to the edge and I had to pay him back," Caleb admitted. "I know I didn't go about it the right way."

"Not by a long shot! Don't you know when you're angry at a person you don't just pick up a rifle and aim it at him?"

Caleb lowered his head and nodded. "Yeah. I went overboard this time."

"You went overboard one time too many as far as I'm concerned. Hopefully, that type of behavior is behind you. You're starting a new page in your life. So this time, do it right."

"Jenny, keep Brother Solomon awake," Caleb said, glancing at her in the backseat. "I'll sleep."

"Better sleep while you've got a chance. 'Cause I figure you'll have to study when you start to school. I'll try to think of something to say so

Brother Solomon'll stay awake. I may compose a poem and recite it to you."

"That should really keep me awake," Brother Solomon teased.

Maybe a poem about orphans. Or sick people. Or crippled people.

"Why is life so unfair?

"Why don't rich people care?"

Not bad, Jenny thought. I can write about us lonely people. If everybody knew how we felt, life would be different. Okay, next line.

"Will kids at school make fun of me?" Caleb interrupted, turning toward Jenny. "I'm older than they are and crippled, too. Will they tease me?"

"Yes, they probably will," Jenny answered, not waiting for Brother Solomon to speak. "That's just the way people act. They all jump on the underdog. They've—"

"But you've been through a lot already, Caleb," Brother Solomon said. "You know how to deal with anger. You've had to be a fighter all your life in order to survive."

"How would you know? You set behind a desk at school all day and order people around," countered Caleb. "You don't have no idea what it's like to set around all day, staring at your feet wrapped up in tow sacks."

I wonder if I should 'a stood up for him? Jenny thought.

She watched Brother Solomon put his fist to his mouth and he coughed loudly. Jenny believed his response held back the angry words he wanted to say.

"No, I don't know what it's like to stare at crippled feet. Hopefully, I do know how to keep from spouting out filthy language," Brother Solomon answered after he cooled off. "Caleb, you're going to have to be careful with that mouth of yours."

"Says who? You ain't my boss. I ain't got no boss." With a catch in his throat Caleb added, "My folks are probably dead and I don't have to answer to nobody."

"You have to answer to God," Brother Solomon said softly.

"And I don't want to hear none of that God business," Caleb snarled.

"I've heard that all my life and look at me, I'm still crippled. And I don't have a home—"

"Yeah, and why don't I have a mama and daddy?" Jenny pitched in. Maybe if she complained, Caleb would see how stupid his words sounded.

"Not you, too, Jenny." Brother Solomon turned to glance at her.

"Yeah, but you did have a mama and daddy for a while," Caleb answered over his shoulder. *"I never had any parents."*

"That's why our tribe provides orphanages," Brother Solomon said. "That's why we furnish boarding schools—for orphans or kids who couldn't go to school otherwise."

"Do I have to set in class?" Caleb persisted. "Can somebody come to the dorm to teach me? You know I can't set in a chair like the others."

"You will go to class tomorrow. We'll find some place for you to sit," Brother Solomon said. "No use to put it off. It'll become harder the longer you wait."

"Look at my feet!" Caleb scuffled his feet in the floorboard. "You know the kids'll laugh and point at 'em."

Jenny peeked over the seat to look at Caleb's feet the best she could.

"Some way, we'll straighten everything out. You could sit in a wheelchair in class and cover your legs and feet," Brother Solomon suggested.

"Like a papoose wrapped in a blanket!" Caleb said. A string of vile words finished the sentence.

Jenny covered her ears and closed her eyes. Yeah, she had made a mistake.

Brother Solomon jerked the steering wheel and the sedan skidded to the side of the road. It stopped with a thud. Jenny almost flew into the front seat.

Brother Solomon turned to face Caleb. "Words like that are not permitted at Clear Creek," he said slowly and evenly. He pointed a finger at the end of Caleb's nose. "Even grown men who curse at the drop of a hat don't do it in front of women and girls. Understood?"

I never saw Brother Solomon so mad, Jenny thought.

"Yeah. Maybe I ought to jump out right now, 'cause I probably can't live up to your rules at school." Caleb reached for the door handle. He swung one foot around.

"Yeah, Brother Solomon, let him out," Jenny said, leaning over the seat. "I thought he was a fighter. I must have been wrong. Let him take the easy way out."

"No, I will not!" Brother Solomon said, pounding the steering wheel. "I said he'd learn to read and write and, I promise you, he'll have the chance to write a letter to that obnoxious woman."

Jenny slid further behind Caleb's bag of clothes. "That woman is really mean."

I hope this works out. Only God can get everything going right, Jenny thought.

"She needs the Lord in her life, Jenny," Brother Solomon said. "She's probably got problems of her own."

"Yeah, I imagine so," Jenny agreed.

"Back to you, Caleb," Brother Solomon said, turning his gaze on the young man. "Are you going to control your tongue? If not, you'll have to stay some place by yourself so the students can't hear you."

"Where would he go, Brother Solomon?" Jenny asked.

"I don't know. Maybe sleep in the loft at the dairy barn. That's my first thought."

"How would he climb up the ladder?"

"We can manage that," Brother Solomon replied. "But I'd much rather Caleb associate with the older boys at school." He turned to face Caleb. "You've never been around boys have you?"

"Those people who raised me have a boy named Levi," Caleb answered. "Mostly, he ignored me."

"Are you going to control your tongue?" Brother Solomon persisted.

"Okay. I'll try to control my mouth. But I'm not making any promises."

"Trying is a good start," Brother Solomon said and shifted the gears for

44

a bumpy start. "It won't be easy, son, but you've got to take advantage of this opportunity to learn."

Brother Solomon called him "son." He must like Caleb.

"It hurts to be kicked out of the only home I've ever known," Caleb said. He covered his face with both hands and sighed deeply. "Especially I hate for Mama to be hurt."

"Your mother is a wonderful person," Brother Solomon said. "I can almost promise you she'll help you some way.

"Jenny, why don't you sing a song so we can drive along in peace?" Brother Solomon asked.

"Okay, I'll try 'Amazing Grace'," Jenny answered. She cleared her throat and searched for a note, then started singing.

"That's good, Jenny," Brother Solomon said, putting his left hand over his shoulder, searching for Jenny's hand.

Jenny put her hand on the back of the seat for the tight squeeze Brother Solomon offered.

For several miles down the road, Jenny sang "Amazing Grace" in Choctaw. She realized she must try to keep harmony between Brother Solomon and Caleb. She helped Caleb come out of the smokehouse. She must work hard to keep the peace.

The group was nearing the outskirts of Piney Ridge when Jenny heard the wailing of a siren.

"What's goin' on?" she asked.

"The sheriff is after someone," answered Brother Solomon. "Surely it's not me." He pulled the sedan to the side of the road to let the car pass. Jenny gasped when she saw the vehicle marked "Sheriff" screech to a stop in front of Brother Solomon's sedan.

A man stepped from the car. A holster with a pair of pistols dangled from his waist. He smiled as he swaggered toward the sedan.

"What's happening?" Jenny asked.

The sheriff stood before the window of the sedan. He tossed his car keys in the air and caught them. "Who's that man beside you?" he asked pointing toward Caleb. His wide smile seemed to indicate a pending arrest, triumphant in nature.

45

"Caleb Wade. I'm taking him to Clear Creek Boarding School," answered Brother Solomon. "What's the problem?"

"I got a report that Caleb is wanted for holding a preacher at gunpoint—"

Oh, no. This will throw a monkey wrench into everything, Jenny thought. She sneaked a look at Caleb. He sat as straight as a pine tree, staring into space.

"May I ask who filed the report?" Brother Solomon asked. He gripped the steering wheel till his knuckles turned white. "Surely it wasn't Paul Wade, the man who raised Caleb. He gave me permission to bring him with me."

"No, it was a woman," the sheriff responded. "She seemed to be pretty upset. Like she'd been setting at gunpoint all night."

Brother Solomon laughed. "Oh, that woman dressed like a flapper."

Jenny breathed a sigh of relief and glanced at Caleb. It seemed as if the sheriff's words clipped the cords of terror. He started to relax a bit.

"Dressed like a flapper ?" the sheriff echoed.

"Yes. That woman back in town who seemed to want Caleb punished. She was in a word fight with us—heckling, and trying to stir up the crowd. Probably just wanted to take revenge because she lost the battle." Brother Solomon's shoulders slackened and he breathed deeply. "Here's Caleb." He pointed toward the young man.

The sheriff walked to Caleb's window and peeked in. "Did your pa release you to this man?"

Caleb nodded.

"Where you headed?"

"To boarding school."

"Ain't you a little old for that?"

Brother Solomon leaned toward the sheriff. "He never attended school," he said. "I promised him I'd find someone to teach him. That's where we're headed."

The sheriff took off his hat and scratched his head. "Puts me between a rock and a hard place," he muttered. He pointed toward Caleb's feet. "But

since you're a cripple, I don't see no harm in letting you try to learn." He chewed the eraser on his pencil for a moment. "I'll tell you what I'll do. I'll let you go on to school, but I'm keepin' your name in mind. Don't go pushing your luck." He nodded toward Brother Solomon, "He's your responsibility."

"Thank you," Caleb said. Jenny felt a warm feeling toward Caleb, because she knew humility wasn't high on his meager list of virtues.

"Thank you very much," Brother Solomon said, stretching his right arm across Caleb to shake the sheriff's hand. "I'll do my part."

The sheriff started to walk away, but stopped. "Oh, by the way, that woman you was speaking of—well, she's my sister. I wouldn't be running people down that way if I was you."

When the sheriff left, Brother Solomon's head fell on the steering wheel and he exhaled a long sigh. "Thank You, Dear God," he said. He ground the starter and stomped the clutch. "Let's leave before the sheriff changes his mind." The sedan lurched onto the road. Jenny heard gravel spinning from the rear tires.

After a while, they drove onto the school grounds. Brother Solomon steered the sedan as close to the high school boys' dorm as he could park. He helped Caleb climb out. Then he led him through the door and they disappeared.

Jenny crawled out of the sedan and hopped toward the junior high girls' dorm.

CHAPTER FOUR

Will I make it? Jenny wondered. She raced across the pasture, wanting to dash inside the cabin to let down the window she'd left open several weeks ago. Her wounded foot healed, she almost could outrun a jackrabbit. Near the cabin, she paused for a moment to listen to a banging sound.

Ghosts?

She told herself ghosts didn't live in the cabin. Her mind liked to play games.

She rushed to the porch to see the door swinging back and forth. A big gust of wind slammed it against the wall like it was made of cardboard. She dashed into the cabin and closed the door, pushing the big rock against it. She leaned over for a moment to take in a breath of fresh air. Rising, she turned to the window, but found it already closed. A pretty blue floral curtain covered the glass panes.

Wait a minute! What's going on? Curtains and a cot with a mattress?

Winded from the mad dash across the pasture, Jenny fell onto the bed to rest while she looked at the additions to the cabin. She yearned to snuggle in the feather mattress, but gave herself only a moment's rest. She wanted to celebrate the transformation that had taken place since she left.

She sat on the bedside to survey the room. A chest of drawers stood against the wall. A cot with the feather mattress, pillow, and clean sheets filled half of another wall. A blue floral cloth that matched the curtains covered the table. A Bible rested on the table.

"I'll bet Louisa came to fix up the cabin. It had to be Louisa," Jenny said, walking around the room. She went to the chest and opened a drawer. She reached in to pull out a soft downy garment.

"Diapers and gowns!" she exclaimed spreading a gown on top of the chest. "And baby blankets! This'll sure help some girl who has a baby."

Listening to the rain splash against the window, she turned toward it. She lifted the curtain and watched the big drops make ever-changing designs on the clean glass like the scenes of a kaleidoscope.

Kind of like us human beings. Everybody's different.

The cabin awaited the next person who came to hide from the public,

however unique she might be. It provided comfort for the girl, but Jenny felt sorry for the next frightened Indian maiden who came here to take shelter.

She folded the gown and blankets and stuffed them inside the drawer. She decided to lie down and rest while she waited for the rain to stop. She pulled off her new patent leather slippers, so sand wouldn't sift on the sheets. Before lying down, Jenny glanced at the foot of the bed to see the quilt she'd lain on when she took refuge in the cabin weeks before. She lifted it to notice it had been washed. It smelled of lye soap. She noted that the edges weren't ragged. Someone had sewn up the rips.

The soft snuggly mattress seemed to invite Jenny to take a nap. Her eyelids started to droop and she fought to stay awake. She knew she couldn't allow herself to doze off, so she rose up to sit on the side of the bed. She thought of Caleb's behavior since he'd been at school. He showed off a lot and acted like a raging bull most of the time. She wondered how Sister Wade would react if she knew Caleb teetered on the edge of being kicked out of school. But, he was learning to read and write.

Jenny glanced out the window to see the sun peeking through the rain clouds. Making sure she left everything in place, she slipped on her shoes and pulled the door shut. She tied the leather string to a nail, and pulled hard on the door, to be certain it stayed closed. Now, the wind couldn't whip it back and forth.

Jenny hurried across the pasture toward the boarding school. She wanted to share the secret of the cabin improvements with another person—not for attention—but for giving out information. Brother Solomon, maybe?

Nearing the chapel, Jenny glanced up the road to see two unfamiliar women walking toward the school. Faded cotton dresses seemed glued to their bodies. Strings of hair stuck to their faces. Each woman carried a soggy bag. Jenny couldn't help but gaze at the ladies, comparing their appearance to drowned rats.

"Jenny, is that you?" called one woman, and hurried toward her.

"Yeah it's me, but who are you?" Jenny answered, walking toward the women. Stepping closer, she stopped, shocked to see Sister Wade.

"Sister Wade! What are you doing here?" Jenny called. She ran to meet the women.

"I came to see Caleb," Sister Wade answered. "Watema and me rode the train. Got caught in a shower on the way out."

Sister Wade turned to the woman beside her. "This is Junior's mama, Watema Maytubby. She came along to keep me company."

"Well, if that don't beat a goose 'a gobblin'," Jenny said, trying not to stare at the empty spaces in Watema's teeth. "Y'all come to the dorm with me and dry off. I know Caleb will be glad to see you."

She shuddered at the thought of having to tell Caleb's mama the truth about his behavior.

The women followed Jenny to the dorm. The damp clothes in their bags weren't fitting to wear yet, so Jenny ran off to ask Miss James for help. She wanted to borrow outfits for them to put on while their clothes dried.

"Has Caleb's mother come to take him home?" Miss James asked, frowning. "I sure hope so. We can't tolerate his outrageous behavior much longer."

"I doubt it, Miss James. I think Watema 'n her just came for a visit. Sister Wade has been Caleb's mama all his life. Paul Wade ran Caleb off—that's why Brother Solomon brought him here with us," Jenny said, breathlessly. "Caleb's supposed to learn to read and write."

"Well, I'll see what's going on," Miss James said. She reached into a closet and pulled out wrappers for the women. In a few moments, the three women stood facing each other.

"Miss James, this here is Sister Wade, Caleb's mama. And the other lady is Watema Maytubby, Junior's mama." She turned to the visitors. "And this is Miss James, the matron."

Watema twiddled with the straggles of hair hanging around her face. Sister Wade gazed at a puddle on the floor while she squeezed rainwater from the hem of her dress. Both women mumbled apologies for their appearance.

"We got caught in the rain," explained Watema.

"Ladies, you can step over there and put on the wrappers," Miss James said pointing to a corner. "I'll come in for your wet clothes when you're finished. Just peek out the door and let me know.

"Jenny, come out with me. Let them have their privacy."

Miss James pulled Jenny down the hall. "What are they doing here?" she demanded.

Jenny shrugged. "Beats me. I just noticed them walking down the road while ago."

After a few moments, Watema opened the door. "We're dressed," she said.

Miss James entered the room, and Jenny followed her. "What brings you two out on such a rainy day?" Miss James asked, smiling. Jenny hoped the matron's face wouldn't crack.

"I got lonesome to see Caleb," Sister Wade answered, timidly. "He's lived with us ever since he was a tiny baby. I wanted to see how he's doing. Papa don't know I came. I have to go back home before he catches me gone." She looked at the door. "Watema came along to keep me company."

"I'm sure you're lonesome to see your son. I never had any children, but I know a mother's love is important. With all these children around here crying for their mothers, believe me I know," said Miss James, and sighed loudly. "It'll be time for lunch after a while."

Jenny believed Miss James was struggling to keep from talking about Caleb's bad conduct. Or maybe she wanted to reveal the facts and he'd leave the school for good.

"By then, your dresses will be dry and you can come to the dining room to eat with the students, including Caleb," Miss James continued, her gaze on the bunk beds. "While you wait, I suppose you can stay in the dorm. Maybe Jenny can bring you up to date on Caleb. Later, you can visit in the parlor."

Jenny squirmed. Miss James wasn't playing fair.

"I'll see you ladies at lunch," Miss James said and she disappeared out the door carrying the wet dresses.

"Is Caleb learnin' to read and write?" Sister Wade asked, smiling.

"Yeah, he's learning some," Jenny said, searching for words. "But I just as well tell you, he's causing a lot of trouble."

"How? In what way?"

"He cusses a lot," Jenny said, afraid to look at Sister Wade.

"Oh, no!" Sister Wade exclaimed.

"And he talks back to the teachers," Jenny continued.

"You don't mean it!" Watema said.

"And he keeps the boys in the dorm awake at night when they're suppose to be sleeping." She wanted to add, "Telling ugly stories," but she didn't dare to over do it.

"Oh, my! How can he act like that?" Sister Wade asked, wringing her hands.

"He's teetering on the edge of getting kicked out," Jenny ventured. "I never heard Brother Solomon say so, but I know it's true. Caleb causes lots of trouble."

"He can't leave!" Sister Wade exclaimed. "He don't have no where to go. Papa won't allow him to come home." Tears overflowed and ran down her cheeks. She felt around the wrapper for a handkerchief, but she found none.

"Here, I'll find a handkerchief in my drawer," Jenny said, scurrying to her spot in the dorm. "While you're waiting for your dresses to dry, why don't you lay down? Sister Wade, you can use my bed, and Watema, you lay on the bed next to mine." She pointed to two lower bunks. "I'll go tell Brother Solomon that you're here for a visit." Jenny slipped out the door before the women could protest.

Jenny scurried across the grounds to the chapel, hoping to find Brother Solomon in his office. She knocked at the door and without waiting for a reply she stepped inside.

Brother Solomon looked up, a frown on his face. "Jenny, are you supposed to walk into my office uninvited?"

"No. But this is a emergency."

"Seems like your life runs from one emergency to another. What's the problem now?"

Jenny recognized the irritation in his voice. She must make this convincing.

"Sister Wade came to visit Caleb," Jenny said, watching Brother Solomon

lift his eyebrows in apprehension. "And she brought Junior Maytubby's mama, Watema. What you gonna tell 'em?"

"What can I tell them except the truth? Caleb is misbehaving. Maybe God sent Caleb's mother so she can take him home," Brother Solomon said, sifting through the papers on his desk.

"He can't go home. You know that," Jenny protested. "Miss James said the women can visit Caleb at lunch. What else can they do?"

"Visit with me. Bring them to the office," Brother Solomon said evenly. "We've got to settle Caleb's case."

"Do I have to bring 'em?"

"What did I say?"

"Go bring 'em. I'll do that, but they need to wait till their dresses dry."

I don't want to do this but I will.

Dragging out her steps, Jenny returned to the dorm.

* * *

Brother Solomon sat at his desk, dreading the moment when Watema and Sister Wade stepped inside his office. Perhaps the dresses would take a long time to dry.

"Dear Lord, what do I tell Sister Wade? Please give me an answer," he prayed. "Do I send Caleb home with them? What do I do?"

Much too soon, he looked out the window to see the two bedraggled Indian women coming to the office, escorted by Jenny. He listened to Jenny's knock at the door.

"Come in, ladies. Please be seated. Jenny, you're excused," he said, nodding toward the door.

"But let me interpret for them," Jenny pleaded.

"I don't need an interpreter. Goodbye, Jenny," Brother Solomon said, with finality.

"Sister Wade, glad to see you," Brother Solomon said, extending his hand to shake hers. He watched her stare at the floor.

"And you're Watema?" he asked the other woman.

"Yeah. Junior's mama," Watema answered.

"I performed the wedding for Junior and Hallie," Brother Solomon said, at a loss for words.

"I heard about that. Kind of surprised when Junior came home with a wife and a baby."

"It was a rough time around the school, keeping Louisa and Maria hidden in Betty's room," Brother Solomon said. He noticed her missing front teeth. *She must have been a beauty once, but the empty spaces draw attention from her better features. I think I've seen her before.* "Maybe you can meet Betty while you're here."

"Maybe," Watema answered.

"Now, what can I do for you?"

"Nothing much. We came to visit Caleb," Sister Wade answered, twisting her handkerchief into knots. "Papa's gone out of town and I slipped off to see Caleb. That's all. I need to be home before Papa comes, though. He'd be mad as a' old wet hen if he knew I was here."

"Oh? Paul hasn't gotten over Louisa's problem, has he?"

"He won't listen to nobody," Sister Wade said, shaking her head. "It's already ruined his preaching. He don't preach no more."

Poor woman. She's suffered too much already.

"If he would rely on God, he could keep preaching, but I think he's full of anger and unforgiveness," Brother Solomon ventured. "If Paul doesn't forgive Caleb and Louisa, he may ruin his health."

"And a bunch of other people's health," whispered Sister Wade. "Mostly, Papa just stays closed up in the house. He don't say much, and when he does, he fusses. He wouldn't believe the reason Louisa gave about Caleb being Maria's daddy."

"And now he has Caleb's situation on top of everything else," Brother Solomon added. "Paul does have a heavy load, but God can help him bear it."

"If he just would let God help him," Sister Wade whispered, and dabbed at her eyes.

"He's wallowing in self-pity," Brother Solomon said. "Really, Louisa's

burden is heavier than his—the way she lived in the cabin trying to keep him from finding out the truth."

"Yeah, but you can't tell him that," Sister Wade replied.

"You need to whop him up the side of the head," Watema said. "Wake him up."

Sister Wade laughed. "You don't know Paul Wade, Watema."

"So, have you seen Caleb yet?" asked Brother Solomon, eager to talk about someone else.

"No, we got caught in the rain and had to take time for our clothes to dry," Watema said.

"We are having some problems with Caleb," Brother Solomon admitted, and then he lowered his voice. "He's older than the other students and he knows more about the ways of the world than they do." He hoped Sister Wade didn't hear. He changed the subject abruptly.

"You found him on the steps of the porch one Sunday after church?" Brother Solomon asked.

I knew nothing about it, but I should have.

Sister Wade nodded. "No name, no nothin'. Just a baby wrapped in flour sacks, with his feet tied up in rags. Papa named him after Caleb in the Bible," she said. "We've had him ever since. I guess we spoiled him because of his clubfeet. He didn't want to go to school and he couldn't work, so he just laid around the house. Our other kids helped take care of him."

Brother Solomon watched Watema fidgeting in her chair and gazing out the window. He said, "It's too bad Caleb didn't go to school," he almost choked on the words. He swallowed hard to continue. "He may have learned a trade so he could help pay his way."

He looked at the clock above his desk. Good, time for lunch. He couldn't take much more of this conversation. He saw Jenny dashing across the lawn. He stood to open the door.

"Ladies, Jenny is here to take you to lunch. We'll talk after you've finished eating," he said, relieved to excuse the women. "I'll eat later. I need to study for a while."

Brother Solomon watched Jenny lead the women out the door and head toward the dining room.

What now, Dear Lord?

He picked up a scrap of paper and folded it into a kite shape and sailed it across the room. He watched it fall to the floor.

That's how I feel right now—like a kite, destined to crash land. I'll fail after while unless I come up with a place for Caleb to stay.

Walking to pick up the paper kite, he noticed a piece of jewelry on the floor. Looking closely, he noticed it spelled "Mother" in fancy letters. Leaves were intertwined in the letters. He lifted the inexpensive pin and looked it over. The bent clasp wouldn't stay fastened.

He knew why someone had lost it—the loose fastener. Perhaps it belonged to Sister Wade. Maybe one of her grown children gave it to her. It could be Watema's but probably not. Did Junior give the pin to her?

Brother Solomon scrutinized the piece of jewelry carefully and slipped it into his pocket. His fingers touched a chain. What could it be?

He lifted the chain to withdraw the necklace he'd borrowed from Hallie.

"Oh, I forgot the locket! I'll have to give it back to Hallie." He opened the locket, hoping to see his smiling face from long ago. He felt his heart sinking when he gazed at two empty spaces. He snapped the locket shut and looked at the engravings on it -flowers, leaves, and a fancy border. "This is the locket I bought for Alta. Too bad the pictures are gone." He dropped the necklace back into his pocket. "I must not misplace this again," he reminded himself.

When the women returned from lunch, he'd show the pin to them to see if one of them had lost it. He sat in the chair before his desk. Thoughtlessly, he picked up a pencil and began to doodle.

After drawing hearts with flowers on the paper, he pulled the brooch from his pocket and tried to copy "Mother" in the same decorative letters. Neither of the mothers who just left seemed to fit the elegant writing. They were plain, simple, hard-working women, who'd sacrificed to buy tickets. They rode the train to come visit Caleb while they had a few spare hours. He knew Sister Wade risked a lot to come. If Paul returned home before she did, she'll be in for a tongue-lashing. What if she went home with Caleb and they both got thrown out?

Brother Solomon dropped the pencil in disgust. He would not send Caleb back to an anger-filled home. Caleb overflowed with rage even now. No, he must be placed in a peaceful environment so he could recover from the trauma in his life.

But where would he put Caleb? Not in the hayloft because he couldn't climb up and down the ladder. Nor in Betty's room, like Louisa did. No, that wouldn't be ethical. But if Betty moved in with someone else, Caleb might sleep in her room for a while. Brother Solomon walked to the window to gaze out. The tall pines stood motionless and the petunias bloomed brightly, washed clean by the rain. On the surface everything appeared peaceful, but he knew a battle raged in the hearts of at least two people. A lot of the blame lay on his shoulders.

Why not take him into your bedroom? The Holy Spirit nudged.

Brother Solomon wondered how to accomplish his duties if he slept in the hayloft, but refusing to keep Caleb was not an option. Caleb could stay in his apartment like Junior and Hallie did when they married. That answered the question. He'd invite Caleb to live with him. They'd grow better acquainted. Brother Solomon breathed a sigh of relief and raised his hands in victory. Now, to go eat lunch with the women. He wouldn't mention thinking about sending Caleb home.

He closed his eyes and prayed aloud, "Thank You, Lord. You are in control."

Brother Solomon hurried to the dining room. Right off, he saw Sister Wade sitting beside Caleb, smiling at him. Watema sat on the opposite side of him. Caleb looked from one woman to the other, scowling at them. Brother Solomon slid onto a bench across from the trio, feeling comfortable about joining in on the conversation.

"Are y'all having a good visit, ladies?" He turned to Caleb. "I'll bet you're surprised your mama came to visit you."

Caleb grunted, then stuffed a large piece of sweet potato in his mouth.

"After you've finished eating, we'll all go back to my office and talk," Brother Solomon said. "Caleb, I want you to come with us."

In a few moments, Brother Solomon sat at his desk, across from the three people. He cleared his throat and launched into his speech. "I have decided that you, Caleb, will move into my apartment for a while."

Sister Wade gasped and covered her face with her hands. "Thank You, Lord," she whispered. "Caleb don't have to go home."

Caleb frowned. "Why stay with you?" he asked.

"Because you say words that our boys don't need to hear."

"I don't say nothing they don't know already," argued Caleb.

"Yes, they may know them, but they aren't allowed to use them while they're here. I want you to stay with me till you can clean up your language," Brother Solomon answered evenly. "I'll ask an older boy to take your things to my apartment after a while.

"And now, ladies," he asked, reaching into his pocket to lift out the pin, "did either of you lose this when you were here earlier?" He held the brooch in his hand.

"It's mine," Watema said, reaching for the pin.

"No, it's mine," Sister Wade argued. "Louisa gave it to me for Christmas last year."

"Junior gave it to me last Christmas," Watema said.

"Wait a minute," Brother Solomon interrupted. "Did you both bring the pins with you today?"

He watched both women nod.

"I had mine pinned on my dress right here," Sister Wade said. She touched a place on her garment. "See, it's gone."

"I had mine in my pocket," Watema said. She reached inside her pocket and shamefacedly, lifted out the pin. "Why, I still have it."

"I told you it was mine," Sister Wade said, with a twisted smile. "I'm sure glad you found it, Brother Solomon. Maybe Papa can straighten the fastener so I won't lose it again." She reached for the pin.

"I'll fix it," said Caleb and grabbed it from Brother Solomon. Before anyone could protest, Caleb twisted the clasp off the pin and threw it across the room.

"There. It's fixed," he said, glaring at Sister Wade.

"Caleb! Why'd you do that?" Sister Wade asked, tears welling in her eyes.

"Are you through with me?" Caleb asked. His icy black stare drilled a hole through Brother Solomon's heart.

My son, my son.

"I'm leaving this council meeting." He grabbed his crutches and pulled his body upright. Awkwardly he clomped out of the office.

Brother Solomon watched Caleb leave the room. He sighed wearily and slumped forward in his chair. "Sister Wade, you see what we're putting up with. Caleb is not cooperating."

Sister Wade stood, gathering her skirt about her. "I guess we've done all we can. I finished losing a son. Watema, let's go catch the train. Come on."

"Wait a minute," Brother Solomon said, raising his hand. "Didn't you bring some things in your bags? Don't forget them. While you walk over to pick them up, I'll bring my sedan and then drive you back to the depot."

Jenny ran across the lawn to stop him. "What's Caleb going to do?"

"For the time being, he'll stay with me," said Brother Solomon. "It may not work, but I must try it."

"Maybe it will," Jenny responded and ran toward Brother Solomon's housing.

Later, when the women climbed into the sedan, Brother Solomon noticed Sister Wade still clutching the pin with the fancy letters and vines entwined on it.

Poor Sister Wade. She's had too many burdens on her shoulders.

CHAPTER FIVE

After he returned from the depot, Brother Solomon found Caleb.

"I promised Sister Wade you'd stay with me for a while," he said. "So let's get you moved."

He walked beside Caleb as the cripple dragged himself to the preacher's apartment. Brother Solomon felt the air around them saturated with dissension, ready for lightning to strike at any moment.

"This is my set of rooms," Brother Solomon said, stepping ahead of Caleb to open the door. "You sleep in that room over there." He pointed to a door to his right. "When my relatives visit, that's where they sleep. Make yourself comfortable. I need to go to the office."

Brother Solomon left Caleb alone while he returned to his office. He made an attempt to straighten the papers on his desk, but the scene between Caleb and the two women kept playing out before him. Caleb damaging Sister Wade's pin. Caleb's hostility toward the two women. Sister Wade's sacrifice to ride the train to Clear Creek to visit with Caleb and he treated her like dirt. It pained his heart.

Caleb's moving in with him probably wouldn't work. What else could he do? He believed the young man was his son and he had a responsibility to help care for him.

The preacher picked up the piece of paper on which he'd written "Mother" in fancy scroll. Copying the same style he wrote, "Father." A lump moved into his throat. Fine father he'd been. He'd run out on Alta and never looked back. *Never?* He had reflected on his actions often. Wonder where Alta lived today? Probably the mother of a dozen kids. Maybe some even attended the boarding school. He needed to look closely at them to see if any resembled Caleb.

"Not in behavior, please Lord," he prayed.

He feared Caleb was determined the arrangement wouldn't work. Brother Solomon was determined it would work. He'd just have to steel himself against the sarcasm and the cursing. Surely there'd be an opportunity to emphasize the need for living a purer life. Caleb would watch every move Brother Solomon made. And then ridicule it. He looked up to see Jenny dashing across the lawn, followed by several other wide-eyed students.

"What's she up to now?" he asked, rising from his chair. He stepped to the door to learn the nature of the problem he'd face next.

"Brother Solomon, hurry! Caleb's tearin' up your apartment," Jenny shouted and ran back toward the building.

"What's going on?" Brother Solomon asked the students who lingered near.

Eugene shrugged. "We don't know. We just heard a lot of noise in your rooms."

"Yeah. Loud banging noises," added Pauline.

"Thanks, I'm on my way," Brother Solomon said and trotted toward the dorm.

He pushed the dorm door open and he heard loud whamming sounds resounding through the hall. What was Caleb up to now? He ran the rest of the way.

When he opened the door, he saw Caleb swinging a hammer, beating on a chair. Caleb didn't stop hammering, just continued to wham, wham away at the chair. The seat bounced in the air after each pounding.

"What are you doing?" demanded Brother Solomon, reaching for the hammer.

"Oh, no you don't," Caleb responded, pulling the tool from Brother Solomon's reach. "I don't want to stay here. I'm just showin' you what you're gonna have to put up with. And I ain't givin' up, neither." He swung the hammer again. A wicked grin covered his face. "Don't come any closer. I'll smash your face in." He held the hammer up, waving it back and forth.

Brother Solomon raised his hands in surrender. "Okay, okay. The message is clear. You don't want to live in the room with me. But you must stay somewhere. Even if it's in the county jail."

"Did Mama tell you they found me on the steps of the church? Did she say I was wrapped in a flour sack?" Caleb demanded. He held the hammer close to Brother Solomon's face. "And that I had rags wrapped around my feet? Did she tell you that? Why would anybody in the shape like I'm in want to live? Tell me." He raised a tow sack-wrapped foot to emphasize his problem. "Just look at that."

"You didn't get off to a good start," Brother Solomon admitted. He watched for a chance to grab the weapon. "But just think. Sister Wade loved you. You know that. I'm sure she did lots of special things for you, like make cherry pies. I know you like those."

"Everbody likes cherry pie. So name something else she did for me."

"I figure she rubbed your feet when they hurt. Didn't she?"

"Yeah. I have to admit she rubbed these crippled feet," Caleb answered, sighing.

"And she read stories to you. She protected you from people who teased you and made fun of you like—"

I have an idea that may work. Can we fool him? He's pretty upset.

"Don't leave, I've got to see someone for a minute," Brother Solomon said, stepping out the door. He found Jenny in the hall where he suspected she'd be. He motioned for her to step inside the next room. He put his finger to his lips. "Sh-h-h," he whispered. He pulled Jenny to his side.

"Remember that flapper back at the smokehouse? I want you to stand in the hall and yell things like she did," Brother Solomon whispered. "Pretend you're that woman."

Jenny nodded.

"Maybe you can bring Caleb to his senses. You've got to try. Do your best, Little Lady."

"I don't know if I can," Jenny protested.

"And I don't either, but we've got to do something. So, put on the best show of your life out there in the hall," begged Brother Solomon.

"Okay, I'll try."

Brother Solomon stepped back inside his room. "Why don't you lie down across the bed and try to control yourself?" he asked Caleb. "You're all worked up."

"Why don't *you* lay down across the bed?" Caleb asked, mimicking Brother Solomon's speech. "You're—." Loud giggling in the hall interrupted him.

Thank you, Jenny.

Caleb looked toward the door.

"Yeah. I think you're right, Cowboy. Got yer rope handy? Step in the door and rope that cripple. He ain't good fer nothin'. Such as him needs to be locked in the smokehouse and left to—"

"Who's that?" Caleb asked, cocking his head.

Brother Solomon shrugged. "Sounds like that smart-aleck woman who said you couldn't learn," he answered.

Jenny giggled loudly. "Yeah, it's me. You told me that cripple was gonna go to school and learn to read and write and then he'd write me a letter. I ain't got it yet." She giggled again.

"Get her out of here before I come after her with this hammer!" Caleb yelled.

"Ha! You couldn't ketch me. And you couldn't throw straight. Come on, cowpoke, start swingin' yer rope," Jenny mocked. "I ain't got my letter yet. He promised to send me a letter."

"And I asked if you could read," Caleb yelled. "Have you learned to read yet?"

"As much as you have," Jenny answered, giggling hysterically. "Where's that Miss Priss who was tryin' to set you free back at the smokehouse? I wish she was here. I wish I could see her smilin' face, I'd bash it in. I'd tell her a thing or two."

"Oh, yeah? Somebody go find Jenny and let her set the lady straight," answered Caleb.

Jenny, can you play both parts? I hope so.

"I think Jenny's somewhere around. See if you can find Jenny, somebody," Brother Solomon called.

"She's afraid to show that skinny face," Jenny answered, imitating the voice of the flapper. "If she was here I'd show her a thing or two. You said you was writin' me a letter. When should I look fer it?"

"Like you said, when Red River freezes over in July. Go back to your cotton pickin' business," Caleb said.

"Where's that gal? I want a' see her. Is she still tryin' to pretend she's clubfooted?"

"That girl is my friend, so shut your mouth," Caleb answered. He handed the hammer to Brother Solomon. "Here. Take the hammer. I'm tired of listening to that sassy woman. I'm going to tear her apart with my bare hands." He grabbed for his crutches.

Brother Solomon reached for the crutches before Caleb got to them.

"That won't work. It'll just get you deeper into trouble. Let me handle this." Carrying the crutches, Brother Solomon stepped into the hall. "I'll send that woman 'a packing." He yelled, "Leave right this minute. And don't you or your cowboy friend come back. Jenny, ask some senior boys to escort her off the school grounds."

Brother Solomon stepped back into his room and retrieved the hammer. He glanced around; aware if Caleb wanted to use another weapon he'd find something, if nothing more than the leg of a chair.

"Why don't you rest a while, Caleb? You've been through a lot. I'll be back after while. I'll see to it that the lady leaves the school property."

"After what I've been through, you think I can rest?" Caleb asked. "You rest for both of us. You're a old man."

Brother Solomon felt resentment rising in him. After all he'd done for Caleb, why didn't his son show appreciation? *Why didn't I show concern for him earlier?* He chose to ignore Caleb's sarcasm and stepped into the hall to see Jenny. He winked at her and motioned for her to follow him. Outside, he gave her a tight squeeze. "Perfect, Jenny, just perfect."

Jenny returned the hug and smiled broadly. "You think we fooled him?"

"It worked, didn't it? This time."

What about the next time?

When Brother Solomon returned to his room, he smiled to himself. Caleb was lying on the bed with his eyes closed. The tow sacks lay in a heap on the floor. Seeing his grotesque bare feet pointing in odd angles caused Brother Solomon to wince in pain. He looked from the misshapen feet to Caleb's robust arms. In them, his son held a wrinkled envelope. Looking closely, he noticed it was a letter from Sister Wade. What kind of heart beat behind that hateful mouth?

Please God, let it be gentle.

CHAPTER SIX

"I need to study for the sermon Sunday morning," Brother Solomon prodded himself a few days later. "The last few weeks have been so hectic, I can't think about preaching."

He thumbed through his Bible, searching for an appropriate text. He wanted to teach the students the importance of showing kindness to those who weren't shaped from the same mold as them. Crippled, high-strung folks, like Caleb.

Brother Solomon knew everyone is different in some ways. Like Jenny with mood swings from happiness to depression. If he scanned the list of students, he'd see that everyone had his own quirks. But Caleb bothered him the most. If he kept on having temper tantrums, somebody would be hurt. And the sheriff might come without anyone needing to call him.

He glanced down at a page of his open Bible. He read a few lines, when a verse, like a bolt of lightning, struck him between the eyes. Slowly he read, "'Master, who did sin, this man, or his parents, that he was born blind?'"

This man was born blind! Caleb was born a cripple!

"Master, what sin caused Caleb to be born a cripple?" Brother Solomon prayed softly. "I know both parents sinned, but why did he have to be a cripple?"

He read the next verse. "Neither hath this man sinned, nor his parents: but that the works of God should be made manifest in him."

Brother Solomon expelled a tremulous breath. "For the works of God to be made manifest would take a miracle! How can they be made visible in Caleb? A colossal change must occur for Him to be evident in my son."

All things are possible if you only believe.

"Yes, Lord I know that," Brother Solomon answered. He cradled his head in his arms to mull over the words. For God to be displayed through Caleb would require a personal experience to take place between both parties. Caleb would need to be born again.

"These words are straight from God," he said, folding his hands in a prayerful pose and raising his eyes heavenward. "Thank You, Dear Lord."

The pastor felt the purpose Caleb lived with him was for his son to see a higher standard of living, encouraging change. Brother Solomon knew he must be careful the way he acted so that Caleb saw his actions, instead of listening to talk.

Brother Solomon slowly turned the pages. He wanted to read about handicapped Bible characters. He found several verses, but the one he wished to find was about the man who was cripple from birth. After a while, he found the section in Acts 3:2-6 and read silently.

"H-m-m-m, a man lame from his mother's womb—just like Caleb. He was healed. He praised God. That's what I'm asking—for Caleb to praise God. Can Caleb do that without a physical healing?" Brother Solomon meditated on the verses for several moments, then closed his Bible. "Thank You for the lesson today," he whispered.

He chose to preach this Sunday on the Golden Rule. "Do unto others as you would have them do unto you." He believed he could go any direction with the verse.

Quickly, he wrote an outline for the sermon, closed his Bible and walked toward his apartment. What should he expect? Had Caleb been on a rampage?

He was almost to his room when he felt a tug on his sleeve. He turned to see Jenny.

"I know a place for Caleb to stay that won't cause you as much trouble as it is for him to live here," Jenny said.

"Where's that?"

"In the cabin where Louisa stayed," Jenny answered.

Brother Solomon smiled. "Now, Jenny, that doesn't make sense," he said.

"Maybe not. But I ran over there one mornin' before it started rainin'. I had to let down the window. And guess what?"

"I can't keep up with you," Brother Solomon said, and smiled. "What do you mean?"

"The cabin is neat and clean and there's a bed and lots of stuff for the next girl who stays. But why couldn't Caleb live there while he's tryin' to work through his problems?"

"I'll need to look into it. You went over because of the rain?" Brother Solomon asked, furrows wrinkling his brow.

"Yeah. I remembered I'd left the window up that day I jumped out and cut my foot. And I—"

"Okay. You went over to close the window and saw a lot of nice things?"

"Louisa has probably been over there fixin' it up," Jenny said.

"I wouldn't be surprised, but why didn't she visit me? Maybe I was away. But, let's sleep on it. This has been a long tiring day and Caleb's settled down for the moment," Brother Solomon said, frowning again. "He was asleep when I left."

"After class tomorrow can we go and look the place over?"

Jenny, will you ever grow up?

"Yes. We can," Brother Solomon said.

"You did good on your flapper act. The next time we have a play, you need to be in it."

"You really think so?" Jenny wrapped her arms around her waist, swaying from side to side. "If you do, I'll ask to be in the next play production."

"You were outstanding. Good evening, Jenny."

* * *

A few days later, Brother Solomon was sitting at his desk when Jenny dashed in, unannounced.

That girl! Always needing attention.

"Brother Solomon, guess who's coming down the road? It's a woman and it's not Sister Wade. Who do you think it is?"

"The only other woman I can think of is Watema."

Watema! But why her?

In a few minutes, someone knocked at the door of his office. Brother Solomon raised his eyebrows and whispered, "Watema?"

Jenny nodded.

Brother Solomon answered the door. "Watema, what a surprise! Come in and have a seat."

Watema perched on the edge of a chair and dropped the paper bag she carried. Wordlessly, she dug inside her pocket and pulled out a letter. She handed it to Brother Solomon.

"Jenny, you're excused. Leave us alone," Brother Solomon said. He glanced at the piece of jewelry pinned to Watema's dress.

Mother

He turned toward Jenny. "Go back to the dorm. I have business to attend to."

Jenny's shoulders slumped; her body drooped like a stalk of wilted celery. Slowly, she backed out of the office.

Brother Solomon opened the envelope and read the message.

"Let Watema stay in the cabin and take care of Caleb if that's all right.

Yours truly,

Sister Wade."

"This is news! How does Sister Wade know about the cabin?"

"Louisa."

"Why did you and Sister Wade decide for you to stay at the cabin with Caleb?" he asked.

"Sister Wade knows Caleb's a big problem. He can't move back home. I don't have no man, so she asked me stay at the cabin and see after him—if that's okay," Watema said.

"If that don't beat a goose 'a gobblin' and the hens 'a peckin'." exclaimed Brother Solomon. "I don't know what to say. You caught me by surprise. Let me think this over." He pulled his handkerchief from his pocket and mopped his brow.

"I'll need to talk to Miss James, the matron, about it. For now, leave your bag here and I'll take you to the kitchen to meet Betty."

Brother Solomon arose and waited for Watema to follow him. They started toward the dining room.

In a few minutes, Brother Solomon was introducing Watema to Betty. "Watema wants to help with Caleb. So, why don't you bring a cup of coffee for yourself and her, and you two get acquainted? I need to check with Caleb's teachers."

He left to call together the teachers, but not before he heard Betty say, "You don't know what you're askin' for. That Caleb is a problem."

Turning back, he saw Watema smiling and nodding. "Yeah. I hear he's a wild buck, but I'm ready to try. I have a son. His name is Lewis Maytubby, Jr."

"Oh, the boy who married Hallie. So you have a granddaughter, don't you?"

"Granddaughter a big surprise—"

Brother Solomon heard no more. After a quick meeting with Miss James and a few other teachers, he found all in agreement with the arrangement. They seemed relieved that Caleb be removed from the younger students. "There are some problems we'll need to work through, but maybe this is an answer to prayer."

He pulled Miss James to one side to speak with her privately. "Miss James, I was looking at this necklace when Caleb was causing trouble. I forgot to return it to Hallie. Will you keep it in a safe place till I have a chance to return it?"

He handed her the locket.

"I'll put it away," Miss James answered.

Now, to send Watema to the cabin.

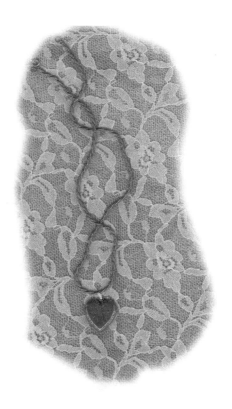

CHAPTER SEVEN

The next day, Watema watched Jim pound nails into the walls at the cabin. He twisted a wire around them to partition off a section by hanging a sheet across the room. Behind the sheet was a space for Caleb's cot. Jim tromped to the wagon to unload the cot and set it up. He brought in food supplies while Jenny waltzed around, showing Watema the chest of drawers for storing her belongings and Caleb's clothes, and other important items in the shanty.

This furniture is better than any thing I ever saw, Watema thought.

"Do you have any questions before we leave?" Jim asked.

"None that I know of," answered Watema.

"Okay, Jenny, let's go."

"But I don't want to go," Jenny objected. "I want to help Watema put everything up."

Jim put his hands on his hips and heaved a sigh. "Brother Solomon said for you to come back with me."

"Oh, all right. I guess some teacher will either come over to teach Caleb or take him to class," Jenny said to Watema as she climbed into the wagon with Jim. "Bye Watema. Bye Caleb."

Watema watched the wagon until a grove of trees enveloped it. A squeamish feeling flitted around in her stomach. How would she and Caleb accept each other?

With that high temper of his, there's no telling how we'll make it. But I promised Sister Wade I'd give it a try.

"How you going to spend your time when you ain't studyin'?" Watema asked. "Would you like for Brother Solomon to bring a hound over so you'd have a dog for a pet?"

"What's it to you, Ol' Snaggletooth?"

A pain like an icicle shot through her heart. She dropped to her knees before Caleb. "Hold it, Crip. Don't you dare call me Ol' Snaggletooth again. You hear?"

"With your front teeth gone, I'd say you was a snaggle tooth," Caleb answered. He laughed sarcastically and threw a stick into the yard.

A twinge of sorrow melted the icicle. "I can't help it because my teeth are out," she said, covering her mouth. "Treat me like you would talk to your mama."

"I don't know how'd I treat my mama since I never saw her to know who she is."

"How would you treat Sister Wade?" Watema paused for a second, and then she frowned. "Maybe that's not a good idea. You yanked the fastener off her pin the other day and throwed it across the room. You didn't know that Junior gave me this pin and Louisa gave Sister Wade a pin just like it for Christmas, did you?" She touched one of the flowers decorating the pin fastened on her faded dress.

"What do I care? What did I get for Christmas? Clean rags to tie around my feet?"

"Sister Wade said they gave you a carvin' knife to use in your whittling."

"Yeah. Gettin' me ready to set out on the street corner holdin' a tin cup and sellin' whistles and flutes."

"Ever time I go to town, I see a crippled beggar settin' on the street. It's nothin' to be ashamed of." Watema arose and walked to the chest of drawers. She set her clothes on top of the chest and she started sorting through them.

"It'll just give more people a chance to see my crippled feet and gawk at me," Caleb answered and choked.

This hurts him real bad. Wonder why his feet turned out like they did? Watema thought.

"It looks like we're gonna have some deep discussions while I'm here, so I guess I better put on my thinkin' cap," Watema said. She opened a drawer and slipped her underwear inside.

"If you can answer my questions, you're a genius."

"You know I ain't no genius, but while you're whittling, I'll be thinkin'. Which reminds me, we'll need to ask somebody to bring some holler sticks for you to whittle on. What do you make?" Forgetting to cover her mouth, Watema smiled.

"Whistles and flutes, mostly, Ol' Sn—,"

Watema bounced in front of Caleb's face. "What did I tell you? You don't be callin' me bad names. Look at—." She covered her mouth.

I almost called him a cripple.

"Look at what, Ol—?"

Watema stood up and walked to the chest of drawers. "Sorry. We both got off on the wrong foot, Caleb. Don't talk about my missin' teeth and I won't mention your crippled feet." She touched the drawer below hers. "This is where you keep your clothes."

Caleb nodded.

"Let's set out on the porch for a while. Maybe we'll see some deer," Watema said, reaching for a chair. She started pulling it through the door. "Do you want a chair or are you gonna set on the floor?"

"I'm used to settin' on the floor, so that'll do. When somebody brings the sticks, I'll probably set out here and whittle or set under that tree," Caleb said, nodding toward a pine tree.

* * *

Jenny felt a bitter taste rising in her throat as she bounced along in the wagon. Why couldn't she stay around at the cabin to help Watema and Caleb adjust to living there? It wasn't fair to be shut off from the excitement. Hadn't she told Brother Solomon about the cabin being fixed up? Wasn't she the one who saw Sister Wade and Watema walking down the road that rainy day? Didn't she take them to the dorm and help them find dry clothes to put on?

She knew that's the way a few grownups treated orphans who didn't have parents to take up for them. Everybody picked on her, including Brother Solomon. He was good in his way, but sometimes he didn't treat the students fair.

"You need to go back to school, Jenny," Jim said, slapping at the horses with the reins. "No use to sulk. You've been out of class for an extra hour already."

Who said I was sulking?

Jenny folded her arms across her chest and stuck out her lower lip. She felt it trembling but she didn't weep. She wouldn't give Jim the satisfaction of seeing her cry. She'd wait till she got to the dorm to start sobbing. Then

75

she'd show Brother Solomon. She'd do something to make him sorry he picked on her. She tried to think of the wildest way to protest. If she ran away and hid and went missing like Hallie, Brother Solomon would organize search parties to look for her. Perhaps she'd slip back to the cabin tonight, but walking in the dark might be scary. Lots of ideas played around in her head while she finished riding to the boarding school. It was just a question of choosing the one that shocked Brother Solomon the most. She'd decide . . .

She jumped from the wagon before the horses completely stopped. Like a frightened rabbit, she dashed to her room and jumped on her bunk. She dove under the quilt then she covered her head and lay still for a few moments, trying to decide on which plan to scare Brother Solomon the worst. What would make him sorry he picked on her? Nobody really liked her anyway. Why should she even try to help Watema and Caleb?

She tugged at her pillow, and stuck a clenched fist under her cheek. Soon, she felt tears trickle down the side of her face. That's the way orphans got treated. Other students received attention before the strays. If her brothers lived here, they'd take up for her. But they stayed at another boarding school for boys. Why study and make good grades? Didn't Brother Solomon appreciate the act she put on to fool Caleb? He said he did.

Relaxing her fist, Jenny stifled a yawn. She wouldn't let herself go to sleep in the bunk bed. She'd go somewhere and hide, right now. Jumping from the bed, Jenny darted out the door and down the hall. She headed for the dairy barn. No use to worry about being found. The dairy boys would see her when they clambered to the loft to throw down hay. In a few moments, Jenny climbed the ladder. She felt around for the softest spot in the straw and lay down to go to sleep, but the worrisome thoughts came back like mice nibbling on cheese. She had nothing to live for really. Maybe it would scare the teachers if they found one of the students not breathing. Perhaps they'd treat the others with more love.

I'll just hold my breath till I die.

Jenny inhaled a deep breath, determined not to take another. While the students looked under the shrubs and behind the trees, she'd be lying in the hay no longer breathing. She could just see Brother Solomon climbing the steps and stopping in disbelief when he found her. He'd grab her wrist and feel for her heartbeat. He'd put his finger below her nose to feel her breath. She'd be lying there, unmoving, pale in death. Oh, it was awful. She let out a heart-wrenching sob. Unintentionally, she inhaled another breath.

One more breath won't hurt.

She took another huge breath, determined that it was her last. After a few seconds, her insides started to ache. She felt as if her lungs would explode.

Is this what it feels like when a person is smotherin' to death?

Her head started getting dizzy. She sat up, trying to glance down at the floor. One last look before she died. Strange, she hadn't planned for her last scene to be a dark old smelly barn. Well, one place was as good as another. She fell back, holding her breath. This was it. She felt tears trickling down her cheeks.

Jenny told herself, they'd be sorry when they found her. But who would preach her funeral? Her brothers wouldn't know how to handle the arrangements. Maybe Samuel—he preached Mama's funeral service. She knew her brothers would really be crying. They'd fall on her grave after the services. Then who would be left to take care of them?

More tears streamed from her eyes. She started to sob, unexpectedly taking another breath. She fell back on the hay. She cried and sobbed till she felt exhausted. Maybe she should keep on breathing for her brothers' sake. So far, no one had come looking for her and she was still alive. Maybe she should put this off till another time. Well, next time she'd be certain the students would search for her. Better go back to her room now. Wiping away the traces of tears, she climbed down the ladder and out of the barn. She slipped from one shrub to the other till she reached the dorm. She sneaked to the room. Falling into bed, she didn't try to stifle the yawn. She curled up, ready to go to sleep.

* * *

Brother Solomon arose when he heard a knock at the door. Opening it, he saw a distraught Miss James. She alternated between wringing her hands and clasping her cheeks.

"What's wrong, Miss James?"

"The teachers say Jenny hasn't come to a single class today. Do you know where she is?"

"She went with Jim to take Watema and Caleb to the cabin," Brother Solomon said. "I told her to come back with Jim. You don't suppose she slipped out and ran off to the cabin?"

"I don't know. Should we send someone over to the cabin to check? She is so unpredictable, I never know what she'll do next."

"She hasn't gotten completely over her mother's death. We need to make allowances for that," Brother Solomon said, rubbing his brow. "When she does show up, let me take care of her. I think she'll be here in time to eat."

"And on your way back, stop at the dorm. She's probably in her bed sulking. Jim told me she seemed upset because he made her come back with him."

"Thank you, Brother Solomon."

"Jenny, what are you up to now?" Brother Solomon asked aloud, after the door closed. He paced back and forth for a short time. "Just to be sure, I'll go see for myself."

In a few moments, Brother Solomon saw Miss James backing out the door of the dorm room. She nodded and smiled.

"Sleeping like a baby," she whispered.

CHAPTER EIGHT

Brother Solomon handed Jenny a bundle of reeds.

"Take these to Caleb over at the cabin. They're for him to use in his whittling," he said. "Be back in an hour."

"Thanks. I'm glad to go see Watema and Caleb," Jenny replied, taking the bundle from the preacher.

In no time, Jenny waded through the tall grass, trying to keep goat heads from clinging to her clothes. She walked briskly, wondering about her next challenge. She wanted to teach Caleb to read and write, but Brother Solomon had chosen Mr. McElroy to do that.

I know Caleb can be downright ornery when he sets his head to it. Like when he don't get his way, he'll pitch a fit. If a person wants to hit it off with Caleb, they have to play by his rules.

Walking so fast caused Jenny to work up a sweat. She decided to rest under a cedar while she thought out the next move she'd take. She leaned low to creep under the sweeping branches of the tree. Suddenly, she felt her eyes bulging almost out of their sockets. Before her lay a sleeping child curled up in the shelter, holding a stuffed bear. A piece of stiff paper lay on the ground beside him. Strings had been poked through holes in the paper and a message was written on it. Jenny grabbed the paper. She sank to the ground to keep from falling. Her hands trembled, causing the words to dance like Indians at a Pow Wow. Slowly, the message came into focus, but the crudely scrawled lettering was hard for her to make out.

Name: Austin Lincoln.
Born: September 29, 1919

After figuring a few moments, she realized the boy was five years old—too young to go to school. What was this all about? She noticed a bag stuffed with clothes thrown nearby. Had Austin run away from home? What was going on?

The paper fell from Jenny's hands. Her heart started running away with itself. What should she do? Hide the boy? Take him to Brother Solomon? She felt tears stinging her eyes because the sleeping child reminded her so much of her youngest brother, Kenny. Did Kenny ever become so lonesome he wanted to run away? No one from his school had told her if he ever tried to slip away.

Jenny touched the dark hair curling about Austin's ear. His thick eyelashes lay like a tiny fan on his dark-skinned cheek. He moved. Turning loose of the bear, he tucked both hands beneath his face while he lay on the side of his head. Such a sweet boy! How did he end up under the cedar tree? What should she do with him? Take him to the school or to the cabin? She sat under the bows and thought for a while.

What if I hadn't taken that breath while I was in the hayloft? I couldn't have helped Austin. I'm glad I'm alive. I'll try to treat him like he's one of my brothers.

After a while, Austin stirred. His long eyelashes fluttered open and he turned to look at Jenny.

"Am I at school?" Austin asked, pushing himself to a sitting position.

"Yes, you're close. What are you doing here under the tree?"

"I was 'fraid." His lower lip trembled. Tears shimmered on his eyelids.

"It's okay," Jenny said, taking his hand. "I'll take you to school. Why do you have this piece of paper?" She picked it up.

"It's got my name on it to give to the teacher."

"Your name is Austin?"

Austin nodded in agreement. He wiped tears from his cheeks with his free hand.

"Lucy put me on a bus and sent me to school. Said give the paper to teacher. I brought my clothes." He reached over and pulled the bag toward him.

Jenny's heart felt like a horse was stampeding across her chest. What should she do? She looked at the bag of reeds for Caleb. Maybe she and Austin should go to the cabin first. "We'll go to school, but first I need to take these sticks to somebody at a cabin. You can leave your clothes here."

Austin picked up the paper and pulled the string over his head. He grabbed his bag of clothes and the Teddy bear.

"Why don't you leave those here till we come back?"

Austin shook his head and squeezed the bag to his chest. "No. Lucy'll get mad."

"We'll come back and pick them up in a few minutes. Leave them here."

"No. Lucy said give them to teacher." He started to whimper.

"Oh, all right, but they'll be real heavy before we go back to school," Jenny said, giving in.

As they walked past a clump of Indian paintbrushes, Austin stopped to break off a few stems. He dropped the flowers on top of the clothes in the bag.

"For teacher," Austin said. He smiled hesitantly. "Does teacher like flowers?"

"She'll like them," Jenny said, nodding.

Several minutes later, the two reached the cabin. Jenny saw Caleb sitting on the porch. Watema sat in a chair nearby. It looked as if Caleb were whittling. The big question in her mind was: Will Caleb pitch a fit? Will he calm down when he sees I've brought some reeds for him to whittle?

When Watema looked toward Jenny and Austin, she jumped from the chair and ran toward them. "Who's this?" she asked, touching Austin's head. He shrank away from her.

"Tell Watema your name," Jenny instructed.

"Is this the school? Are you my teacher?" Austin asked. He stared at Watema.

Jenny snickered "No. This is Watema. And that's Caleb sitting on the porch," she said, pointing toward Caleb. "They live here. Tell Watema your name."

"Austin. Lucy sent me to school." Austin squeezed the bag of clothes to his chest. An Indian paintbrush bounced out. When he leaned over to pick up the flower, the rest of them tumbled out.

"Let me have the flowers," Jenny said, scrambling for the long-stemmed plants. "I'll put them in some water." She ran toward the cabin, dropping the bundle of reeds beside Caleb as she entered the door. "Brother Solomon sent these to you."

"Who's that boy?" Caleb called.

"Just a minute and I'll tell you." Jenny found a metal cup and stuffed the flowers inside. She shoved the cup against the wall to keep the flowers from falling out. She grabbed a piece of cold fry bread for Austin. When she

walked out the door, Watema and Austin stepped onto the porch. Watema tried to take the bag from Austin, but he shook his head and squeezed the clothes to his chest.

"Tell us about the boy," Watema said, looking toward Jenny with questioning eyes. She lifted the stiff paper from Austin's neck. "What's this?"

Austin scooted closer to Jenny. She handed him the fry bread and patted his shoulder. "Brother Solomon sent me over with the reeds so Caleb'll have something to whittle on. I got hot and was gonna rest under a cedar tree for a minute. When I saw this boy laying there asleep, my eyes almost popped out of my head. I just let him sleep for a while. When he woke up, he asked me if he was at school," Jenny said, pausing for a breath. "I said I'd take him to school after while."

"If that don't beat all," Watema said, rubbing her hands together. Turning to Austin she asked, "Your mama sent you to school? How'd you get here?"

"Rode the bus. The bus driver told me which road to take. I took off walking. Lucy said for me to go to school."

"Well, you're at the right place," Watema said. She held the paper out a ways so she could read the handwritten message. "Austin Lincoln, born in 1919. H-m-m. How old are you suppose to be to go to school?" She asked Jenny.

"Six."

"He ain't old enough. What do we do, send him back?" Watema asked.

Austin sank deeper into Jenny's arms. She felt his body trembling. She saw a tear slipping down his cheek.

"I got to go to school. Lucy said, 'Go to school.'"

"We have lessons here," Caleb said unexpectedly. "I go to school here. Let Austin stay with us. Mr. McElroy can teach him when he teaches me."

"You go to school?" Austin asked, looking at Caleb's wrapped feet. "What's wrong with your feet?"

"He was born with crippled feet," Jenny answered, hoping to intercept any anger Caleb might hurl toward Austin. "He never went to school, so

the teacher comes over here to teach him."

"Yeah, boy. I ain't never learned to walk the way other kids like you do. Just have to set around and keep my hands busy," Caleb said. He blew on a whistle he had finished.

Austin stared at the whistle. "Can I have it?" he asked.

Jenny felt herself wanting to draw up into a knot. What if Caleb mistreated Austin?

"I'm making 'em to sell, but you can have one. Just one." Caleb answered. "Come look at 'em."

Jenny knew she should leave for school. Miss James would be upset if she spent too much time at the cabin. "Austin, decide on which whistle you want because we've got to go. Grab your clothes and the paper that's got your name on it. Let's leave."

"Let him stay with us today," Caleb insisted. "He's got the rest of his life to go to school. He's tired and needs to sleep. Go on. Me and Watema will take care of him."

"What do you think, Watema?" Jenny asked.

I don't want to leave him. He can take the place of Kenny.

"Leave him here for now. He might be scared when he sees all the other students. Let him get used to us first," Watema said. She hugged Austin close. "Just don't mention him to Brother Solomon or Miss James."

"I'm afraid I'll get in trouble. What if I get campused?"

"What's that?" Watema asked.

"It's where a student can't leave the dorm except to go to church or to class. And if I got campused, I couldn't come over here."

"You really think Brother Solomon would do that?" asked Watema.

Jenny nodded. "Yeah, he does it to students who disobey the rules."

"You won't get into trouble for helping this little boy," Caleb argued. "Go on. We'll take care of him."

Austin blew a whistle. "I like this one," he said.

"We'll watch him," Watema promised.

"Okay, but I don't like this idea," Jenny said. She started back to school, feeling like a bone had lodged in her craw. What if Caleb threw a fit while she was away?

What if Brother Solomon does campus me? I'd have to slip out of the dorm. I must see about Austin.

Jenny walked toward the school. Thoughts of punishment mushroomed in her mind. If Brother Solomon learned about Austin staying at the cabin, she'd be restricted from nearly all activities. The sweet boy would miss her. She slipped under the limbs of a cedar to think. She couldn't go off and leave Austin. How could she take care of Austin and still pretend nothing unusual was going on? Oh, this was too much! She needed to decide on the best way to protect Austin. Yeah, she trusted Watema, but she wasn't so sure of Caleb's actions. He might get mad all of a sudden.

I've got to do the right thing! Even if it means getting in trouble at school. Wonder if I have enough money to buy a train ticket for Austin and me? We can go to White Rabbit's for a few days while I think this over. I'll go to the dorm and count my money.

She scooted from beneath the cedar and ran toward the school. If she could slip into the dorm and count her money, she was home free. Approaching the school, Jenny noticed Brother Solomon walking toward the chapel. She hid behind a pine tree, hoping she was hidden. When Brother Solomon closed the door to his office, she raced on toward the dorm.

In the dorm, Jenny shook her change out of a bag onto the bunk. She stacked the coins into piles. "Yeah, I believe I've got enough to buy a ticket for me. Maybe Austin won't need one since he's just five."

So many questions darted around in her brain. When did the train leave? How much did a ticket cost? How would she sneak Austin away from Watema and Caleb without causing a fuss? If Brother Solomon saw she was missing, would he call the sheriff?

Jenny lay on her bunk, trying to think through the problems. Really, she needed to go to class first so no one would be suspicious of her. She decided to attend the next class. She'd think while she pretended to listen to the teacher. She glanced at the clock. Enough time remained for her to grab her books and hurry to class.

In history class, Jenny's mind drifted away from the subject the teacher was talking about. Abraham Lincoln and the Emancipation Proclamation

were far from her mind. When the teacher asked her a question, Maggie, the student behind her tapped her on the shoulder and whispered, "Wake up. Miss Brewer is talking to you."

"Jenny, who signed the Emancipation Proclamation?"

"Austin Lincoln," Jenny answered. Right away, she knew she'd made a big blunder, because all the students hooted at her and giggled.

"Austin Lincoln! What are you thinking about?" Miss Brewer asked, frowning.

"Abraham Lincoln," Jenny corrected, feeling her face grow warm. "Sorry, I know a boy by that name." Now trouble stalked her.

"Is he your feller?" Maggie whispered, poking a finger is Jenny's back. Then Maggie snickered.

"Be quiet," Jenny whispered.

After class, Maggie made a beeline toward Jenny. "That was funny when you said 'Austin Lincoln'. Who is he, anyway?"

"A boy I once knew," Jenny fibbed.

I can't let anybody know about Austin till we've decided where he'll stay.

"That name sounds familiar," Maggie said, rubbing her forehead. "I've heard it before, but I can't think where. If I remember, I'll tell you about him."

"Are you sure you don't mean Abraham Lincoln? Your friend's not the one I used to know. That's for sure."

He better not be. What am I doing with Austin? I'll sneak to the cabin before dark. Maybe I'll ask Watema what time she caught the train; then I'll know when to leave and take him to White Rabbit's. Can I slip Austin away from the cabin tonight? He slept under the cedar last night, so more 'n likely, he's tuckered out.

As soon as Jenny felt it was safe to sneak away, she raced toward the cabin. The meeting would only take a few minutes—just long enough to ask Watema and Caleb to have Austin ready to leave the next day.

When she approached the cabin, she saw Austin marching around the porch, blowing on a whistle. She breathed a sigh of relief. Perhaps the shanty felt like home.

Looking up to see Jenny, Austin started running toward her.

"Are you taking me to school? Can I see my teacher?" he asked. He put his hands on his knees, acting like that flapper did, the last time Jenny saw her. Has he seen someone doing the Charleston?

"You need to stay all night with Caleb one more night," Jenny said, tousling his black curls.

"Why? Lucy said for me to go to school."

"The cabin is your school right now," Jenny replied. She turned to Caleb. "How'd y'all make it today? Uh-oh, did Mr. McElroy come to teach you?"

Icy fear chilled her heart. If the teacher came, he'd wonder about Austin. He might ask questions.

"We made it okay. Watema took Austin for a walk while I was having school," Caleb answered. "Mr. McElroy didn't see him. He's safe for right now,"

"I am so glad," Jenny said, expelling a long breath. "But what about tomorrow and the next day? We have to do something or else I need to take him to school." Turning to Austin she asked, "What did you learn today?"

"Caleb showed me how to make a big A," Austin answered. He ran into the cabin and brought out a piece of paper covered with squiggly A's "He said Austin starts with A, didn't you, Caleb?"

"Those letters are good," Jenny said, looking at Austin's work.

We're still gonna have to do something with Austin.

"Go put your paper away," Jenny said, handing it to Austin. "Where's Watema?"

"She went out to look for berries," Austin answered. "She went out that way." He pointed toward the north.

"I'll go see if I can find her. You put your schoolwork up and stay with Caleb. I'll be back in a few minutes. I'm in a hurry."

Jenny dashed off to look for Watema. "She's probably wearin' that faded dress she wears all time," Jenny mused while she searched for a whitish dress. Soon she saw Watema bending over berry vines. "Watema," she called. "I need to talk to you."

Watema rose up and rubbed the small of her back. "Be right there," she called. She pushed back her bonnet and started toward the cabin.

Jenny and Watema sat on the edge of the porch near Caleb. "We need to have a talk about Austin. Can he have some berries to eat, Watema?"

Watema nodded and handed the bucket to Austin. She walked into the cabin to return with a pan of water.

"Go set under that tree while you eat some berries," Jenny said. "And wash 'em before you eat 'em."

After Austin walked to the tree, Jenny spoke in a low voice, hoping he wouldn't hear. "Austin is too young to go to school and I've been thinking about what to do with him," she began.

"He's okay right here," Caleb said.

"I know that, but what if Mr. McElroy comes to teach and he sees Austin? What then? You know he's gonna ask questions," Jenny said.

"We can manage to have him out of sight," Watema said.

This ain't gonna be easy.

"I know you both like Austin, and I do, too. Can I borrow him for a day or two and take him to White Rabbit's while I think this through?"

Watema frowned and stood up. She walked toward a tree. She yanked a small twig from a limb and peeled it. Then she stuck it between her teeth on the side of her mouth.

"Bring me one," Caleb said.

Watema plucked off another twig and peeled the tender bark for Caleb. The two sat silently, chewing on twigs.

"What I'm thinking about doin' is catchin' the train and Austin and me goin' to see White Rabbit for a day or two. Maybe she can help decide what to do with Austin. What do y'all think?"

"I said I'd take care of him," Caleb argued. "He's like my own boy. I'm callin' him Buck."

He's like my brother, Kenny.

"Hiding him till school's out is gonna be hard to do," Jenny said.

"Do you think living with this ain't hard?" asked Caleb, raising one foot. "I know what it's like, dealin' with bad situations. I say we can do it. What about you, Watema? Are you willin' to help take care of Buck?"

"'Course I am," Watema answered.

This ain't workin'. I'll have to do something behind their backs.

"Okay. You've got to take good care of Buck," Jenny said, hoping Watema and Caleb believed she agreed to their plan. *Which I don't really like at all.*

"Austin, come here," she called. When he came to Jenny, she said, "I've got to go back to school. I'll see you tomorrow, maybe. And when Watema and Caleb call for Buck, you answer. That's your new nickname."

"Okay," Buck answered, then stuffed another berry into his purple-stained mouth.

CHAPTER NINE

Jenny stayed awake for hours scheming, trying to decide on a workable plan to take care of Austin.

If I can take him to White Rabbit's house, I know they'll help me decide what to do with Austin.

Her conscience bothered her. Why not ask Brother Solomon? He's worked with kids for years. He should know what to do.

"Yeah, but what if he says to send Austin home? I feel like he's taking Kenny's place for me now, and if Brother Solomon sent him home, I'd be all alone again," she whispered to herself.

You should ask Brother Solomon.

At last, Jenny dozed off only to awake with a start. Someone was shaking her, trying to awaken her. She focused on the face leaning over her. "Who is it?" she whispered.

"Rachel," the girl answered. "I need to talk to you outside. Put on your clothes. Hurry."

Jenny almost could hear the tears in Rachel's voice, causing Jenny to slip out of bed and into her clothes. What was so wrong they needed to discuss it in the middle of the night? The two girls sneaked down the hall and to the front doors. Rachel eased a door open and stopped outside. Jenny followed Rachel to a bench under a tree. They dropped onto the bench.

"What's wrong?" Jenny asked, watching Rachel cover her face with her hands. Her shoulders quaked while she wept noiselessly.

"I did something bad," Rachel said, sobbing. "Real bad."

Why did you wake me up? I can't solve your problems.

"What am I supposed to do? Why are you asking me to solve your problems?"

"Do you promise to keep this a secret?"

"I don't know. What if you did something against the law? You know I'd have to tell," Jenny answered. She laughed because she knew Rachel would never break the law.

Rachel began to cry even harder. "How-did-you-know?" she asked, almost hysterically.

She broke the law! Now she's headed for trouble.

"Rachel! How do I know what you've done? I was just teasing you. Maybe you didn't really break the law; maybe you're panicking."

"No. I stole something expensive," Rachel confessed.

"What did you steal?" Jenny lowered her head while she fiddled with a curl hanging on her forehead.

I hope it wasn't money and she's already spent it.

"You promise not to tell?" Rachel asked again.

"I can't promise that. Just tell me and I'll decide what I'll do."

"It was a locket that belonged to Miss James. I thought it was so pretty and she left it where I could just reach over and pick it up," Rachel said, crying harder.

"Rachel, if you don't be quiet, the whole dorm will know. So hush your bawling if you want to keep this a secret," Jenny said. "I can't help you tonight. Let's go back to bed. I'll think about your problem and we can talk about it later. Okay?" Gently, Jenny touched Rachel on the arm. "Usually my problems seem worse at night. I'll sit with you at breakfast and we'll talk. By then, I may have a plan."

"You promise?" Rachel asked, digging her fingernails into Jenny's shoulder.

"I promise to think about your problem," Jenny answered, pulling away. "Let's go to bed."

After Jenny fell back into bed, she couldn't sleep. Her concerns about Austin and Rachel hippety-hopped back and forth in her mind. How could she help both of them? Rachel stole a necklace. Austin might go away and leave her. What did they have in common? Nothing really.

All at once she had a wonderful thought. Rachel's problem could be used to Jenny's advantage. Maybe if she put pressure on Rachel to help with Austin, both problems could be solved.

No sooner had Jenny fallen asleep, she felt Maggie shaking her. "You're late. Wake up, so we can eat breakfast."

"I don't want to eat. I want to sleep," Jenny fussed. She covered her head with a pillow. She was almost asleep when she recalled her promise to talk to Rachel at breakfast, so she jumped from the bunk and dressed hurriedly, paying scant attention to her appearance.

Jenny stepped into the dining room while the pianist was playing and the students were lined up to march in. In a second, someone slid in line behind her and Jenny felt hands on her shoulders. Rachel?

Seated at the table, Jenny tried to talk in codes to Rachel.

"Last night left me in the dark," she said.

"Yeah. It was dark. The moon wasn't shining," Rachel agreed.

I don't mean that. I meant I was in the dark about how to solve your problems.

"It's bright today," Jenny said.

"The sun is really shining," Rachel said, nodding.

Trying to talk in codes reminded Jenny of how Tobias talked about the Choctaw Indians known as Code Talkers during the World War.

I sure couldn't be a Code Talker with Rachel. I couldn't make her understand what I meant.

"Meet me out in the road after your last class," Jenny whispered, abandoning the code talk. "We'll go sit under a cedar tree and talk."

All day Jenny thought about how to put pressure on Rachel to force her to help with Austin. It would be perfect if she could persuade Rachel to pose as Austin's sister who had come for him, but how could she push Rachel to promise to pretend to be Austin's sister?

You're not being fair with Rachel, her conscience nagged. *You should try to help her. You aren't supposed to think about yourself all the time.*

"Oh, yeah?" Jenny said aloud. "How can a orphan help somebody else?"

Later, the two girls met and sneaked to the cedar. They bent low and pulled the swooping branches apart as they inched closer underneath the tree. Jenny smoothed the dirt for them both to sit.

"What did you decide?" Rachel asked anxiously.

"Do you have enough money for a train ticket to go home with me?"

"I guess I could scrape together enough," Rachel answered.

"Are you a good actress?"

"I guess I can try, but why?"

"First, you must promise me you'll keep this a secret. Do you promise?"

"Yeah. I have to. If you'll help me," Rachel answered.

"I want you to pretend to be a five-year-old boy's sister."

"Why?"

"I'm getting to that. There's a cabin off in the pasture," Jenny explained, pointing toward the north. "I found a boy the other day sleeping under one of the cedars. He came here to go to school, but he's not old enough, so he's staying in the cabin. I want you to pretend to be his sister."

"But what does that have to do with me stealing Miss James' necklace?"

"Not much," Jenny answered. She looked away and laughed nervously. "But I'm not involved with your taking the necklace either, so we're even."

I don't think this is working.

"I want to take the boy to see White Rabbit so she can help decide what to do with him. If you'll pretend to be his sister, Watema and Caleb will have to let him go with us."

"Yeah, but he'll know I'm not his sister. So how does that work?"

"We'll just have to take a chance, that's all I can say," Jenny admitted. "Will you go along with my plan?"

"I'll try if it'll solve my problems. This is the worst puzzle I've ever had to try to figure out," Rachel said, choking back the tears.

"We'll leave school just before sunset. By the time we reach the cabin, it'll be almost dark and maybe Austin can't see to tell who you are. If Watema and Caleb agree to let him go, I'll go for him tomorrow morning and we'll catch the train to go see White Rabbit. Agreed?"

Rachel frowned. "This sounds risky to me. I don't want to get into more trouble."

"Mama would say we're jumping out of the frying pan and into the fire," Jenny said. "But sometimes we have to take risks. This is one of those times. We both need help."

"I'm afraid I'm already in enough trouble. I'm not going to pretend to be that boy's sister. That's lying and I'm already guilty of stealing," Rachel said. She touched Jenny's arm and asked her, "You know what I'm talking about, don't you?"

Just what I thought! She wants my help, but she won't give me any.

Jenny jerked her arm away. She got into Rachel's face and screamed at her. "You wanted my help, but you don't want to help me! That's not fair. Go back to school, but don't expect any help from me. I'll take care of Austin someway. He's-he's-like one of my brothers who's off at Blue Valley Boarding School," she ended in a sob.

"I'm sorry but I just can't get in trouble any deeper than I am now," Rachel answered and she started to crawl from beneath the cedar tree.

Jenny grabbed her arm. "Let me see your hand," she demanded.

Rachel held out her hand. Jenny grabbed Rachel's pinkie and pushed it back on her hand.

"Stop it! That hurts," yelled Rachel trying to pull her hand free.

Jenny held Rachel's finger pressed backward. "Not till you say you'll help me." She put more pressure on Rachel's finger. "Give up?"

That's the way my brothers did me. I know it hurts.

"Two can play that game," Rachel shouted. She grabbed a crop of Jenny's long black hair. She jerked on it till Jenny's head pulled backward.

"Okay, okay. I give up," Jenny said, releasing Rachel's finger. Rachel wrenched another handful of Jenny's hair and pulled harder.

"You're sure?" Rachel asked, trying to pop Jenny's neck.

"Yeah. Stop pulling my hair. You don't have to pretend to be Austin's sister."

Jenny wiped tears from her eyes.

"I guess we're even now. I'll solve my problems and you can solve yours," Rachel said, scrambling from beneath the cedar. "I'm through with you."

"Good riddance," Jenny yelled, twisting her neck around, trying to recover from the hair-pulling episode. She fell back under the tree, breathing deeply. She sobbed for a while before she came out from the cedar limbs.

"I guess I'll go on to the cabin and see if I can take Austin to White Rabbit's tomorrow."

Several minutes later, Jenny saw the dull light shining through the cabin window.

She stood straight and pulled her shoulders back, ready for another fight. A word fight. She banged on the door. Watema opened it. Jenny felt her heart drop to the floor when she saw Austin already asleep on a pallet.

"Is Austin sick?" Jenny whispered.

"No," Watema answered, stepping out onto the porch. "He's just tired."

Caleb followed her out.

"Have y'all changed your mind about letting me take Austin to see White Rabbit? We've got to do something with him. There's no parent's name on that piece of paper. We don't know who he belongs to."

"That's just the point," Caleb said. "Where would we send him?"

"He's too young to know who his mama is," Watema said. "It'd be a shame to put him on the train and send him off to who-knows-where."

"Yeah. I don't want him to grow up to be like me. Never knowin' who his real parents are," Caleb said.

"I can't see that keeping him here will help decide who his parents are," Jenny argued.

They sat on the porch, watching fireflies flitting about. In the distance an owl hooted sending shivers up Jenny's back. "Well, I need to walk back to the dorm before Brother Solomon sends out a search party. Take care of Austin."

Caleb pressed a reed whistle in Jenny's hand. "Take this to Brother Solomon and show him how the new reeds are working out."

"See y'all tomorrow, maybe," Jenny said, and she took the whistle. Enveloped in darkness, she started to the dorm.

CHAPTER TEN

Brother Solomon frowned when he heard a knock at his office door. Usually, he studied at night without interruptions. Question marks jumped around in his mind when he saw Rachel.

"What's the purpose of your visit, Rachel?" he asked. "Couldn't you wait till morning?"

He was startled to see Rachel pull a necklace from her pocket and slam it onto his desk. He picked it up to look at the flowers engraved on the heart-shaped locket.

Hallie's necklace! What's going on?

"I'm here to turn myself in and take my punishment," Rachel said. Her lips trembled and her black eyes swam in pools of tears. "Miss James laid this necklace on her desk and I picked it up to look at. I decided not to put it back. I know I did wrong. So, I'm ready to be disciplined." She wiped the tears from her eyes.

Brother Solomon placed a gentle hand on Rachel's shoulder. He smiled at her, trying to reassure her of his gratitude because she told him the truth. "You did the right thing. You will be punished, but it will be less than if you hid the locket and kept this to yourself." He held the chain and watched the locket sway back and forth.

"You see, this is an important piece of jewelry. Years ago, it was brought over the Trail of Tears by a Choctaw whose descendents I know. I'm sure the owner would be frantic if she knew it had been lost. Thank you for turning it in to me. Miss James and I both have been careless in the handling of this necklace. Have you lost any sleep over committing this act?"

"Yes, Sir," Rachel answered, covering her face with her hands. "Lots of sleep."

"Tonight you'll be able to sleep, because of your honesty. So, go on back to the dorm. I'll talk to you later about the punishment."

"But I wanted to tell you about Jenny . . ."

"Jenny's always into something. She can wait," Brother Solomon interrupted, opening the door for Rachel. He ushered her out. "You can tell me tomorrow."

"Okay," Rachel said, looking over her shoulder as she walked away. "But I tried to tell you . . . "

"Later, Rachel," Brother Solomon said, dropping the locket inside his pocket.

I must put this in the safe tonight. What if Rachel hadn't been honest with me? I would be the guilty party.

He shuddered in disbelief. He closed the book he was studying and straightened his desk. Perhaps he should go by Jenny's dorm. She might have a real problem.

Is she on a high or a low?

He needed a woman to go with him. Since Betty went to bed early, he'd ask Miss James to accompany him. He hurried to her room and knocked on her door.

"Sorry, Brother Solomon. I wasn't feeling well, so I've already retired. I'll change into a dress if you want me to go with you," Miss James called through the crack in the door.

"Don't worry. I'll check on Jenny tomorrow," Brother Solomon said and hurried to lock the necklace away—this time for sure.

* * *

Jenny left the cabin wondering why she stayed until after dark. She held both hands in front of her to feel for low hanging limbs and bushes. She clasped the reed whistle in one hand.

"Rachel was right. It was dark last night and it's darker tonight. Hope I can find my way back to school," she whispered to herself.

She shivered with fright when an owl hooted in a nearby tree. What if the coyotes came out on their nightly run across the pasture? Would they know she was a human being? She started to run. In the daylight, she knew where to step to avoid holes and rough spots. She saw the vines and briars. In the dark, would she remember when to slow down? Before she had time to answer the question, she stepped into a hole and fell flat. She lay on the soft ground for a few moments, trying to catch her breath and calm the wild beating of her heart.

Why did I wait till dark to go to the cabin? Why did I cause a fight with Rachel? Why can't I live a life like other kids who have a mama and a

daddy? She swallowed back a big lump working its way up her throat. *Why am I being punished?*

She arose to a sitting position; a feeling of frustration controlling her She gripped long strands of hair in both hands. She yanked on her hair— fussing at herself while she tugged angrily at the curls. Why did she act like this? Why did she feel sorry for herself? Her neck ached because Rachel had pulled her hair with brute force and now she was adding to the pain. Her tender scalp ached with every tug.

Jenny forced herself to stop pulling at her hair and she tried to collect her wits. She must compose herself. Peaceful feelings must take over.

Please help me to calm down, Dear God.

In a short time, a sense of urgency pushed her on. She arose and eased forward. She put one foot in front of the other and felt around with her toes before she stepped on the ground. At this rate, she might walk to the dorm by daylight. She should just sleep and try to wake up with the first beam of sunlight.

Still determined to move on, Jenny calculated the firmness of the soil before she placed her foot down. Intently, she inched forward. After a while, her eyes adjusted to the darkness and she realized she was near the cedar tree where this wild escapade began hours earlier.

Jenny hurried on toward the school. Wonder if Austin would wake up early? Could she lure him away from the cabin? She knew what she'd do. She'd nap for the remainder of the night, then go to the cabin and snatch him away. They'd leave for the train depot without even returning to the school. She'd need to remember to take her money to buy tickets. If she didn't have enough, maybe she could talk the agent into letting her buy Austin's ticket on credit, if he needed one. Sure, the man would recognize her plight and let her and Austin ride home. Having decided on a plan, she sneaked into the dorm and dropped into bed.

The warm rays of the sun roused Jenny from her sleep. She arose and grabbed her change purse and the reed whistle as she sneaked from the dorm. She might need the whistle to entice Austin to follow. Now, the holes and vines that kept her from moving at a fast pace last night didn't bother her. She saw them and slipped around them. She arrived at the cabin quickly.

Jenny tiptoed onto the porch and opened the door a crack. Just as she

hoped. Austin lay on the pallet. He clutched the bear in his arms. How could she awaken him without Caleb or Watema's knowledge? She stepped out into the yard looking for a twig long enough to reach Austin's hand or foot. She couldn't find one, but she picked up the longest reed from Caleb's bundle. Kneeling down before the opening in the door, she slid the reed toward Austin's foot. He squirmed, and gripped the bear tighter.

Again, she poked the reed through the crack. Austin's big black eyes opened. He looked around wildly. Jenny put her fingers to her lips to shush him and beckoned him to come out.

"Did you come to take me to school?" Austin whispered, when he was on the porch.

Jenny smiled and nodded.

He knows to be quiet. I'll just tell a white lie. It's for his good.

She guided him from the cabin and whispered to him. "Come with me. We're going on a trip."

"I don't want to go on a trip," Austin protested. "I want to go to school."

"There's a school where we're going," Jenny said. She reached for his hand and half dragged him along. A pain shot up her back to her neck, but she needed to take Austin far enough away from the cabin so she could speak aloud. She ignored the pain as she pulled Austin along.

When they were out of Watema's earshot, Jenny knelt before Austin. "We're going to take a train ride." *I hope.* "We're going to see the people I live with when I'm not in school."

"Why?"

Jenny fumbled around with her list of excuses for taking Austin to White Rabbit's. "These people are older than we are and they had two boys. They'll know what to do."

"Why wouldn't Watema and Caleb know what to do?" Austin asked, unmoving. He folded his arms across his chest.

"Come on, Austin. We'll miss the train. We'll talk about it when we get on board," Jenny said, pulling on his arm.

Austin dug his heels into the soft earth and refused to move. He glanced over his shoulder toward the cabin. "Where's Teddy?"

"Oh, you left your bear. Can't you go without him?"

"No, I can't."

"I know what. I'll buy you a new Teddy bear. How's that?"

"I want *my* Teddy; not another one," Austin argued.

"Austin! Schoolboys don't take their bears with them to class. If you don't go without Teddy, you can't start to school."

"Why'd Lucy send Teddy with me if I can't take him to school?"

"To sleep with, I guess. Come on, we've got to go. We'll miss the train." Jenny leaned over to lift Austin. "I know. You can ride piggyback. Did you ever do that?"

"No. Let's go to school. Which way?"

"This way. Just follow me," Jenny answered leading the way across the pasture. Hopefully, they were headed toward Piney Ridge. Jenny half-pulled Austin across the bumpy pasture. She had no idea if she was bound for town or not, but she trudged on.

What would White Rabbit think when she showed up at the door with a boy? White Rabbit loved boys. She had two of her own, so Jenny knew she'd welcome Austin.

Would Tobias let Austin stay? Not only did she worry over the reception from the Grant family, her stomach growled with hunger. She hadn't eaten for a long time. What would she do when Austin started begging for food? She looked around for berry vines or wild plum trees. Seeing none, Jenny quickened her steps toward a stand of trees. Maybe she had reached a fencerow. Dropping Austin's hand, she ran toward the trees to see what lay ahead. A sagging fence.

Jenny crawled through the fence and stepped out onto the dirt road. Wonderful. They were walking in the direction toward Piney Ridge. Jenny turned back for Austin, but he had disappeared.

"Austin! Quit playing games! You come here right this minute. I found a fence and we can crawl over it and get on the dirt road."

When Austin didn't come out of hiding, Jenny decided to handle him like her mama used to treat her brothers.

"Okay, I'm going off and leave you," Jenny called loudly. "You'll be

out here all by yourself and no telling what will happen. Bye, Austin, I'm leaving."

Jenny shielded her eyes with one hand from the rising sun. She looked in different directions trying to see Austin's small figure rushing away from her. "Now what have I done?" she asked, choking back a sob. She started running toward the path through the weeds they had just carved out. Panic gripped her chest as she zigzagged from one cedar tree to another, lifting limbs searching for Austin.

She turned to stare at the fence row behind her. She counted seven pine trees and in the middle grew a large oak. She must keep this spot in mind. She couldn't let herself lose sight of it. The road led to freedom. She might catch the train to a different town.

Jenny walked toward the pines. She slowed down enough to yank a few Indian paintbrushes by the roots. She twisted them together into a bundle and wrapped them around a piece of barbed wire. There—she had marked the spot to help her find the road.

Now she must find Austin. "But why?" she asked, stopping for a moment. Austin refused to go with her. He wanted to stay with Caleb and Watema until he could start to school.

"Why am I worrying about that stinking boy anyway? I'll just go catch the train and run away." She turned back to face the fencerow.

She gripped a strand of wire to crawl through, but a barb pricked her palm. Looking at the blood seeping from the cut, reminded her that her conscience wouldn't let her leave Austin wandering around in an unfamiliar pasture. She must find the boy and be sure of his safety. The train could leave without them, if need be. Losing Austin would hurt her as much as losing Kenny.

"Austin! Austin!" Jenny called. He couldn't have gone far. No telling what story she'd have to concoct to tell Brother Solomon about this reckless prank. It didn't matter; she must find Austin before he really got lost.

Why did he go back, anyway? Did he want his Teddy bear enough to run to the cabin to find it? Jenny didn't know the reason for Austin's disappearance, but she must be certain of his safety before she left to catch the train, to a new destination. As she ran from one possible hiding place to another, she tripped over a root and stumbled forward several feet before she landed on the ground. When she sprawled on the dirt, she heard a cracking sound in her neck.

Maybe because Rachel yanked my hair so hard. Or I caused it myself. She twisted her head, hoping nothing serious was wrong. *It's a wonder I'm not baldheaded.*

"Okay, forget the pains in your neck and your hand. Start looking for Austin," Jenny told herself, rising from the ground. "I guess I'm just going to have to admit that he's lost and go ask Watema to help me find him. That ain't gonna be fun. Watema can be mean and so can Caleb."

Slowly, Jenny tramped toward the cabin. She knew Watema would give her a good tongue-lashing for sneaking Austin away. No telling what Caleb would do.

Was Austin back at the cabin, snuggling Teddy while he lay on the pallet? If he was, she'd wasted all this time hunting for him. She walked along, arguing with her self.

Look for Austin. No, go catch the train.

Her seesawing thoughts came to an abrupt halt when she saw Austin standing at the well, playing with the rope. If he tried to draw a bucket of water with that ragged cord, no telling what might happen. He could fall into the big dug well. Jenny began to run.

"Austin! You're too short to draw a bucket of water," Jenny yelled. "Let me do it for you."

Austin turned toward Jenny. "Look at me. I'm strong enough to climb up the well," he called and pulled on the rope.

"Please, God, keep Austin safe," Jenny prayed as she ran toward the boy.

Fear paralyzed Jenny as she watched Austin jumping toward the rock well, trying to hang onto the rim with his arms.

"He's gonna fall into the well," Jenny predicted, quietly. She took a deep breath and started running toward Austin. He was inching his way up the side of the well, pulling himself up with his arms and pushing with his feet.

"Look, Jenny. Watch me climb to the top of the well," Austin yelled.

Jenny stopped short. "No, I will not watch you," she shouted, angrily. "You're acting just like Kenny. He was always pulling stupid pranks. You climb down right this minute."

Austin turned toward Jenny, a look of bewilderment covering his face. Her harsh voice seemed to flabbergast him. He shrugged, then began climbing up and pulling himself closer to the top of the well. In a split second, his body was hanging over the top of the well. He stood on the edge, holding onto the rope, and leaning backward to take a big swing.

Jenny covered her face, not daring to look. "Dear God," she prayed, "why do I always end up in so much trouble? Please save Austin's life." She jumped when she felt a hand clamp onto her shoulder. Was she going to be punished, already?

Turning around, she saw Caleb, a triumphant look covering his face. "Did you see that? Buck's learning to swing across the well. I taught him how to do that."

"You taught him to almost kill hisself? What are you talking about?" Jenny demanded.

"The rope's okay. I fixed it. It won't break," Caleb said.

"Yeah, but what if he turns loose? He'll fall in the well."

"No, I put some boards over it. He'd just scrap his knees or his elbows," Caleb said.

Jenny felt as if all her backbone had turned to jelly. Unable to stand, she sank to the ground in gratitude for Austin's protection.

"Thank God you didn't teach him to hang over the well without a cover," she said, weakly. "Caleb, you're gonna have to realize Austin is not as old as you are. He's just a child, not even old enough to go to school." Her strength began returning, and she stood, placing her hands on her hips confronting Caleb.

"Yeah, but I want to teach him all the things I missed out on. Having these crippled feet has kept me on the ground all my life. Buck's like my own son."

"And he's like my brother Kenny," Jenny answered, "but that don't mean he needs to go swingin' across a open well."

"It's not open any more, Jenny," Caleb said. "I can't use my feet, but at least give me credit for using my head."

"I'd rather see him swing from a tree. Maybe we can ask some boys from school to fix a swing for Austin." She sniffed as a delicious odor

wafted through the breeze. "I smell food cookin'. I ain't had nothin' to eat since lunch yesterday." Jenny said, twisting a lock of hair around her finger. "Ouch, that hurts."

She turned to Austin. "Come on, Austin, let's eat breakfast. It smells like Watema's cookin' something good, maybe fry bread."

At the table a few moments later, Jenny sat squirming, She wasn't in the habit of saying grace, but today she must thank God for His protection. At last she asked, "Can I say grace, Watema? I'm so glad Austin is safe, I want to thank the Good Lord that he's okay. And for this good food."

CHAPTER ELEVEN

Jenny glanced out the window of the dorm to see Rachel sitting under a tree with Nathaniel. She watched as they hit at each other, playfully, then laughed. Rachel hadn't been campused as long as Jenny. Her restrictions were over and she seemed to be enjoying life. She didn't let the locket problem bother her outlook on life, or so it appeared to Jenny. Jenny still had a few more days to stay in her section of the dorm during hours when classes weren't in session. Gazing at the frolicking of the carefree couple caused Jenny to steam with anger. It wasn't fair. Rachel had stolen a locket and all Jenny had done was try to take Austin to visit White Rabbit. The worst part of her punishment was an order from Brother Solomon restricting Jenny from visiting the cabin.

Even at fifteen, Jenny had lived long enough to realize that life doesn't treat everyone the same. It's hardly ever fair. She had no parents and her brothers lived at Blue Valley Boarding School. A loud sigh slipped from her lips.

"What's wrong with you?" asked Mary, who was staying in the dorm because she felt bad. "You act like a baby calf, searching for its mama."

"I couldn't be looking for my mama, 'cause I don't have one," Jenny answered. Under her breath, she muttered, "For five cents, I'd crawl out this window and run away. Maybe I'll go to the cabin. Or to the depot."

"You don't need to be plannin' to run away. That's what got you here in the first place."

"Don't be sticking your nose in my business," Jenny said. She fell back onto her flimsy mattress, and picked up a book she was reading. In her heart Jenny realized being confined to the dorm for two weeks wasn't a cruel punishment. Not being allowed to return to the cabin—that was pure cold-heartedness.

It was okay, however. For, if Austin had fallen into the well, she'd have a reason to worry. She didn't mind being stuck in the dorm for a while longer. She needed to study and take her mind off her problems. The book she was reading for Bible Class wasn't all that bad.

Jenny glanced toward Mary. She needed to ask her forgiveness for being harsh with her. "Have you read the book for Bible Class?" Jenny asked. She examined the cover of the black book. "*In His Steps*," she read aloud. "Do you like it?"

"Yeah. I'm readin' it. I have to, if I want to pass Bible," Mary answered. "It's a good story, but I sure couldn't do what these people are doin'. It might help some people I know, though." She looked at Jenny and frowned.

A rush of anger flew through Jenny. Already, she had read the section about a group of Christians who, for one year, pledged themselves not to do anything before first asking the question, "What would Jesus do?" and then act as Jesus would. How dare Mary suggest she should make a vow like that? She forced herself to tighten the grip on her emotions before she answered.

"I know somebody who did something like that. Tobias Grant, the man who is kind of like a papa to me . . . he offered his first son to be a preacher or missionary."

"How come?" Mary asked.

"The way they told me, Tobias was condemned to execution. A man took his place and Tobias was so glad about it, he vowed to give his first son to the Lord. The first son was the oldest one of a set of twins. And the twins got mixed up, so it took years to find out which one was supposed to be a preacher."

"Sounds interesting. But when there's just one, there ain't no way of making a mistake. So if anybody said they'd ask what Jesus would do—there wouldn't be no room to wonder who should do it."

"Yeah. I guess so," Jenny answered. She picked up the book and started reading.

Wonder what Jesus would do with a boy like Austin?

Jenny's heart thumped loudly and she felt flushed. Maybe she shouldn't be thinking these deep thoughts about Austin. An answer came, however.

He'd love Austin and do what's best for him.

Jenny covered her head with her pillow, trying to blot out the thoughts, but she couldn't escape the message. *Jesus would love Austin and do what's best for him.*

"Do you have any brothers?" Jenny asked, tossing the pillow aside.

"Yeah. They're a bunch of wild bucks," Mary answered.

"I've got three brothers, but they all go to a school for boys. I'm homesick to see them all the time."

"Good riddance, I'd say," Mary said.

"You don't mean that, Mary," Jenny said. "If you had to go without seein' them, you'd miss 'em, even if they are mean to you."

"They're mean to me—fastening me up in the smokehouse or in the pen with the hens and that fightin' rooster. Yeah, I like my brothers, but they're always doin' mischief to me.

"Why don't you read your book?" Mary asked wearily. "I'm in here because I'm sick."

"Okay," Jenny said. She picked up the book and began reading, but the words *"He'd love Austin and do what's best for him,"* kept dancing before her eyes.

Jenny tossed the book aside and reached for her pencil and tablet. She drew a picture of a five-year-old boy. He held a Teddy bear and a bowl of berries sat on the floor beside him. A reed whistle lay nearby. Jenny's eyes started stinging. The tears were about to flow. "Watema is taking the place of a granny," she whispered, rubbing her eyes. "And Caleb is sure trying to be a papa to him, even if he don't know how to do it."

Jenny scratched her head with the pencil. *Caleb seems to like Austin. I just hope everything's okay while I'm penned in here.*

With her pencil, she added some grass and flowers in the background. Underneath the picture, she printed "Austin." She tore the page from the tablet, and slid it under her pillow.

The next day in Math class, while Jenny was filling in more details to Austin's picture, Maggie leaned over her shoulder to peek.

"How do you like it?" Jenny whispered.

"It's good. You need to take Art class," Maggie answered. "Let me see it."

Jenny was handing the picture over her shoulder to Maggie, when Mr. Bacon walked down the aisle. The picture fluttered to the floor. Mr. Bacon stooped to pick it up. He said nothing, but slipped the picture inside his math book. Jenny kept her eyes glued on her math paper. She tried to hold her pencil steady while she pretended to work the problem. How dare Mr. Bacon keep her picture? She'd tell Brother Solomon about his actions next time she saw the preacher. She tried to act normal during the rest of the class, but inwardly she fumed.

Maggie and Jenny walked into the dorm after class. "Why'd you drop the picture, Jenny?"

"You think I did that on purpose? Well, you've got another think coming. It slipped out of my hand. Now, what's gonna happen to Austin's picture?"

"You mean like Austin Lincoln? Remember that stupid answer you gave in history class the other day?" Maggie asked. She fell onto the bed giggling.

"Hush up," Jenny said and swatted at Maggie's leg.

"This is serious business with you, ain't it?" Maggie asked, rubbing her leg. "Well, I was only teasing. You did real good on drawing the picture. I'm serious about that. Who is this Austin, anyway?"

"Just a kid I saw a while back. He's about five and he's really cute."

"But there's more to it than what you're tellin' me. Is one of your brothers named Austin?"

Jenny breathed a sigh of relief. Now she could change the subject. "No, my brothers are Kenny, Benny, and Lennie."

"And you're Jenny, so all the names rhyme," Maggie said.

"Not really. Kenny is Kenneth, and Benny is Benjamin and Lennie is Leonard. And my real name is Jennifer. My parents just shortened our names when we were babies."

"And Austin is . . . ?"

Oh, no. The subject wasn't changed after all. "Austin is Austin as far as I know. He's just a cute boy who reminds me of my baby brother, Kenny."

"I still think you need to take Art class next year," Maggie said.

"Maybe I will."

Later in the day, Jenny walked down the hall to class. She paused to glance at the bulletin board to see if any new announcements had been posted. She felt her face grow warm with embarrassment when she saw the picture she had drawn fastened to the board. How many students and teachers had seen the picture? Maybe they wouldn't make a connection between her and Austin. Maybe, just maybe . . .. Hurriedly but carefully, she removed Austin's picture and raced to the dorm to hide it. She had to see

Austin, even if it meant breaking the rule Brother Solomon had enforced.

Jenny fell across the bed, her thoughts dwelling on Austin's safety. The longer she pictured Austin taking dangerous risks, the more her heart ached to see him. What if Watema took the boards off the well when she drew a bucket of water and forgot to replace them? What if Austin decided to swing out over the open well? Without a doubt, he'd fall in the water. Visions of Austin dropping into the well danced before her eyes. She must see about him. She must beg Brother Solomon to send some boys to the cabin to hang a swing in the nearby tree. If she asked him to do that, then he'd find out about Austin. How could she take care of Austin without breaking the rules?

Slowly, it dawned on Jenny that Austin actually filled the need to be with her brothers.

Maybe I could ask some boys to sneak over to the cabin and put a swing in a tree.

While the boys are milking, I'll go to the barn and ask two of the dairy boys to help me.

During the afternoon milking, Jenny walked to the barn to set up the right time. Maybe they could even find a rope in the barn to use. She walked over to stand beside Nathaniel, Rachel's feller.

"Nathaniel, would you do me a favor?" she asked.

"I doubt it," Nathaniel answered, frowning. He squirted a stream of milk toward Jenny's feet. She jumped away.

"Stop it!"

"You and Rachel got into a fight, remember? She'd be mad it if I did a favor for you. And if you mess around with me, I'll turn you in to Brother Solomon for keeping that boy at the cabin. *And for trying to force Rachel to pretend she's his sister."*

"You wouldn't dare!" Jenny yelled, backing away hurriedly. So Nathaniel knew about Austin.

"Just try and see," Nathaniel said, aiming another stream of milk toward her feet.

"Okay. I'm leaving," Jenny said, jumping away. She looked toward the loft, where a few weeks ago she had tried to hold her breath till she passed

out. Perhaps she should try that again. Nobody liked her and if the news got out about her keeping Austin hidden, no telling what would happen.

"What are y'all doing over there?" asked the boy in the next stall.

"Playin' 'dodge the milk'," Nathaniel answered. He laughed. "She's pretty good at it."

"Guy Ray, would you help me?" Jenny pled. "I need somebody to build a swing in a tree."

"You don't want to be involved with helping Jenny," Nathaniel warned. "She's bad medicine."

"Why?" asked Guy Ray.

"She got into a fight with Rachel. Rachel was just trying to help Jenny and they had a big fight. You try to help her and you'll find out what she's up to," answered Nathaniel.

"Sounds interesting. I always did like a good fist fight," Guy Ray said. Then he glanced toward Jenny and laughed cynically.

"Nathaniel is just makin' a mountain out of a mole hill," Jenny said. "All I want is a swing built for a . . . "

"Maybe I better not take a chance," interrupted Guy Ray. "I'm already skatin' on thin ice with low grades."

"Oh, forget the whole thing," Jenny said in disgust. Slipping off and catching the train might be easier than asking some boy to be tangled up with her problems. She'd catch the train; that's what she'd do. She walked back to the dorm before the evening meal. After everyone went to bed, she'd sneak out and walk to Piney Ridge to catch the train—alone. Or else, she'd wait till almost daylight. It would be safer that way.

CHAPTER TWELVE

The next morning, Miss James called Brother Solomon to the phone. "It's the ticket agent from the depot," she whispered. "He said a student was asking him to let her buy a ticket on credit."

Brother Solomon took the receiver from Miss James. "Brother Solomon speaking. How may I help you?"

"There's a girl from boarding school wanting me to sell her a ticket on time. I thought you ought to know," said the agent. "She's got a young boy with her."

"I'll drive up to Piney Ridge in a few minutes. Thanks for the tip." He looked toward Miss James. "Would you check the classes to see if Jenny is present today? I would guess the girl in the depot is Jenny Blackwell."

"Jenny was not at breakfast this morning," Miss James answered. "She's absent today."

*　*　*

Jenny squeezed Austin's hand when he tried to pull away and dart out of the station.

"I want to watch for the train," Austin said, giving his hand a yank.

"I'll go with you, but you can't turn loose of my hand. We have to stay together."

They walked outside. Austin gazed at the railroad tracks. "I wish I had come to school on a train," he said. "Lucy made me ride the bus."

With his free hand, Austin touched his chest. "Oh, I left my tag at the cabin. I'm supposed to wear that around my neck so people will know where I'm going."

"I know where you're going, so that's all that matters," Jenny said. She forced a smile toward Austin. "I'll take care of you."

I wonder if the agent has made up his mind about letting me charge the ticket. I think Austin can ride free. Why did I forget my money?

"We can't go, because I forgot Teddy," Austin said suddenly. "Let's go back to the cabin and get him." He pulled Jenny toward the road. Jenny held onto Austin, but her body swayed toward him.

"You're strong. Did you know that?"

"Yeah. That's what Caleb said. And I was getting stronger, swinging on that rope."

"What you need is a swing fastened to a limb. I asked some boys at school to come build you a swing, but they wouldn't do it," Jenny said. She looked down at Austin. He needed someone to love him. Back at the cabin, she, Watema, and Caleb loved him, but he needed to be close to his mama, whoever she was.

Maybe his mother loves him, but what mother would put a five-year-old on a bus and send him off to school with a tag around his neck? I know Jesus loves Austin and wants what's best for him. Well, I do, too.

Jenny looked up to see a sedan veer into the drive. Inside sat a man dressed in a suit who looked a lot like Brother Solomon. Gazing at him closely, Jenny recognized Brother Solomon. How did he find out about her slipping away to the depot? Did Watema go to school and tell him?

Brother Solomon eased his long frame out of the sedan and started walking toward her. He stopped suddenly. "Who's the boy, Jenny?"

"This is Austin Lincoln. I'm taking him to stay with White Rabbit and Tobias because he's not old enough to go to school."

"Hello, Austin," Brother Solomon said. He extended his hand to shake Austin's. "Come sit in the car with me and we'll talk this over." He turned to Jenny and said, "Run tell the ticket agent you've changed you mind. You don't want a ticket."

"Yes, Sir," Jenny said. She surprised herself by speaking so meekly and obeying so quickly.

"Austin, climb in the car with Brother Solomon. I'll be back in a minute. Brother Solomon runs the school." Jenny dashed into the office and waved to the ticket agent. "We're not going. But thanks, anyway."

Sitting inside the car, Brother Solomon sat tapping his fingers on the steering wheel while Jenny climbed in. "Well?" he asked.

"Austin's mama sent him to school a while back. I found him asleep under a cedar tree. He had a tag around his neck with his name and birthday," Jenny said, sneaking a look at Brother Solomon's angry face. "Don't be mad at me. Austin's not old enough to go to school and I didn't

112

know what to do with him. He's been staying with Watema and Caleb."

"Why were you taking him to Tobias' house?"

"So him and White Rabbit could help me decide what to do with him."

"That's the reason you've been slipping off from class so much lately—checking on this boy?"

"Yes, Sir," Jenny admitted, twisting a curl around her finger. Her scalp was still tender. "You see, he's kind of taking the place of my brother, Kenny."

"Austin, do you know sheriff Lucky Lincoln?"

"He's my uncle."

"Who's sheriff Lucky Lincoln?" Jenny asked.

"The sheriff who stopped us the day Caleb came to boarding school. His name was on the side of his car."

"Is he your papa?" Jenny said, looking at Austin with a broad smile. "He didn't look Indian to me."

"He's my uncle."

"Your uncle? Wonder why he didn't come looking for you?"

"Lucy told him not to."

"Who is your mama?" asked Brother Solomon.

"Lucy."

"Lucy Lincoln?"

"Yes. That's my mama—Lucy Lincoln," Austin replied.

Jenny sat wondering what was taking place. Sheriff Lucky Lincoln's nephew had been put on a bus and sent to boarding school, even though he was too young to enroll. Lucy must be his mother, because Austin often mentioned her name.

There's more to this than meets the eye, Jenny thought.

"I respect you for protecting Austin, Jenny, but you know that the teachers at school would have known more about taking care of him than you do."

"I know that, but I didn't want you to send him home. Watema makes a good grandma and Caleb is like his papa," Jenny defended. "Caleb nicknamed him 'Buck'. Bein' around Austin is really helpin' Caleb."

"I'm getting stronger every day," boasted Austin. He flexed a muscle for Brother Solomon.

"Sh-h-h," Jenny whispered. "Don't tell that." She sighed deeply. "Just as well to tell. I've got a confession to make, Brother Solomon."

"What's that?"

"I asked two of the dairy boys to sneak off and build a swing for Austin. They wouldn't do it and I got mad and ran away."

"So that's why you were at the depot trying to take Austin to Tobias' house?"

"That's it exactly." The stinking tears were stinging Jenny's eyes. "I need Austin to be my brother. I thought if he had a swing, he'd be satisfied till school starts later this year. If you want to give those boys a merit or something for staying out of trouble—they're Nathaniel and Guy Ray."

"I'm pleased that they didn't leave the campus--which a certain student I know does quite often. When we get back to school, I'll have a team hitched to a wagon and we'll go to the cabin. I need to see about Caleb, anyway," Brother Solomon said. "Didn't I tell you I was making plans to move you to a school closer to your brothers?"

"Yeah. But I just about gave up on that," Jenny said.

A while later, the wagon rattled to a stop at the cabin. Austin climbed out first and raced to see Caleb. The others followed behind.

"Watema, come here!" yelled Caleb. "They've found Austin."

Watema peeked out the door. Her eyes were red and swollen. It seemed to Jenny that she'd been crying. Not tough Watema—her eyes didn't cry tears; just shot black daggers when she grew angry.

"Austin! Where you been?" Watema asked, hugging Austin.

"Where's Teddy?" Austin asked.

"He's on my bed, waitin' for you," Caleb answered. Austin raced inside and returned squeezing his bear.

Brother Solomon sat in a chair on the porch while he, Jenny, and Austin took turns telling about their adventure. After a while, Brother Solomon looked at Caleb's school papers and listened to him read.

"You're really learning, Caleb. I'm proud of you," Brother Solomon said, as he shook Caleb's hand.

"I'm teaching Buck, too," Caleb said and he smiled.

Jenny decided Caleb would be handsome if he smiled more and wasn't cranky. He just needed his feet fixed and he'd be normal.

On the ride back to the boarding school Brother Solomon sat rigidly in the seat as he drove the wagon. Jenny thought he looked awfully stern. She braced herself for the harsh discipline he would dole out.

When Jenny was ready to crawl from the wagon, Brother Solomon held her by the arm for a moment. "I am sorry to tell you this, Jenny. You are campused till school is dismissed. Perhaps you can learn a lesson in the next three weeks of confinement. Austin will be cared for; don't worry about him. Now go to the dorm till it's time to eat."

CHAPTER THIRTEEN

"Brother Solomon may think I'll stay fastened in the dormitory for three weeks, but he's wrong," Jenny muttered while she hurried to the junior high girls' dorm. "I'm leaving, once and for all."

She jerked the door open and walked to her area of the room. She started grabbing her personal belongings and tossed them onto the mattress. She made two piles: one to keep, the other to leave. She couldn't take a lot of possessions—just the necessities.

She picked up her comb and brush, her precious mirror, and her face powder. While she prowled through her belongings, she picked up the packet of sleeping powder Mrs. Coleman had given her the day Caleb was holed up with Brother Wade.

"I may need this," she whispered. "I might want to take a long nap." She tossed the packet of powders in her keeper side. She blinked back the tears and added, "A long, long nap."

She picked up a reed whistle, which she pitched in with her possessions. Carefully, she laid the picture she'd drawn of Austin in the stack to take.

"They'll help me remember Caleb and Austin," she said. She wiped tears from her cheeks.

As she was scrounging through the school papers, she picked up the small package in which she'd kept the two pictures she found the day she ran away to the cabin.

"I don't need those. I'll let whoever cleans this up have them. I know somebody would like to have them, so that's my gift to the school history," she said. She put the package in the pile she was leaving behind.

Jenny felt like a hobo. Lots of men roamed around asking for handouts. If she just had a stick to sling over her shoulder, she'd fit into the group right well.

Finally, she had her most precious belongings sorted and packed. They didn't amount to much. She decided she needed to take paper and pencil, should she think of a poem to write while she was hiding. She picked up her copy of *In His Steps* to use for a support for her paper while she wrote.

Now, everything was arranged. All she had to do was choose the right hour to leave the dorm and she'd be on her own.

I may try to find Blue Valley Boarding School.

* * *

The night was dark and Jenny lay in a barn, trying to find a comfortable sleeping position. Running away hadn't been filled with as much excitement as she had anticipated. Really, it was dreadful. She hadn't eaten much that day. Her stomach was growling and she certainly could use a drink of clean water. Tomorrow, at daylight, she'd count her change and see if she had enough to ride the train somewhere. Maybe she'd go to Blue River Town where the boys lived.

I might go see Louisa and Sam in Durant.

She lay on the hard ground, squirming. She needed a pillow. Why hadn't she put her belongings in a pillowcase along with the pillow? She'd been too upset with Brother Solomon to think straight. Looking back, Brother Solomon hadn't been all that mean. Probably, the discipline was less than she deserved. She felt around in the dark, hoping to find a pile of hay. Finally, she gave up and tucked her hands under her cheek. Hopefully, this was a good position for dreaming. Fanciful, wonderful, pleasant dreams—not nightmares.

Jenny opened her eyes to a bright shaft of sunlight streaming through a crack in the door. She turned her head away, trying to go back to sleep. The adventures she had experienced in her dreams caused the night to pass too quickly. In her dream, she visited with her brothers. She talked with her parents. They were well and healthy. She yearned for more time for dreaming before she started out walking. She needed food, too, but that was another fantasy.

After a while of trying to go to sleep, Jenny knew she was wide-awake. She propped up on one elbow to look at her surroundings. Hay! She had slept just a few feet from a pile of hay. No reason to cry over that now, but she wondered how many times a dream had been within reach and she gave up just inches away from it coming true?

She dug inside her bag for her coin purse. How much change did she bring with her? Frantically, she searched for the bag. Had she forgotten her change? Each object she touched added to her fears—she had run off without any money. She lifted out her mirror, her face powder, Austin's picture—but no purse.

Her fingers rubbed against the packet of sleeping powders. Just feeling the packet sent shivers up her hands and arms. Should she take the medicine and go back to sleep? Should she take all of it and go to sleep for a long time? Jenny lifted the parcel, pulling it almost to the top of the bag. It felt as if she were holding a live coal; she dropped it. Then her hand sought the packet again. Why should she try to keep struggling against life's problems? No one understood her, not even Brother Solomon: a preacher. She started lifting the packet to the opening. No. She must think this over. She must make the correct decision, after all; how would this affect Kenny, Lennie, and Benny? Did they care?

"They wouldn't care," she said. "They have each other."

Before she had time to renege, Jenny pulled the sleeping powders from the bag. She walked out of the barn to look for a well or a creek. Jenny ran frantically searching for water so she could swallow the medicine before she backed out. She kicked at a discarded rusty kettle that possibly had been used to hold water for a cow, but it was bone dry. Could a spring of water be near like the hay, within spitting distance, but she didn't see it? She saw a log cabin squatting in a pasture. She'd have to go begging for a drink.

Jenny stared at the sagging fence surrounding the cabin. *Drooping, like I feel.*

She walked through the opening that may once have held up a gate, and then she followed a path of rocks buried in the ground. Springs of grass grew between the rocks. Ants scurried across the rocks, searching for seeds to carry back inside their holes. Sidestepping the ants, Jenny bumped into a scraggly rose bush. A thorn pricked her leg.

"Ouch," she whispered, pulling her skirt free from the thorny bush. She gazed at several ragged bushes on which a few faded yellow roses halfheartedly clung to the branches. Jenny decided they should quit holding on and drop to the ground.

They're just like me. Dried out and faded.

Jenny knocked on the door and peeked inside. She saw an old granny hobbling toward her. Her faded apron had worn places through which another contrasting color stuck out. A bonnet partially hid the granny's face. The lady stopped at the door, waiting for Jenny to speak.

"Could I have a drink of water?" Jenny asked. "I need to take some

medicine and I don't have any water to help wash it down." She held out the packet of sleeping powder to show the elderly woman.

The granny nodded silently and limped toward the kitchen where a bucket of water sat on the table. Silently, she pulled out an enamel cup from a safe and poured in a small amount of water.

Jenny's hands trembled when she tore open the packet to empty about half the contents into the liquid.

Maybe I should take just part of it.

She folded the packet and stuffed it into her pocket.

"Thanks," Jenny said to the granny and then she swallowed the water in several big gulps. She smiled at the lady and walked to the door.

Jenny trudged down the road a short distance to throw Granny off track, should she be watching. Then Jenny doubled back, slipping behind trees, till she reached the barn where she'd slept the night before. She tossed the hay, trying to add body to it so it would provide a more comfortable place for resting. While she waited for the medicine to put her to sleep, she decided to write about her adventures of being out on her own. She felt around in her bag for a pencil. Placing the paper on the book, she dampened the lead with her tongue and wrote the title.

On My Own
By Jenny Blackwell (Age 15)

What's it like to be alone
When you're fifteen years old?
It's like you're lost and wandering afar
Looking for the rest of the fold.
You look to the left,
And you look to the right,
'Cause you just woke up
From a long lonely night.
But no one's around,
And it makes you feel
Like falling to the ground.
And crying . . .

As if she needed a touch of realism to embellish her writing, Jenny felt the tears springing to her eyes. She fell over and wept for a long time.

Nobody cares.

She folded the paper and put it in her bag. Then she took out the picture she'd drawn of Austin. Sweet boy! Wonder what he's doing this morning? Eating fry bread while he's sittin' at Watema's lopsided table? Hopefully, not swinging across the well, but Caleb seemed to be taking precautions for Austin's safety.

"I can't help Austin while I'm way out here at this jumpin'-off place, so I'll try to think about something else." She thumbed through the pages of *In His Steps* to find the place where she stopped reading. She'd read while she waited for the sleeping powders to put her to sleep. She propped her head on a pile of hay and stared at the page. In a strange way, she felt a connection to the poor sick man who died in the story. Yeah, he was no longer in his misery. He must feel comfortable now—away from the problems that beset him on every side. He told the preacher as much. She read the last words he spoke.

"You have been good to me. Somehow I feel as if it was what Jesus would do."

The lonely man had been misunderstood almost to the very end of his life, but just before he died, he saw a picture of how Jesus treated people.

Will I see a glimpse of how Jesus would treat me?

Jenny swallowed a lump working its way up her throat. Being misunderstood most of the time caused tormenting feelings. No one knew how she felt, without a mama or papa, and her brothers off in another school. What was the reason to keep on living?

A voice seemed to whisper, *What about Austin?*

I wonder about the boy whose mother must not care a lot about him. If she did, why'd she send him away to school even before he was old enough to go to class? Some days, he may feel like I do. I could help him if I'd try.

Did the Lord expect her to help Austin when he experienced rough times?

Why did I take that medicine? Austin needs somebody to love him and do what's best for him. I ought to walk back to the cabin, but I'm too drowsy. I'll read myself to sleep.

She turned back to the book. She scooted closer to sunlight streaming in

the cracks to see more clearly. Again, she read the instructions the preacher gave to the group who pledged to ask the important question "What would Jesus do?" before they made decisions. The minister told them they must not sway from one extreme to the other in their reactions. They should be " . . . free from fanaticism on one hand and too much caution on the other."

She paused to think over the directions the preacher gave. What did "fanaticism" mean, anyway? She wished she had a dictionary. She tried to reason out the meaning. If, in her case, too much caution meant acting melancholy, then fanaticism must mean just the opposite. Maybe it meant going to extremes or getting too excited. Did the preacher mean don't go to extremes at all? Jenny remembered Mama talking about religious fanatics. That was it—going overboard both ways!

Sometimes it seems like I do that. My feelings go too far when I feel sorry for myself. Like right now. I'm by myself in a barn because I got too excited over the punishment Brother Solomon gave me. And I jumped out of the frying pan into the fire.

She felt like a knife pierced her heart. Is that the way she behaved? Sometimes, like when she was five and flew high in a swing trying to touch the limbs of the tree or other times she pouted, and sat in the swing hardly moving? Suddenly, she realized that her responses to life situations were either too fanatical or too restrained. She overreacted without thinking, like when she raced off to the depot to catch a train if she got upset. Or on the other hand, she ran away from life like when she hid in the loft. Yeah, she wouldn't be a good candidate to answer, "What would Jesus do?".

Her conscience started gnawing at her insides. Mostly, she thought of herself and her feelings. She had been too self-centered. Those Christians who took the pledge were saying they'd follow the commands of Jesus rather than listen to their own thoughts. "But I wanted Austin to be safe," she soothed her inner voice. "I was trying to take care of him."

Is that true, Jenny? You didn't know Austin when you hid in the cabin or the barn loft.

"Forgive me, Lord," Jenny prayed. "I was thinking of myself and no one else. If it's not too late, I'll change my ways. I'll think of others first, but I may have waited too late."

Jenny rubbed her eyes. Was the sleeping powders putting her to sleep?

She felt her head drooping and her eyes closing. She closed the book and folded her hands under her cheek, ready to fall asleep.

* * *

Early in the morning, Brother Solomon heard a loud banging at his office door. "Who is it?" he asked, rather grouchily.

"Rachel. Let me in!"

"What's going on now?"

"Miss James sent me over to tell you we think Jenny ran away—again."

"Again is right. What's the emergency this time? She's probably at the cabin."

"She cleaned out her belongings. She left some, but the important things she took," Rachel said, stopping to breathe. "Miss James wants you to come over right now."

"I should send someone to the cabin, just to be sure she's there before I take any further action. See if you can send a boy to find Jim. Tell him to go to the cabin and see if Jenny is there. Tell him to hurry."

Brother Solomon arose from his desk and walked toward the junior high girls' dorm. He knocked on the door and Miss James admitted him. He noticed her face was white and her lips trembled when she spoke.

"Jenny's gone for good."

"Why do you say that?"

Miss James took his hand and led him to a bed on which Jenny's belongings were piled. "If she didn't plan to leave, why didn't she take this?" She picked up a stack of letters tied with a ribbon.

Brother Solomon examined the envelopes. They were from White Rabbit. "Maybe she went to see White Rabbit and Tobias. I'm sure she did, if she took that young boy with her."

"What young boy?" Miss James asked, raising her eyebrows.

"Oh, just a little fellow she goes to the cabin to see about." His heart did a flip-flop. Jenny wasn't all bad; she loved Austin as if he were her brother. "There's a child too young to attend school who lives in the cabin with Watema and Caleb. His mother sent him to school with a tag around his neck. Jenny found him and she's been protecting him like he was one of her brothers."

"If done correctly, that's an admirable quality," Miss James admitted, "but hiding him out with Caleb . . . that could be dangerous."

"I'm guessing she did the best she could, considering the emotional state she's in most of the time," Brother Solomon conceded. "But the boy was safe a day or two ago, and I'm praying he still is." He dug through the pile of items Jenny had left. He lifted her textbooks, one by one, and flipped through the pages for messages Jenny may have left.

"I don't see any notes she left."

He lifted a coin purse and shook it. The loose coins rattled. "She must have been in a big hurry to leave without her money. She may not have gone to the depot." He touched the small bundle containing the pictures Jenny had found in the cabin. "Wonder if there's a message in this package? Or maybe some money she had hidden?"

Frank Solomon opened the packet. Two heart-shaped pictures fluttered onto the bed. He picked up one picture to look at. A fiery hot feeling like a poker pulled from the fireplace shot through his heart, and the heat coursed through his veins. He reached for the bed railing to keep from falling to the floor. He lifted the other picture to look at. Then, he sank onto the mattress when a smothering fog enveloped him.

CHAPTER FOURTEEN

Brother Solomon sat with his head in his hands for a few seconds. He shook his head as if trying to get out of the fog. When the smothering feeling lessened, he tucked the pictures in his pocket and ordered, "Go stop Jim. If he hasn't left for the cabin, I need to go with him. Hurry, Miss James, send someone to see if Jim is hitching up a wagon. I must go with him. This is an emergency."

Miss James ran from the room as fast as her high heels would allow.

Brother Solomon could hear her calling to the students from the front door. Warily, he took the pictures from his pocket and examined them. One bore his likeness; there was no doubt. The other was Alta. He remembered the day they'd had those pictures made. He had bought the locket from Randall Grant. When they saw the traveling photographer, Frank paid him to take their picture. Later, when they received the picture, Alta had cut it into heart shapes. Frank Solomon had inserted them into the locket himself.

He slipped the pictures in his shirt pocket. He held onto the wall as he tried to walk through the fog that hovered around him and was smothering the breath out of him. He staggered to the front of the building to wait for Jim. Brother Solomon had just seen himself twenty-five years ago. The picture left him reeling.

Jim pulled the wagon to a stop. Still in the clutches of fog, Brother Solomon, climbed into the driver's seat to sit beside Jim. "Hurry, Jim. Jenny is missing."

"Again?" Jim asked. Then he laughed. "She sure runs away a lot these days."

"This time it's serious business. So drive me to the cabin as fast as you can."

Moments later, Jim pulled back on the reins and the wagon bounced to a stop. Brother Solomon jumped down and ran toward the porch. Caleb sat out front, whittling.

"Did Jenny spend the night over here? Do you know where she is?" Brother Solomon asked as he stepped onto the porch.

"No. Ain't seen Jenny since she sneaked off with Austin and took him to the depot. Is she gone again?" Caleb asked.

"She's missing. Is Austin here?"

"Yeah. He's still asleep on his pallet." He put his hand to his mouth and called, "Watema, is Austin still asleep?"

Watema poked her head out the door. She put her finger to her lips and she nodded her head. "How come you're over here, preacher?"

Brother Solomon fell into a chair and dropped his head in his hands. He sighed deeply. "Jenny's run away again. I campused her till school is out," he admitted. "That's three weeks from now. I guess she couldn't face being away from Austin. She's gone."

He turned to Jim. "Jim, take the wagon to school. I'll walk back. Thanks for bringing me over."

"At your service," Jim responded and started climbing into the wagon.

"And Jim, tell Miss James she needs to call the students together in the chapel to start praying for Jenny's safe return. I'll be there soon."

Jim nodded his head and slapped at the horses. They headed back to school.

After Jim was out of sight, Frank Solomon tried to explain about Jenny. The constrictions in his throat kept him from making himself clear, but after a while he muddled through giving his excuses.

"Should I get in touch with White Rabbit and Tobias or call the sheriff or what? Y'all know Jenny as well as I. You've been around her more than I have."

At the mention of "sheriff," Austin poked his head out the door. "Is Uncle Lucky coming to get me?" he asked.

"No," Watema answered. "Jenny's run away and we're thinking about telling the sheriff, that's all."

"Where'd she go?"

"Nobody knows," Caleb answered. "But you're safe, Buck. She didn't take you with her, so we're glad about that."

"If you were looking for her, Watema, where would you start?" Brother Solomon asked, staring into Watema's black eyes. In a moment, he turned to Caleb and asked the same question.

Both adults sat in stony silence. At last Watema ventured a guess. "Maybe she went to see White Rabbit and Tobias," she said.

"I thought so, too, but she left her money at school. Last time, she asked the ticket agent to charge a ticket so she could go home. If she'd done that again, the agent would have called, I believe," Brother Solomon said. "No one saw her leave, so we have no idea which direction she took."

"I'll bet I can find her," Austin said. "She was always trying to take me to school."

"You sure may help find her," Brother Solomon agreed. "We'll go looking after a while. Watema, what do I do first? Contact White Rabbit? Get out a search party or what? I feel responsible for her. After all, I did campus her till school is out."

"Call out a search party," Caleb said.

"And I'll go," Austin said. "Let's go." He reached for Brother Solomon's hand.

Brother Solomon stood, shifting from one foot to the other. "I'll take Austin with me. He may know some of the places Jenny stayed when she was running away. Is that okay?" He looked from Watema to Caleb for their responses.

"I want that boy back," Caleb said. "He's my buckaroo. You understand?"

"I do, too," Watema said. "We can't make it without Austin. He's the light in this dark cabin."

"I'm not promising he'll be back tonight. If a search party is out after dark, Austin may be helping us. Is that okay?"

Caleb and Watema looked at each other with questioning looks. Slowly, they nodded their heads. "Go in the cabin and get your whistle," Caleb directed Austin. "That way you'll know where you belong."

Austin returned with his whistle and his tag hanging around his neck. "I want to wear my tag. I may see a teacher," he said. In his arms, he clutched Teddy.

Brother Solomon and Austin started walking toward the school. When they passed the cedar where he spent his first night, Austin pointed beneath the swooping limbs. "That's where Jenny found me," he said.

"You were almost at the school," Brother Solomon said.

We need to find Jenny. I have other accounts to settle, thought Brother Solomon.

* * *

Brother Solomon put his fingers to his lips to quiet Austin when they entered the chapel. Miss James stood at the pulpit, telling the students about the importance of praying for Jenny's safe return. She looked toward the door when Brother Solomon entered. A questioning look covered her face when she saw Austin accompanying the superintendent.

Brother Solomon walked directly to the pulpit. "Miss James, I want you to write down the suggestions the students give. We need to investigate the possible places Jenny may be hiding." He turned to the students. "Raise your hand if you can think of a place where Jenny may have gone to hide."

One student said, "The hay loft."

Miss James wrote down the suggestion.

"Nathaniel, you and Guy Ray go search the hay loft," Brother Solomon directed. The boys scurried away immediately.

"The cabin in the woods," Mary said.

Brother James shook his head. "I've already been there."

"Somewhere in the dorm, like under the bed," another student ventured.

Again, Brother Solomon shook his head. "We've looked in the dorm."

"Hiding up in a tree," suggested a boy. Most of the students giggled softly. "Well, it's possible, if you know Jenny like I do," the boy shot back.

"Any place is a possibility," Brother Solomon answered. "Billy, take five boys and go out to start looking in trees. While you're walking along, look behind bushes."

"In a barn," Austin spoke up.

"You are right, Austin. Or she could be in someone's house," Brother Solomon agreed. He noticed the students, hands to mouths, whispering to each other. They didn't recognize the new boy.

"Students, this is Austin Lincoln. He knows Jenny. He lives in a cabin off in the pasture," Brother Solomon said, pointing toward the cabin.

He watched Maggie open her mouth and cover it quickly.

Does she know something?

"Now, we will divide into groups. The groups will go in all four directions. Look in every barn, however rundown it is, but be careful. Knock on every door. Look in ditches, under bridges. I'll ask Bob to have someone from the band to blow a trumpet when it's time to return. When you hear the sound, come back to the school grounds. But first, we will pray before we leave."

Brother Solomon led in a short prayer, asking for success in finding Jenny. Then the teachers divided the students into groups and pointed them in the direction to search.

"I want to go with you," Austin said to Brother Solomon.

"Yes, you'll stay with me. We can't afford for you to wander off, too. Mary, see if you can find Jim. Tell him to bring the wagon and team to the chapel so we can start another search."

Soon, Brother Solomon, Jim, and Austin were riding along following a narrow road. Brother Solomon stood in the wagon, looking to the left, while Jim stood and looked to the right. Austin looked in all directions.

After a while Austin began playing with his whistle. As he rode along, he tried to play a tune. The wagon lumbered over a decrepit bridge. When the horses kept plodding along, Austin yelled, "Stop. You said to look under bridges. I'll look under this one."

"Good for you. Stop the team, Jim. Let Austin see if Jenny's under this bridge."

Austin scooted from the rear of the wagon and hurried down the edge of the creek. Brother Solomon watched Austin stoop down to look under the bridge. Austin came back from underneath the bridge shaking his head. "She's not there."

He climbed back into the wagon. The team started off again. Each time they crossed a bridge, Austin insisted he should investigate to see if Jenny were hiding there. He had no success. After they rode for several miles, Brother Solomon decided they should retrace their tracks and return to the boarding school.

"Where's Jenny?" Austin asked.

"You know we haven't found her, but some of the students may know where she is," Brother Solomon replied.

I wish I believed that.

When they drew near to the school, Brother Solomon heard the sound of the trumpet. The students were being summoned to return. As the tired youths stumbled onto the lawn of the school, none reported seeing signs of Jenny. It was time for the evening meal and the students' appetites were ravenous. The students sat quietly discussing the possible whereabouts of Jenny. All teachers and students were exhausted from their explorations of the day. Several boys shook their heads in disbelief.

"We looked everywhere," one boy said, summing up the feelings of all.

Brother Solomon took Austin to spend the night in his apartment. Austin asked, "Is this school?"

"Yes. This will be your first night to spend at school."

After Austin fell asleep, Brother Solomon slipped from bed and went to sit in a chair. He had some serious thinking and praying to do. With the picture of that woman in his possession, he believed he had found Caleb's mama. What did he do about it? He must seek God's wisdom in this critical hour.

* * *

When Jenny awoke from her sleep, she was enveloped in darkness. She must have slept all day, but she was alive. God gave her an opportunity to make things right with Brother Solomon and the others she had wronged. She lay still, marveling in her newfound freedom.

"Thank You, God, for the chance to straighten out the mistakes I've made, like telling lies, sneaking off and hiding, and picking a fight with Mary, " she prayed. She could hardly wait to set the record straight, but what did she do now? Spend the night in the barn or try to find her way back to the school? She must take care of mistakes she'd made. Should she do that tonight or wait till morning?

Her better judgment told Jenny she should stay in the safety of the barn, but the night would be so long. She'd slept most of the day. Those sleeping powders really worked.

"I'm so glad I didn't take all the medicine Mrs. Coleman gave me. I may not have woke up." Jenny shivered at the thought of the discovery of her lifeless form lying in the barn. She stood and stretched. Her legs and arms ached from lying in one position for long hours. She jumped up and down, trying to work the kinks out of her muscles.

Tonight will be long, but after all the problems I've caused, I should lay here and think about trying to make things right with everyone.

Mentally, Jenny went through many of the offenses she had committed. She had been angry with Brother Solomon and Mary. She had told lies to several people, especially in regard to Austin. She had fought with Rachel and shoved her finger onto the back of her hand. Jenny had a lot to ask forgiveness of.

After hours of waiting for daybreak, Jenny saw the first crack of daylight peeking through the door. She collected all her items, including Austin's picture, the book, *In His Steps,* the poem she wrote, which now would need a different ending, her reed whistle, and other things she had been looking at during the day. Carefully placed them in her bag. She no longer felt like a hobo. She was making a new start on life. Today, she'd write the first page of her new experiences. The first sentences would be a bunch of words all jumbled together because getting back to school might take a long time. She'd run away in the darkness and didn't even know whether to go to the left or the right, the north or the south. Maybe she should go ask that old granny who gave her a drink for advice.

Jenny set out for the cabin. She hoped Granny could tell her which direction to follow. She trudged along slowly. She hadn't eaten for a long time and just had a few sips of water. Entering the yard, Jenny couldn't keep her gaze from the faded yellow roses growing on the thorny branches. At one time, Granny must have enjoyed the beauties of nature.

When I was a girl, I would have had a good time hopping on these rocks, she thought, as she looked down at the carefully laid-out path.

Long ago, somebody cared for this place.

She knocked at the door of the sagging cabin. No one answered, so she yelled, "Halito." Jenny stood at the door calling for several moments, but no one answered.

"I know I'm not supposed to go inside a stranger's house, but I need a drink real bad," Jenny muttered, pushing on the door. The door was

fastened on to the frame with leather strips. The nails were loose and the door barely attached to the leather. It might even fall off while she opened it, so she scarcely touched it as she entered. She wouldn't have time to try to put the door back, should it fall while she walked through.

When she saw the old woman lying in the floor, Jenny's eyes almost popped out of their sockets. Her heart started beating like a sledgehammer. She clamped her hand to her chest to control the thumping. Was the woman dead or unconscious? Should Jenny touch the woman and try to find a pulse? Jenny hesitated only a moment before tossing her bag aside and falling to her knees to listen to Granny's chest for a heartbeat. She put a finger under Granny's nose to feel for signs of life. In a few seconds, Granny exhaled a breath. She was alive!

"Thank You, Dear Jesus!" Jenny prayed. "Now what do I do?'

Jenny walked to the kitchen table to see if Granny had any medicine she might be in need of. Nothing was laid out, so Jenny stepped to the water bucket to take a gulp of water. Then she took a rag and poured water over it to start bathing Granny's face and brow.

"Come back, Granny. Come back!" Jenny begged. Granny's appearance blurred before her eyes. Jenny saw snuff stains filling the cracks around her drawn mouth. Granny's face turned into a vision of her mama, Inez Blackwell's, haggard countenance. Jenny's breath seemed like it was being pulled out of her chest. She felt helpless trying to save her dear mama from death's clutches, but Mama had died years ago. Jenny couldn't let Granny die. Mama and Papa were gone—there was no reason for another person to die while she cared for them.

Gently, Jenny kept bathing Granny's face, which faded in and out changing from Granny's to Mama's. Jenny couldn't let her heartache over Mama keep her from trying to revive Granny. She shook Granny's shoulders, and tried to hold Granny's arms to her sides. Granny couldn't raise her arms and tell a loved one she was coming to see him. No, Granny must live!

Jenny jumped from her knees and looked around for a pillow. She found a stained feather pillow to stuff under Granny's head. She saw a cardboard fan; she reached for it and began fanning Granny's face. "Granny, Granny, please come back," she begged.

After a long time, Granny's eyelids fluttered, however faintly. Her lips

moved silently. Jenny put her ear to Granny's mouth to hear her words. Granny's fingers were reaching toward her apron pocket. Jenny felt inside the pocket and found a tin of pills.

"How many?" she asked.

Granny raised one finger. Jenny tried to open the tin while she raced for water, and the pills scattered on the floor.

"Oh, no," Jenny exclaimed, picking up one pill. She plunged the dipper in the bucket, splashing water on the table. She tiptoed back, stepping around the medications and placed one pill on Granny's tongue. Then she held the dipper to Granny's mouth for the sick woman to take a drink. Painstakingly, Granny swallowed the water and the pill, followed by a sigh.

"Thank You, Lord," Jenny prayed as she lowered Granny's head back on the pillow. "I think you'll be better in a few minutes," Jenny told Granny. She crawled away to pick up the pills before she stepped on them.

By the time Jenny had found the pills, Granny was struggling to sit up. Jenny helped her to a broken down rocker. Granny's head fell onto her chest and she breathed raggedly. Jenny walked back into the kitchen to again wet the rag. She started bathing Granny's face and hands with the cool water once more. After a few moments, Jenny stepped back into the kitchen, searching for food. Maybe a piece of fry bread would revive Granny.

"Do you have any fry bread?" Jenny called.

"Don't have no vittles," answered Granny. " That's why I passed out."

"We'll have to find something for you to eat. I came out here in the dark and I don't know where the general store is. Can you tell me which way to go and I'll buy some food for you?"

I don't have any money.

"Down the road a piece," Granny answered. She lifted a shaky finger, pointing toward the north.

"Will you promise me to stay in the rocker while I go after some food?"

Granny tried to smile, and she said, "I can't go nowhere. I'm weak as a kitten."

"You hold this cloth and bathe your face. I'll head to the north. But first I need a drink of water." Jenny gulped down another big swallow of water and walked out of the house. She left her bag in the floor.

Jenny felt renewed strength when she compared her problems with the pathetic situation Granny faced. She walked past the barn and toward the north. How far was it to the nearest house or store? She didn't recognize any of the trees or dilapidated bridges, but she kept moving in a northward direction.

At last, Jenny decided to rest a few minutes. She stepped to the creek below a bridge to splash water on her face and to take a drink. While she sat at the edge of the creek, she saw a piece of string tied to a tree limb. Where had she seen a string that color before? Like water seeping through a crack, Jenny slowly realized the string on Austin's nametag was the same shade of blue. She jerked the cord from the limb.

It's from Austin's tag! Where is he? Has he run away, too? Has he run away because of me?

Clutching the string in her hand, Jenny scampered up the side of the creek and back onto the road. As she ran, she glanced from side to side, searching for Austin or a sign of his presence. After a while, she saw a store in the distance. She ran faster and soon lunged through the door.

"Have you—seen a boy—about five years old?" Jenny asked, pausing to take deep breaths.

"What you talkin' about?" a cowboy who was sitting on a nail keg asked.

"A boy! He's not even old enough to go to school. I'm afraid he ran away," Jenny said. She twisted the green string around her wrist.

"Yeah, late yesterday I saw a wagon with two men and a boy ridin' past here," the storekeeper said.

Two men! Brother Solomon and a man from the school, I hope. Jenny felt her face grow warm with embarrassment. *They were searchin' for me. I'll take care of that.*

"Who lives in the house back south?" Jenny asked, trying to sound casual.

"I imagine you mean Granny Wesley," the cowboy commented.

"If it's Granny Wesley, I knocked on her door a while ago and found her passed out layin' in the floor," Jenny said. "When I got her to talkin', she said she didn't have no vittles. I promised I'd bring her some, but I don't have no money. Can you give me something so her strength will come back?" She hesitated. "I hate to beg, but the old woman needs some food."

"You're sure?" the storekeeper asked, looking at Jenny over his round wire-framed glasses.

"Why else would she be layin' out in the floor? I went to ask for a drink and found her. For a few minutes, I thought she was dead," Jenny said, defending her integrity.

"Yeah, I'll give you a few things for Granny." The storekeeper wrapped up a small chunk of cheese and a slab of bacon. He scooped out a pound or so of dried beans into a brown paper sack, and dumped some sugar into another bag. He reached for some flour and peppermint candy.

"The candy ought to revive her, even though she does have diabetes." He turned to the cowboy, "Pete, take this girl and the grub to Granny's house. Thanks for lettin' us know about Granny."

After a wild ride on horseback, the cowboy jumped off and held out his hand to Jenny. He followed Jenny into the house. Granny was slouched in the rocker, pale and shaky. Quickly, Jenny stuck a peppermint in Granny's mouth. She took the food into the kitchen and dropped it on the table.

"Does Granny have any kin folks around here?" Jenny asked. " I hate to leave her like this, but I need to go back to boarding school."

"Yeah. Her lazy grandson lives with her. No tellin' where he is. Off somewhere drunker'n a skunk, I'd say. Why don't you stay with Granny while I go bring my woman over here? She can put on a pot of beans and fry some bacon." Without waiting for a reply, the cowboy raced out the door. Jenny watched him leap onto his horse and head south.

"Granny, would you like to eat a piece of cheese we're waitin' for the woman to come cook something for you?" Jenny asked.

"Yes, I'm starvin' to death," Granny admitted.

Soon Granny was nibbling on the cheese and drinking fresh water.

While the cowboy's wife started picking dirt clods and trash from the

beans, Jenny got ready to leave. Granny pointed to her bag. "Don't forget that. Thanks for bringin' me back from the dead."

"I didn't do that, Granny. Thank you. You did a lot for me, too." Jenny turned to the cowboy. "Could I ask you to take me to school? I can't promise, but I believe the superintendent will pay you for your work."

"Sue, is that all right with you?" the cowboy called to his wife.

"Yeah, I guess, but hurry back."

After she climbed on the horse, riding sidesaddle, Jenny looked one last time at the faded roses. If someone hoed around them and watered them, they'd probably come back to life.

A picture of me?

"What's wrong with Granny's grandson?"

"At one time Bailey seemed to have a good future. He was about to get married, but his girlfriend Sadie fell off a horse and hit her head on a rock and died. That happened just a few days before they were supposed to get married."

"Oh, that must have broke his heart."

"Yeah, it was sad. At first, Bailey tried to make the best of it. He set out those yellow roses in memory of Sadie and him and Granny took good care of them. But I guess he just slipped into a real lonely spell and started drinkin'. He didn't drink a lot at first, but alcohol got a hold of him and took over. He stays drunk most of the time now. Some folks believe he's trying to drown his pain in drink."

"That's a bad way to get rid of pain."

What I did was just as bad, even though my ways was different.

In a short while, the cowboy reined the horse onto the grounds of the boarding school. Jenny marveled at the quiet peaceful atmosphere. Where was everyone? She jumped from the horse and carried her bag toward the chapel. "Follow me. I think Brother Solomon will be in here."

Jenny tapped on the office door. Brother Solomon answered. When he saw her, his smile was full of love and gratitude. He grabbed Jenny's hand. "Glad you're home."

She got right to the point. "We don't have time to talk now, but would

you pay this cowboy for bringing me home? I'll work it out some way," she said. "There's a sick old granny he needs to see about."

"Who is the woman?"

"Granny Wesley," answered the cowboy. "She passed out and this girl found her."

"What about Bailey? Isn't he taking care of her?"

"He was probably out on a binge. After Sadie died, he's turned to drinkin' a lot."

Brother Solomon sighed heavily. "I am sorry. He had so much potential when he was in school. It'd be a pity if he wasted his life."

Reaching for his wallet, he asked, "How much do I owe you?"

"Oh, whatever you think it's worth," the cowboy replied, and he smiled.

"In that case, you owe me," Brother Solomon joked.

The cowboy appeared confused. "How could I owe you for bringing a student back?"

"You don't know this student, does he Jenny?" Brother Solomon asked. He pulled two bills from his wallet and handed them to the man. He shook the hand of the cowboy, who mumbled his gratitude and hurried back to his horse.

"Could I eat something, then take a bath and a nap before you talk about my punishment, Brother Solomon?" Jenny asked. "I've been sleepin' on the ground in a barn and I'm dirty and hungry."

"Go ahead. But you are still campused for the rest of the school year. Running away didn't remove the punishment."

Jenny smiled. "That's okay, Sir. I'm glad to be home."

CHAPTER FIFTEEN

Frank Solomon slipped from bed, grabbing his robe. He wanted to inspect the photographs while no one would be near to question him. "I've got to be sure of these pictures before I take action," he whispered to himself. He reached for the heart-shaped images and went to sit in a chair beside a lamp to better look at them. In his heart, Frank knew the young people. He was the male and she was the female. How did he make amends with *her*?

He recalled a few years ago, at a church service when Samuel Grant preached about Vows, he had uttered a sincere statement. He rubbed his brow, wondering what were his words? No use pretending; he recalled the exact words. "I am asking for prayer that I will have the courage to come clean with a secret I've been keeping for many years."

Now, Frank dropped to his knees. "How, Lord? How do I right this wrong? I know I said I'd work it out in my own way, but I want it to be Your way. Now that there's no mistaking the way, I need courage from You. This could ruin my life as a preacher and a superintendent."

It could lift the guilt you've carried for years.

Frank knelt with his head on the cushion of the chair for a long time, praying and meditating. The golden opportunity to ask pardon for the sins of his youth was within his grasp. He'd asked for forgiveness daily for many years, just between himself and God. If he made it public— what would Jim think—the man who looked up to him when things were not going well? And, Miss James, how would she react? No doubt she felt Frank Solomon was above reproach. As for the other teachers in school—Frank could hear the gossip now. "Did you hear about our *beloved superintendent*? He fathered a son and guess who the son is? That cripple, Caleb." He knew the teachers and students would go on and on, gloating over every word and phrase, exaggerating each syllable to the limit.

Who are you wanting to please? Me or your friends?

"You, Lord, and the others involved. Caleb and *his mother*," Frank replied.

How did he correct the mistakes he'd made with her and Caleb? He was leaving for his new position of superintendent of a different boarding school. How would the board accept a man who had a son with clubfeet and a wife with—well, who wasn't educated and didn't know about the responsibilities of a man in his position? She probably didn't have any

social graces about her. She was just a woman who knew nothing but hard work. She wasn't the best pick to be the wife of a superintendent.

At last he arose from prayer. He knew the next step he must take. Gratefully, school was dismissed. He was preparing to leave for his new assignment. His life could start anew.

In the morning, Brother Solomon found Jenny packing her clothes, getting ready to move to White Rabbit's for the summer.

"Jenny, would you walk with me to the cabin? I want to see Caleb and Watema. Of course, I want to see Austin. No one has sent for him, have they? I wonder about that boy."

"Yes, I'll go with you," Jenny agreed. "If someone takes Austin away, it'll break Caleb's heart."

"We must do what is right for the boy. Next school year, he'll be old enough to start to class."

In a few moments, the two stepped onto the porch of the cabin. Caleb was whittling on a whistle and Austin was practicing writing his A B C's. After they visited a while, Brother Solomon asked Jenny to take Austin for a walk. "Don't run away this time," Brother Solomon added, followed by a chuckle.

Jenny felt her face burning with shame. No, if she retained her sanity, never again would she run away. "Grab Teddy, Austin. We'll go swing on grapevines," Jenny said.

Brother Solomon watched closely as Jenny and Austin left the cabin. He stared at the floor, trying to buy more time. He cleared his throat, searching for the courage to face this formidable task. How did he start the conversation that would end up in his confessing to Caleb that, he, a preacher, was Caleb's father?

"Remember back when you were holding Paul Wade captive in the smokehouse?"

"How can I forget?"

"I'm sure it's hard, but one of the questions you asked was to be told who were—your— parents, right?"

"Yeah, but Mama didn't know. I was left in a basket at the church. I'm sure my real mama was too ashamed of my feet to keep me," Caleb said, lifting a deformed foot.

"I don't know about that, but what if I can tell you who your papa is? How would you feel about that?" Brother Solomon swallowed hard. He watched Caleb clench his fist and hit at an unseen object in the air.

"That's how I'd feel. The same goes for my mama."

"I'd like to see you have a more loving attitude toward your parents. After all, they were probably a couple of scared young adults."

"That don't matter none. They made their bed and in it they should lay. Is that in the Bible? Papa always quoted it like it was Scripture. He always said that when one of us got into trouble."

"I don't think the exact words are in the Bible, but I imagine your real parents have lain in the bed of guilt for a long time. I reckon they were fairly young and gave in to passion," Brother Solomon insisted.

The door opened and Watema stepped out. "I wouldn't say adults, preacher. I was just sixteen when Caleb was borned. I'm his Mama."

"You—a snaggle-tooth old woman—my mama! Go away and leave me alone."

A troubled look covered Watema's face. Frank recognized the appearance as one of years of pain. Watema rushed out the door.

"You're my son, that's for sure," she said, kneeling before Caleb. She stared into his face and pointed her finger at him. "You keep goin' on about me bein' a snaggle-tooth. It's high time I told you why my front teeth's missing. And I want you to listen, too, preacher. I think you'll find this interesting." Watema moved to a chair to sit. She fiddled with the bib of her apron, pushed her hair back, crossed and uncrossed her legs.

She's trying to finish the details of his birth.

"It won't matter none, but have your say," Caleb said. The wood chips flew in all directions while he frantically whittled.

"When you was borned, the first thing we noticed was your poor little crippled feet. I cried over that for a long time. I'd been crying at night for several months as I tried to hide the news that I'd soon be a mama. But at last it couldn't be hid no longer. I never told nobody who your papa was," she continued, and stared at Frank Solomon.

Frank wanted to shrivel into a ball and disappear, but he knew he had to face the truth.

141

Her gaze returned to Caleb. "Anyway, my Uncle Jack told me I had to give you away. I couldn't disgrace the family with not only havin' a baby with no husband, but havin' one with crippled feet.

"Mama and me both said no, we'd take care of you and carry you ever where you needed to go. Uncle Jack caught me out by myself one day. He twisted my arm behind my back and slapped me around, tryin' to make me say I'd give you away, but I wouldn't do it. Nearly broke my arm. I was still weak from your birth, but I stood up to him. I wasn't givin' you away."

"That makes me feel some better," Caleb said, looking up. "But I guess your uncle won out."

"Yeah, he did. But old snaggle-tooth . . . ," Watema covered her face with her hands, and a loud sigh escaped her lips. "Old snaggle-tooth, like you called me, got my teeth knocked out because I stood up for you. Uncle Jack beat me up and hit me in the face with his fist and knocked out my two front teeth." She started to cry.

Frank felt like Uncle Jack was standing over him with an ice pick plunging it into his heart. *Because of my sin. Forgive me, Dear Lord.*

"After Uncle Jack beat me up, Mama and Papa decided it'd be best if I give you away. They was scared that he'd kill me and you. So we got a cute basket and put you in it. I told myself you was like Baby Moses and maybe a princess would find you."

Tears were streaming down Watema's face. Frank wanted to comfort her so much, but how would she react? She couldn't hurt him more that she'd been hurt, so he moved his chair beside hers. Frank took her work-worn hands in his. He turned the palms up and rubbed the calluses in her hands. She had known nothing but hard work all her life. Perhaps he could make life easier for her. He swallowed hard because the real words must come out. Watema had told the truth; he must do the same.

"And in way, a princess did find Caleb. Sister Wade was a princess in her own way. Do you agree, Caleb?"

Caleb frowned and shuffled his feet. "Yeah. She was a good mother. But Brother Wade—he wasn't all that kind to me."

"How long have you known Caleb was your son? He could just be another baby with clubfeet," Frank asked.

"All the time," Watema answered, jerking her hands away. She pulled her handkerchief from her pocket and twisted it. "It would be hard not to know that the baby I left on the church steps was mine. That's why when Brother Wade run Caleb off from his home, I told Sister Wade I'd come take care of Caleb. I knowed he was my son, however mean he is."

"I have ever right to be mean," Caleb said, leaning over to spit off the side of the porch.

It's time, Frank Solomon.

Frank stretched out his hand to Caleb. Caleb dropped the carving knife and the reed and took Brother Solomon's hand. He looked questioningly at the preacher.

"What's that for?" Caleb asked.

"That's a—welcome to the—family from—from—your earthly father," Frank Solomon said, haltingly. He felt a catch in his throat.

Caleb dropped Brother Solomon's hand. "What are you saying?" he demanded.

"I'm your father. I discovered that a while back and have been wondering how to tell you. Now you have no excuses to wonder about your parents. You know who your mama and papa are. We're sitting here with you on the porch."

"Caleb, you have a brother," Watema said. "Junior Maytubby is my boy, too, but I ain't told him about you. I ain't told nobody about you. Not even your papa." Watema raised her eyes and stared at Frank. "I never seen much more of him," she said, nodding toward Frank. "He just skedaddled and run like a scared cat."

Caleb held up both hands. "This is too much for one day. Wait twenty-four years and find out about both parents the same day. This is too much! I'm going to bed." He arose and shuffled into the house.

Frank watched his son work his way through the door and shut it behind him. "I have always felt guilty about our relationship, but I didn't know about Caleb till a few years ago. When I saw the locket Louisa gave to Hallie; I knew Caleb was my son. I've been praying about this all the time. I promised the Lord some way I'd make it right."

"How can you turn back the clock twenty-five years? There ain't much you can do now," Watema said.

Frank reached into his shirt pocket and pulled out the photographs. He handed them to Watema.

"Why that's us, back when we was in love," she said, shaking her head in disbelief.

"Alta Watema, were those really your feelings for me back then? Did you love me when we were out sneaking around at night after church?" Frank asked. He couldn't look into her eyes.

"Yeah. In the way a fifteen-year-old girl can love; I loved you. I knew I shouldn't of chased after you, but you was so handsome and from a good family . . . "

"The good family part is the reason I had to leave town. My papa would have hit the ceiling."

"And knocked out your teeth?"

"I hope not but I'm not through. I have something important to say. I'm moving soon. I want you and Caleb to move with me." Frank knelt on one knee. "I'm asking you to marry—."

Watema lifted her head and covered her mouth with her hand. A tear trickled down her cheek. "What did you say?"

"I want you to marry me. We'll fix this family like it should be."

"I thought I heard you. What made you think of marryin' me after all these years?" Watema jumped from the chair and walked into the cabin. "Come out here. Something big is happening."

"Something big already happened."

"Come on, Son."

In a few moments, Caleb came shuffling to the porch. He sat down on its edge and picked up a flute. He blew a tune. "Music for the family celebration," he said sarcastically. He threw the flute out in the grass. He stared angrily at Watema and Frank. "You're both civet cats."

"Caleb, this is an important time in all our lives," Frank said. "Maybe the most important time up until now."

"Yeah. I agree. I find out who my mama and papa are on the same day. Been waitin' all my life for this day. Don't know how to act. More music!"

He blew on another flute, and then he flung it out into the grass and weeds.

"I know it's a shock, but I had to be sure. I couldn't tell you I was your father if I didn't know for certain. I had to pray for guidance."

"You should have prayed twenty-five years ago. You let me live with Papa, Brother Wade, all these years. Sometimes he was mean to me and all us kids."

"There's no excuse for Paul's actions, but he did take you in and give you a home. It wouldn't be easy to find a home for a baby with crippled feet."

"Don't mention my feet. I got 'em from one of y'all," Caleb growled.

"I don't have any excuses for that, son. I suppose it was God's Will," Frank answered. He looked up to see Jenny and Austin running toward them.

"Did you want us?" Jenny asked, out of breath. "We heard Caleb whistlin'."

"Yes. The whole family should be in on this. Everyone sit down and listen. Whistle another tune, Caleb."

With a flourish, Caleb played a tune.

When he had finished, Brother Solomon knelt on one knee again. Austin cocked an eyebrow at his actions. "What's he doing?" Austin asked.

"Sh-h-h. You'll find out. And so will I," Jenny said.

"Alta Watema Maytubby, will you marry me?" Frank Solomon asked.

"If that don't beat a goose 'a gobblin'," Jenny shouted. She jumped up and put her hands on her hips. "Whoever heard of such?"

"Marry him," explained Austin.

"I can't believe you're asking *me* to marry *you*." She shook her head in mock disbelief. "Thanks for askin' me, but the answer is no. No, no! Do you hear me? I don't take charity. Me and Caleb will make it by ourselves."

Frank felt like he had been slapped with a wet rag. He had wrestled with this problem for a long time. Finally, he did what he felt was right and Watema refused him. She called his proposal charity, but if he knew his heart, it wasn't that. If her answer was no, why was she wiping tears from her eyes?

"Don't I have any thing to say about this?" Caleb asked.

"After while, Caleb," Watema answered. "And now, it's time for me to go off by myself." She arose and walked into the cabin, slamming the door after her.

"What's going on?" Jenny asked. "You asked Watema to marry you? And she won't do it? I can't understand."

"What about me?" Austin asked. "If you get married, where do I stay?"

"Don't you worry none, Buck. You stay with me," Caleb answered, extending his arms to Austin.

"It's all mixed up confusion right now," Frank confessed. "It'll straighten out soon enough. I'll give Watema time to think about marriage." He stood, about to leave. "Jenny, you want to go back with me or stay here for a while?" He looked toward Caleb. "I'm getting ready to move to the new school. You can move with me and, Jenny, you can enroll there if you want to."

"Yes, I want to move to the new school. Right now, I want to stay with Caleb and Watema for a while. I'll be back in a hour or so. And, Brother Solomon, don't worry. Things will work out."

CHAPTER SIXTEEN

"Take your writing book, and go out under that tree," Jenny said to Austin. "Caleb and me have some serious talkin' to do." She watched Austin pick up his pencil and paper and walk toward the tree.

"What's goin' on?" Jenny whispered to Caleb.

"Set down or you'll fall down when I tell you," Caleb advised.

Jenny sat beside Caleb. "Okay. Tell me."

"Brother Solomon is my papa." A dizzy spell enveloped Jenny. Brother Solomon had a son!

"Watema is my mama," Caleb continued. "*He* wants her to marry him and let's be a family. That's about it."

Watema is Caleb's mama! Jenny took a deep breath and she covered her face with her hands. What would happen next?

"That don't solve my problems. I'm still a cripple," Caleb said.

Jenny sneaked a look at Caleb through the cracks between her fingers. Caleb gave a dirty look at Jenny.

"I'm sorry," Jenny replied. lowering her hands. There was nothing more she could say. "I think you have your best chance for happiness now. Wonder why Watema turned Brother Solomon down?"

"Who knows?" Caleb answered.

"I think she's been hurtin' for such a long time that it's real hard for her to even believe she can have a normal life. From what I heard, she raised Junior mostly by herself, 'cause her husband, Lewis Maytubby, was old when they married," Jenny speculated. She sat quietly for a few moments, before she added, "In a way, it's like me. Brother Solomon asked me to start to school in the new place where he's moving. I'm going and y'all ought to go, too."

"It's mostly up to Watema. It's gonna be hard callin' her Mama, but Papa, Brother Wade, kicked me out and I have to stay somewhere," Caleb said, staring across the pasture. He cut a few marks on a flute, before he dropped the stick. "I think I'll like my real papa. Wonder if I have any more kin folks, besides Junior?"

"You've got a sister-in-law, Hallie. This is sure exciting, except for one thing. What happens to Austin? I don't know if his mama or his Uncle Lucky will come after him."

"Don't worry. That will be worked out. Why don't you go talk to Watema?" Caleb asked. "She needs to talk to a woman about now."

Feeling ridiculed at being called a woman, Jenny crinkled her nose at Caleb and stepped inside to speak with Watema. Jenny was shocked to see Watema lying on her cot, crying. She walked over to sit on the side of the bed.

"Why are you cryin'?" she asked, touching Watema's arm.

"How would you feel if you'd just had the superintendent of a boarding school ask to marry you? No good—that's how I feel," Watema admitted.

"Why?"

"Look at me. I had my front teeth knocked out. I have calluses on my hands. I don't have no decent clothes to wear. I don't have no education. I feel so no-account, I just want to lay here and cry," Watema said. She covered her face and started to weep.

"I feel worthless, too. I don't have any parents and I made a big mess of my life by running off and hidin' and tellin' lies, but I'm moving to the new school with Brother Solomon," Jenny said. "I'll spend the summer with White Rabbit. Then I'll start to the school that's closer to my brothers.

"Just think! Our lives can all start over. I asked God to forgive me of all the ugly things I used to do. I'm not gonna go from feelin' high to feelin' low anymore. I gonna stay on the same path all time. I learned about that from reading *In His Steps.* Why don't you read it?"

"How did it help you?"

"The people in the book promised to ask 'What would Jesus do?' before they did anything. I'm tryin' to do that. You could, too." She looked toward the door. "So could that son of yours."

Watema smiled. "What do you think of the news? I'm glad it's out in the open, after all these years."

"Caleb needs some smoothin' around the edges; but we all need that. Yeah, he's got a lot of possibilities. I'm surprised that he's your son. But Brother Solomon's son, too? It's unbelievable!"

Watema took the heart-shaped pictures from her bosom. Lovingly she removed the paper covering them. "Just look at that! We was walkin' in high cotton back then."

Jenny glanced at the pictures. "I found those the first day I came to the cabin. I sure didn't know they were of you and Brother Solomon back twenty-five years ago. God can change anybody's life." She handed the photographs back to Watema. "So why don't you think about gettin' married? We could go to a dentist at Piney Ridge and have some false teeth made for the wedding."

"You think so? Maybe I'd look different if I had new teeth," Watema said, thoughtfully. She held up her picture. "I do look better with teeth. But I don't want teeth for the weddin'. Just for looks."

"I think that would be nice. You wouldn't have to be coverin' your mouth with your hand all time." Jenny stood, ready to leave. "So you've made up your mind? You don't want to marry Brother Solomon?"

"That's right. Just think—me, the wife of a preacher—I don't know nothing. He'd have to be making excuses for the way I look and talk and act."

"All right, if I can't talk you into marryin', it's still been a big day. I need to pack my clothes to take to White Rabbit's for the summer. I'll see about you going to the dentist."

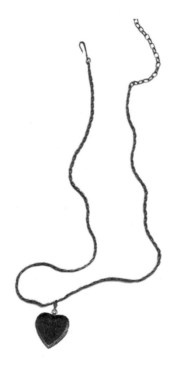

CHAPTER SEVENTEEN

"I wish Watema would marry you," Jenny said to Brother Solomon. They were in his office while Jenny helped packed his books.

The preacher shook his head. "She says she will not marry me. So what can I do about it? I tried to correct the mistakes of my past, but she won't hear to marriage."

"One way you could help is to see if a dentist at Piney Ridge can make her some new teeth. She looked real pretty in that picture back before her teeth was knocked out."

"She was a beauty. I'll see if I can find a dentist to mold some teeth for her. That would be one way of making restitution."

"Thanks for that, Brother Solomon. Before I leave for White Rabbit's, I'd like to go back down south of here," Jenny said motioning in that direction. "I'm not running away and hidin'; I just want to go see Granny. Could Jim take me in the wagon?"

Brother Solomon smiled at Jenny. "At least you are asking to go. Yes, I'll ask Jim to hitch up the team and take you to retrace the steps of your last runaway."

"It was and is my last time to run away. I saw how foolish I had been actin' just because I felt sorry for myself." Jenny rubbed her forehead and she stared at her dress. "I've been wondering, what does fa-nat-i-cism mean?"

"Why do you want to know that?"

"When I ran off, I read some pages out of *In His Steps* while I was restin'. I saw that word. I think I act that way some times."

Brother Solomon reached for the dictionary. "Good thing we hadn't packed the dictionary." After dusted the cover, he thumbed through it and found the page where the word was listed. He put his index finger on the right spot. "I'll read the correct definition for you. It means 'excessive, irrational zeal.' It comes from fanatic or fanatical. That's when someone's too worked up over a cause and doesn't make good decisions. Why did you think it applied to you?"

"You know I used to be all worked up over my parents' dyin' and me

being alone. When that happened, I didn't think of nobody but myself before I took off running away. In the book, it said a Christian should be free from fa-nat-i-cism or not be too cautious in doing what Jesus would do. I think that's what's wrong with me. I acted too wild or too mild. But that's in the past. I'm gonna be on the same path all the time now." Jenny made a straight line with her hand. "Like this."

"You took a big step, Jenny," Brother Solomon said, patting Jenny's shoulder.

"I've been wonderin' about that ever since I read it. I'm glad I was right.

"And now, if it's okay, I'll go to the cabin and bring Austin back to ride with me and Jim."

"Would you bring Watema with you? I'll take her to the dentist's while you're running around."

"Yeah. That's good news."

After a while, Jenny came traipsing across the pasture with Austin and Watema.

"Don't Watema look good, Brother Solomon? She fixed up to go to the dentist."

Watema stared at the ground. "Why don't you keep your mouth shut?" she asked.

Before Jenny and Austin climbed into the wagon, a fancy car whirled in and parked at the chapel. Jenny watched a young woman and a child climb out. The driver left in a cloud of dust. Jenny gazed at the woman for a second before running toward her. "Louisa, what are you doin' out here?" She ran to lift Maria.

"She's too big to carry, Jenny. She can walk faster and run faster than I can. Brother Solomon, how are you?" Louisa extended her hand to shake his. She gave Watema a pat on the back. "Watema, it's good to see you. You look nice. Who's this little boy? He looks about your age, Maria." She reached toward Austin, but he slipped from her grasp.

"This is Austin. He lives in the cabin with Caleb and Watema," Jenny said.

After the jovial greetings, Louisa revealed the purpose of her visit. "I want to go to the cabin. Is it all right?"

Brother Solomon scowled. He kicked at the dirt. "It's all right, but you might not want to go just yet. Caleb is there by himself."

"I'm going to the dentist to see about new teeth," explained Watema.

"Oh, good! I know it will make you prettier than we've ever seen you," Louisa said.

"Why don't you and Maria ride with Austin and me? We're going for one last ride before I leave. Please, go with us so you can meet Granny," begged Jenny. "We ought to come back by the time Brother Solomon and Watema do."

Louisa sighed. "But Jenny, I came all this way to see about the cabin. Why don't you and Austin go back with me and then if I have time, I'll go for a ride with you?"

"That'll be fine," Brother Solomon said. "Jim's got the team hitched up, so he can just go a different direction.

"Jim, take Louisa wherever she wants to go. Jenny, you and Austin go, too."

I wanted to go see Granny Wesley, but I'll do that another time.

As they passed the cedar where Austin slept the first night, Jenny told about finding him there.

"He's not old enough to go to school, so he lives with Caleb and Watema," Jenny explained.

"You'll be old enough next year, won't you?" Louisa asked.

"Yeah, but I don't know what's gonna happen to me," Austin said. "Brother Solomon and Jenny are moving."

"Jenny will you explain that to me while I look at the cabin?"

"Sure," Jenny said, moving up to sit beside Jim. "It would be good if you can take Caleb for a ride. He and Louisa ain't on friendly terms."

"Okay. I'll see what I can do," Jim answered. In a few minutes he pulled the wagon beside the porch so Caleb could get in the back easier.

"Where we goin'?" Caleb asked.

"Louisa wants to look at the cabin. She's the one who fixed it up and put up the curtains and did other things. She wants to see about doin' more work on it. So, Jim is taking you and Austin for a ride."

"And me," Maria said.

"No, you stay here. You've never ridden in a wagon before today," Louisa said, shaking her head at Maria. "You can't go."

Maria started hitting Louisa's skirt with her fists. "I want to go with that boy," she cried, and she pointed toward Austin. She grabbed her mother's skirt and hid her face while she cried.

"No. You cannot go. You don't know how to sit in a wagon. You're used to riding in cars," Louisa said. She waved Jim on. "Go on, Jim. Maria would just cause trouble."

"Are you sure?"

"I'm sure. She can write on Austin's tablet or blow a flute.

"Look at this flute," Louisa said, handing Maria a flute, "You can blow it while they're gone."

The wagon left without Maria. She was screaming at the top of her lungs.

"I said you can play a flute. Now, quit crying and try to make some music. Jenny and I are going in the cabin for a while."

Once inside the cabin, Jenny noticed that Watema had made the beds and everything was arranged orderly.

"It looks fine," Louisa said. She pulled a paper and pencil from her purse and started writing. "The reason I came was because I want to fix it up some more. What's happening with Caleb and Watema now that school's out? Are they going to live here? Is Watema taking Caleb back to her house or what?"

"We haven't talked about that yet. There's been a lot of other things happening. Brother Solomon is moving to Green Briar."

Louisa nodded. "He told me he was going to another school."

"And I'll be going to school there next year. I'm staying with White Rabbit until it starts. I'd like to visit my brothers while school's out. What did you want to do to the cabin?"

"It's so small! I don't see how it will hold more furniture. I can't concentrate, though, because Maria threw such a fit. She can run away from a person before he knows it." Louisa looked out the door. "In fact, I wonder where she is right now. Let's go outside."

Jenny picked up Austin's writing book and pencil. It appeared that Maria had tossed it aside and run away. Jenny shrugged and pointed toward the back of the cabin. She and Louisa walked around opposite corners. They met at the back, but Maria was nowhere to be found. Jenny's mind flew to the well beside the cabin. Surely, she didn't climb up on it! No, she couldn't do that, could she? Jenny ran toward the well, but the boards were untouched. It didn't appear that Maria had been near the well.

"I'd be willing to say that stinker ran after the wagon," Louisa said. A hint of anger colored her words. She looked in the direction the wagon had headed. "Let's watch for Jim. I can think better when Maria's with me."

They stepped back onto the porch. Louisa picked up one of the reeds Caleb had been carving. "Does he whittle all time?" She blew a few notes.

"Yes. He's always whittling on whistles and flutes. I guess he's getting a supply ready to sell when he goes back home. But to who-knows-where? You know your papa still won't let Caleb come back, don't you?"

"Yes. But Papa is furious with me, too. Papa is an angry man. He needs to learn how to forgive. It's really hard on Mama."

"That's the reason your mama got Watema to come stay with Caleb. She knew Brother Wade really had it in for him."

"It gives me the shivers," Louisa said, hugging her body. "Let's walk on and see if we can see the wagon. I have a bad feeling about Maria and that wagon. She's such an energetic child. She can get into mischief before I turn my back."

As they walked along, Louisa confided that she hoped to start another shelter at Green Briar. She said Sammy was graduating and they had saved enough money to build a small structure.

"Oh, I'd love to help fix it up," Jenny said.

"Is that the wagon heading this way?" Lousia asked, grabbing Jenny by the arm and pointing toward it. "Looks like Jim's slapping the reins, making the horses run. Oh, I hope nothing's wrong with Maria. I hope she didn't run catch them and cause trouble."

The horses pulled to a stop and Jim yelled, "Ya'll climb in, quick. There's been an accident. I've got to take Caleb to the doctor. Hurry!"

"We can't leave without Maria!" Jenny cried.

"She's with us. Get in quick!" insisted Jim

Louisa and Jenny climbed into the wagon. Maria was crying and crawled over to bury her head in Louisa's lap.

When she saw blood running from Caleb's mangled feet, Jenny covered her eyes with her hands. Caleb lay in the wagon bed, groaning.

"What's wrong, Austin?" Jenny whispered, uncovering one eye.

"Caleb's legs are hurt bad," Austin answered.

"What happened?" Louisa asked.

"Maria was hidin' behind a tree and she jumped in front of the wagon. Caleb tried to grab her and he fell out. The wagon wheels ran over his legs," Austin answered.

"Is Maria alive?" Caleb asked, turning his head from side to side.

"Yes, she's all right," Jenny answered. She took one of Caleb's hands and began to massage it. "Don't worry about Maria. She's fine."

"I tried to save her . . . " Caleb whispered.

"He saved her life," Jim affirmed. "She jumped out in front of the wagon and scared the horses. I couldn't stop the team. Caleb leaned over the side to catch Maria and fell under the wagon wheels."

When the wagon pulled into the schoolyard, Jim stopped the team. "Jenny, go ask Miss James to send for Mr. Bacon or Mr. McElroy. We've got to take Caleb to the hospital at Piney Ridge quick."

Louisa leaned over Caleb, soothing his brow. "Caleb, I am so sorry. I would never have let Maria out of my sight if I'd known she was going to jump in front of the wagon."

Caleb spoke through gritted teeth. "It's not your fault, but it don't stop my feet from hurtin'."

Jenny heard no more. She raced to follow Jim's directions. Soon Mr. Bacon drove his car near the wagon. Jim helped lift Caleb into the car. "Get a boy to unhitch the team," Mr. Bacon called and he and Jim sped away furiously.

* * *

Brother Solomon sat in the dentist's office, waiting for Watema. He looked up when he saw Jim standing at the door beckoning him to come out. Quietly Jim told the preacher about the accident.

Brother Solomon found the dentist and peeked in. "Is Watema almost ready to go? Or should someone come back for her later? I need to leave for a few minutes."

"Someone can come back in thirty minutes," answered the dentist.

At the hospital, the doctor told Brother Solomon that Caleb needed go to the Indian Hospital at Talihina. The surgeon there could make a better decision regarding Caleb's feet.

"It's my personal opinion that both feet need to be amputated. The quicker the better," he said tersely. "We don't want infection to set in."

Brother Solomon dropped into a chair. *Amputate Caleb's feet? How will he react to the news?*

"I'll give permission for Caleb to be transferred to the other hospital for the surgeon's opinion. I'll bring his mother over soon."

Brother Solomon stepped in to see Caleb for a minute. "They're transferring you to Talihina, Son. I pray all will be well. You were very brave to save Maria." He took Caleb's hand and whispered a prayer. "Watema and I will be there soon."

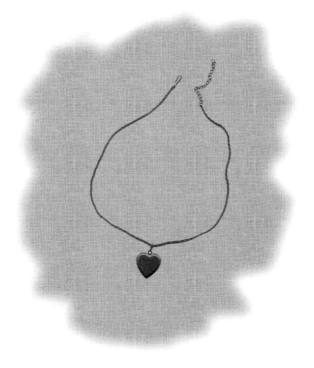

CHAPTER EIGHTEEN

Brother Solomon waited till Watema was in the sedan before he told her about Caleb.

"What do I do now?" Watema asked as she stared out the window, unmoving.

"Well, you ride with me to Talihina. We'll see what the surgeon recommends. And we'll be in prayer all the way," Frank Solomon said. "Are you ready to go? We may be in the waiting room for hours."

"Yeah. I'm ready."

While driving toward Talihina, Frank asked, "Tell me about your life. When did you marry?"

"Me 'n Lewis Maytubby got married at camp meeting at Panki Bok in '99. White Rabbit and Tobias came to the wedding. I wasn't married long. Lewis was a old man when we married. Just married long enough to have Junior. I raised him by myself mostly. Junior never knew his pa."

"You did a good job raising him alone. He was one of the outstanding boys at school. I performed his and Hallie's wedding, but you already know that."

"And was that a shock! Him comin' home with a wife and a baby. When I found out it warn't his baby, I felt better, though. You do know that Maria is my grandbaby, don't you? Louisa don't know that, 'lessen you told her."

Brother Solomon winced at Watema's language. Maybe it was best she refused his proposal. If they married, how would he explain her blunders to visiting ministers? No reason to worry about that now.

"No, I haven't told her. I told her that I was the grandfather, though. Your part in this is all new, but Jenny may have told Louisa. I believe Caleb saved Maria because he loved her, don't you?"

"Yeah, if he's got it in him to love. He's had a hard up-bringin'."

"But God can fix all that, including our relationship," Frank said, touching her hand.

Watema looked at Frank's hand, but did not reply.

"So, how did you support Junior?"

"I raised a garden and kept chickens and pigs. We managed to keep the wolf away from the door. Sometimes he stood outside howling, though." Watema laughed at her joke.

"I'm sure times were hard. Now you've got another rough time ahead. What will you say if the surgeon wants to amputate his feet?" Frank gazed straight ahead. He didn't want to see the pained expression on Watema's face.

"That will be up to Caleb more 'n me," Watema answered. "We've just got acquainted in the last few months. Oh, I kept up with him from listenin' to people talk. And it hurt a lot when they said mean things about him."

Frank squeezed Watema's hand. "Yes, you've carried a heavy load. That's one reason I'm going to see about Louisa and Sammy building a cabin for girls at Green Briar, the new school where I'm moving. My heart goes out to girls in situations like yours and Louisa's."

"What about the boys?" Watema shoved Frank's hand away.

"They need to be held accountable for their actions."

"What about you?"

"I have been punished for all these years. Yes, me." Frank looked out the window. It was getting hot in here. Too hot for comfort. "Let's talk about something else."

"Yeah. Take the easy way out. Don't talk about the men and boys." She laughed cynically.

After a while, Watema dozed off. She hadn't mentioned how long it would be until she got her new teeth or how much they would cost. Frank planned to pay for them.

It was the least he could do.

At last they arrived at the hospital. After they sat in the waiting room a long time, they were permitted to speak with the surgeon.

"If he were my son, I'd have his feet amputated. They were of no use anyway," Dr. Dennis said.

Frank looked at Watema. "I know it's a hard decision. How do you feel about amputation?"

"It's up to Caleb. He's a grown man," Watema said. "He'd have to use

a wheelchair to get around. He could set in a wheelchair while he whittles on sticks. Don't sound too good, does it?"

None of this sounds good, Frank thought.

"Caleb will be asleep for a while. As warm as the weather is, there's a higher risk of infection than if it was cooler. I need a decision now." Dr. Dennis turned to address Watema, "Are you, as his mother, prepared to make the decision? We should take him into surgery soon."

"What would you do, Brother . . . oh, all right . . . Frank? You're as much kin to him as I am. Help me out," she pled.

"Okay. I'm going to say go ahead with the surgery," Frank said. "I'm his father." *I can't hurt my relationship with Caleb any further.*

The doctor raised his eyebrows questioningly. "Are you prepared to sign a release?"

"Yes. I am. Watema, the final say is up to you. Will you sign it, too?"

Watema fidgeted for a moment. "Yeah. I'll sign it."

"Go to the office and I'll have the papers ready for you to sign. We will begin the amputation soon," said Dr. Dennis. "You made the proper decision."

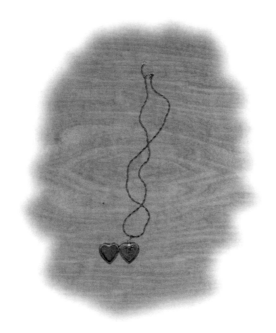

CHAPTER NINETEEN

Jenny and Louisa looked at each other in disbelief. Caleb's deformed feet had been damaged severely by the weight of grinding wagon wheels. What now? Jenny watched Maria and Austin chasing butterflies that fluttered around a bed of flowers. They didn't seem to realize how serious life could be.

That's good, Jenny thought. *I'm glad Maria's not crying over Caleb's accident.*

"I don't know what to do," Louisa said, wiping her eyes. "I feel so responsible. If I had kept my eyes on Maria, this wouldn't have happened. I wish we'd gone for the ride like you were talking about."

So do I, but there's no use cryin' over spilt milk.

She walked over to the flowerbed and picked a daisy, a pure white daisy with a yellow center. Today had been spotless like the petals, till the accident.

"We'll do whatever you want to do," Jenny said, tucking the daisy in a buttonhole.

"I can't leave without knowing about Caleb, even though we're not on the best of terms. Let's go to the office. Maybe someone has called from the hospital."

Miss James was speaking on the phone when they entered the office. The matron held up a finger for Jenny and Louisa to wait a moment. "It's that serious? The girls are here. I'll tell them the news." She put down the receiver and turned to face them. "The doctor at Piney Ridge is sending Caleb to Talihina. He says it's essential to amputate Caleb's feet."

Jenny dropped into a chair and rested her head in her hands. Now what would Caleb do without his crippled feet? She looked at the daisy, already beginning to wilt. Would Caleb's life shrivel up after his feet were cut off?

"Oh, how awful!" Louisa said. "I shouldn't have come today." She started crying,

"Don't blame yourself." Jenny looked up to see Miss James placing her hand on Louisa's shoulder. "We need to rely on God to carry us through this situation," the older woman said.

163

"You said someone is taking Caleb to Talihina. Wonder what Watema and Brother Solomon will do?" Jenny asked, removing the daisy and sniffing at it.

After considerable discussion, suddenly Jenny asked, "Why don't we catch the train to White Rabbit's? You and Maria can stay at your house and Austin and me will stay with White Rabbit. How does that sound? I'm already packed and ready to leave."

"I wonder if I can find the man who drove Maria and me out here? I wonder if Papa will let me stay? I'll need to call Sammy and . . . " In a few moments, Jenny and Louisa decided to visit their families.

After the train ride, they stood at the depot with Jenny's baggage, trying to figure out what to do first.

"Let's walk to your house," Jenny suggested. " I'll leave my bags there and Austin and me can walk on out to White Rabbit's. Is that okay?"

"It's fine. And if Papa throws a fit, I'll go on with you. Maria needs to see all her grandparents while we're here."

As they neared the house, Jenny saw Sister Wade sitting on the porch with a large white cloth in her lap. Drawing closer, Jenny saw the woman was working on embroidery. When Louisa, Jenny, and the two youngsters stepped into the fenced yard, Austin tugged at Jenny's skirt and asked, "Who lives here?"

"My mama and papa," answered Louisa. "That woman on the porch is Maria's grandma. Her grandpa is probably in the house.

"Mama, look who's here," she called. "Maria came to see you. Run see Grandma, Maria."

Maria hesitated, nibbling on her index finger. Sister Wade dropped her handiwork and hurried down the steps to see Maria. Maria turned away from her, clinging to Louisa.

"She don't even know me, Louisa. You need to bring her more often. But what brought y'all here today?" Sister Wade asked. She turned toward Austin. "And who's this boy? I know Maria don't have a brother." She laughed and touched Austin's shoulder. "Come sit on the porch and tell me what's goin' on."

Jenny took over. "There's so much to tell; it'll take a long time. This boy is Austin. His mother is Lucy Lincoln. Do you know her?"

Sister Wade's expression changed to one of scorn. "Most ever body knows Lucy Lincoln. She left town a while back. Why is her boy with you?" She reached for Austin. "Come sit in the swing with me." She smiled at him.

"It's a long story, but the most important thing to tell is that Caleb was in a accident and his feet were run over by a wagon. Brother Solomon—"

"Oh, no. Is it bad? Surely his feet can't get any worse." Sister Wade jumped up and walked to open the screen door. "Papa, come here. We've got company. Caleb's been in a accident."

In a moment, Brother Wade peeked out the door. When he recognized Louisa, an ugly scowl covered his face. "Oh, it's you. You know not to come here," he said, waving her away. He slammed the door and he went back inside.

Jenny noticed Louisa's bottom lip trembling. She walked toward Louisa. "Don't let it bother you. He'll feel better some day," she whispered.

"After all this time? I don't think so. I'll just go on out to White Rabbit's with you." Louisa turned to Sister Wade. "Mama, do you want to go with us? We can tell you about the accident while we walk."

"Yeah, I'll go," Sister Wade answered. She stepped to the door and called, "Papa, I'll be back after while. I'm walkin' with Louisa and Maria to White Rabbit's."

"No, you're not. You will not go anywhere with that girl. Do you hear me? I forbid you to leave the house," Brother Wade yelled. A loud bang erupted from inside, like he might have thrown a book at the wall.

Maria and Austin scooted close to Louisa. Austin looked at Sister Wade with a questioning look in his eyes. "Is he mean?" he whispered.

"Sometimes," answered Sister Wade. She reached into her apron pocket and pulled out a handkerchief. She wiped at the tears starting to flow. "Louisa, I can't go. I have to try to keep peace in the family. You tell White Rabbit ever thing I need to know.

"Maria, come hug Grandma."

Maria shook her head and clung to Louisa's skirt.

"Maybe we'll see you again while we're here, Mama," Louisa said. "We're waiting for news of how bad Caleb's feet are." She took Maria by

the hand and looked back at her mama as she walked away.

I wish I had some of those sleeping powders. I'd sneak 'em in Brother Wade's coffee, thought Jenny. She decided not to leave her bags at this house with that awful man. Just take them on home with her.

Finally, the four weary travelers arrived at the Grant home. The dogs ran out growling and snarling. Maria and Austin clung to Louisa's skirt; they didn't know about the behaviour of the animals. Jenny yelled at them to quiet down. She was hot and sweaty and didn't have time to worry with the dogs. She swung her bags onto the front porch.

White Rabbit peeked out the door. "If that don't beat the hens 'a peckin'!" she said loudly. "Papa, we've got company. Our grandbaby is here. And maybe a grandson we don't know nothin' about."

"No, this is Austin Lincoln. His mama is Lucy Lincoln. He came on the bus to school, but he was too young to go to class. He's been stayin' at the cabin with Watema and Caleb," explained Jenny. "But—Caleb's the real reason we're here. He's been in a accident. A wagon ran over his feet. He's gonna have to have them cut off."

"Oh, that's terrible," White Rabbit said, gesturing for them to enter. "Come on in everybody. Maria, come see your granny. You come, too, Austin. Bur first, you need a drink of water so you can cool off.

"Papa, why don't you draw a bucket of fresh water? It'll help everybody feel better."

Tobias arose from a straight back chair and walked over to shake hands with Louisa and Jenny. Gently, he tousled the curls on the heads of the two youngsters, before taking the water bucket out to fill it.

As they sat drinking the cool water, Louisa and Jenny took turns telling about how Caleb saved Maria from being run over.

"We don't know what's goin' on with him now. Somebody from the hospital called Miss James and told her Caleb's feet need to be cut off. That's all we know. We decided to stay with you till we can find out what's goin' on," Jenny said. "Besides, I was all packed and ready to come home."

"We went to my house first," Louisa explained, "but Papa's still mad at me and Caleb."

"Yeah. He don't preach no more. Tobias is still takin' his place at the

church," White Rabbit said. She stood and straightened her apron. "Let me make some fry bread for you. I'll bet you're hungry."

"Have you had any thing to eat since breakfast?" Jenny asked Louisa.

"No, we left Durant early this morning. You know everything that's happened since we got to school. Fry bread would taste delicious, White Rabbit," said Louisa.

While White Rabbit mixed flour and milk together, Louisa went outside to watch Maria and Austin while they played.

Jenny stayed inside for a few moments. "Louisa is upset about Caleb because Maria slipped off and ran away. She jumped in front of the wagon and Caleb fell out of the wagon, trying to save her. It's hurtin' her on account of she thinks Maria caused Caleb to have the accident."

White Rabbit shook her head in dismay. "Maria's not old enough to understand. She can't be blamed," she said. She reached for a cast iron skillet and poured some bacon grease in it. "I'm glad she's outside playing with that boy. What's going to become of him? I heard tell that his mama left town."

Jenny shrugged her shoulders. "Who knows? Caleb really likes him. Nicknamed him Buck. If Austin leaves, I don't know how Caleb will take it." She stood up. "While the bread's fryin', I'll go see about Louisa and the kids."

Outside, Louisa saw Jenny and she ran toward her. "I've got to do something. I can't just stand around not knowing what's going on," she said. "I think I'll ask Tobias to hitch up the wagon and take me to town. I can call Sammy from the drugstore. Do y'all want to come along?" She twisted a strand of hair around her finger.

"I guess we can," Jenny agreed, slapping at a fly. "We'll have to hurry or it'll be dark by the time we get home."

After everyone ate, Tobias drove the wagonload of folks to town and let them out at the drugstore. "I'm going to see Paul for a few minutes. He helped raise Caleb. I know he's got feelings for him," Tobias said.

"He raised me, too. He should have feelings for me," Louisa said softly.

"He does, child. He's just too stubborn to show them," Tobias said, and he urged the team on.

Darkness had almost set in when the wagon jostled into the yard at the Grant's. The visitors fell into bed, ready for sleep. Austin awakened Jenny in the night, whining for Caleb. Nightly, he slept on a pallet next to Caleb's bed, and he missed his friend.

Jenny, Louisa, and the two children were so tired they slept late. Jenny had just opened her eyes when she heard White Rabbit's loud voice in the kitchen. Jenny hopped out of bed and dressed.

"Sammy, what are you doin' here?" White Rabbit asked.

"Just came to see my family, Mama," Sammy replied. "Papa out at the barn milking?"

"Yes. I'm cookin' breakfast for Louisa and Jenny and the kids."

"Did you say 'kids'? Who's here besides Maria?"

"A boy from school. He's Lucy Lincoln's little boy."

Jenny staggered into the kitchen. "Sammy—I'm surprised to see you. Is there some news about Caleb we need to know?"

Sammy shook his head. "I haven't heard since last night. I thought I'd come on over since Louisa was already here." He walked to the kitchen door, pausing for a second. "I'm going to see Papa. I'll eat with everybody when breakfast is ready. I want to eat your good cooking, Mama."

Jenny walked out the door, following Sammy toward the barn. He stopped for a moment. "Why don't you stay with Mama? I want to talk to Papa in private," Sammy said. He flashed Jenny a reassuring smile.

"Sure," Jenny answered. She felt flushed. What could Sammy want to hide from her? Shamefacedly, she went back into the kitchen.

"I don't know what's goin' on, but Sammy didn't want me to hear what he's talkin' to Tobias about," Jenny confided in White Rabbit.

"Don't worry. Probably talkin' to Papa about his future. Since he finished college this spring, he's got to decide what he's gonna do with his life," White Rabbit said. "Papa's preachin' now, so he may be able to help him decide." She smiled proudly.

She's glad Tobias is preachin'.

After Tobias offered thanks for the food, everyone dug into the pieces of golden fry bread covered with butter and honey. In a while, Sammy cleared

his throat. "Listen. I have an important announcement to make. I believe I can borrow Doc Coleman's automobile."

What for? Jenny wondered. *Is this the secret he was keepin' from me?*

"And if we ask Brother Wade to take his car, we'll all ride to Talihina to see Caleb—"

"I think you're dreaming, Sammy," Louisa interrupted. "Papa almost hates Caleb."

"Paul couldn't take care of Caleb for more than twenty years and not have some feelings for him," Papa said.

"He does have feelings for him," Louisa retorted. "And they're all bad."

"We're going to believe things will work out for the best," Sammy said. Jenny watched him reach for Louisa's hand and squeeze it.

CHAPTER TWENTY

"God can sure do things people can't do," Jenny said to anyone who would listen. God had to have a hand in getting everybody here in two cars, especially the loan of Brother Wade's automobile. When the cars parked under pine trees at the hospital at Talihina, a tired group of travelers crawled out. Brother and Sister Wade and Tobias and White Rabbit, along with Maria got out of one car. Louisa, Sammy, Hallie, Junior, Jenny and Austin climbed out of the other. The men walked around stretching their long legs and the two children ran in circles and somersaulted across the grass. The women folk sat under a tree for a while to take a breath of fresh air.

"There's Brother Solomon's sedan," Jenny commented, after a while. She nodded toward a sedan parked a short distance away.

Wonder how things are working out between Brother Solomon and Watema and Caleb?

In a few moments, Tobias called Junior to him and whispered in his ear. Junior hurried inside the hospital. Soon he returned, followed by Watema and Frank Solomon. After exchanging greetings, Tobias called everyone together. "We need to go off by ourselves. There's some important news we need to tell you."

Jenny's heart started racing. "Is Caleb alive?" she asked.

Brother Solomon nodded. "He's as well as can be expected after having both feet run over by wagon wheels."

"Follow me," Tobias said. He led the group to a secluded area away from the hospital. Most everyone sat underneath two pine trees. Tobias and Brother Solomon remained standing.

"Watema tell us about Caleb. How's he doing?" Tobias asked. Jenny noticed a quizzical expression cover Junior's face.

He don't know Caleb is his brother. Maybe he'll find out today.

"Let Frank tell. He knows those big words better than I do," Watema said.

No one had to beg. Frank Solomon walked to stand before the group. "Caleb had both feet amputated."

Gasps from surprised members of the family filled the air. Sister Wade covered her face with her hands for a short time.

"He will be staying here for a long time as the stumps heal. He's in pain and he's asking for Austin."

"What?" yelled Brother Wade. His face was contorted with anger. "Asking for a young buck he hardly knows, when me and his mama gave a good part of our lives raising him. That's the thanks I get for all that hard work, toting him around because he couldn't walk. Let's go, Mama!" He stood up and jammed his hat on his head. "We're leaving."

"Go ahead," Sister Wade answered in unusual defiance. "I'm not going with you. The poor boy just had his feet cut off and he's probably out of his head. And you are too, Papa, but you don't have no excuses."

That took a lot of nerve to stand up to Brother Wade the way she did.

"Mama! I said, 'Let's go,' and I meant it. So come on right now. I won't stand around another minute watching all these people get the glory because they're helping that-that—"

Watema stood to face Brother Wade. "You think you had it tough, Paul Wade? What if you had to go off and leave your crippled baby on the steps of the church? What if one of your hardhearted kin folks knocked out your teeth and told you that you had to give your baby away? Then you'd know a thing or two."

Paul Wade stared at Watema. "You? You're his mama?"

Other family members looked at each other questioningly, as if they were in a daze. Junior's face turned pale.

"Yes, I am his Mama and it ain't been no picnic for me watching my son from the sidelines," Watema said evenly. She turned to Junior. "Junior, Caleb is your big brother. And Brother Solomon—"

Frank Solomon touched Watema's arm. "I'll take over from here. I am Caleb's father." Everyone but Maria and Austin sat in a state of disbelief. Brother Solomon pulled his Bible from his pocket. He thumbed toward the back and put his finger on a verse. "At a time like this, all I can tell you to do is follow God's word.

"Galatians 6:1-2 *'Brethren'* and Sisters, too *'if a man be overtaken in a fault, ye which are spiritual, restore such an one in the spirit of meekness; considering thyself, lest thou also be tempted.*

'Bear ye one another's burdens, and so fulfil the law of Christ.'

"All of us have our faults and today is a good day for me to get mine out in the open. Maybe some of you, too."

Jenny looked at the ground. *If somebody walks by, what will they think if they see us readin' the Bible?* she wondered. She felt her face growing warm.

A quiet voice whispered to her, *"What would Jesus do, Jenny?"* She felt ashamed that she'd even questioned God. *He'd quote His Father's words, Lord.* She leaned back against the tree trunk to see what happened next.

Brother Wade exploded. "I'm not in on this. I'm not going to have my faults put on display for everybody to laugh at. I'm getting out of here." He jumped from the ground and left. Without looking back, he headed toward his automobile.

"You come back, Papa," demanded Sister Wade. She followed him and grabbed his hand. "I don't think this is gonna' be what you're imagining it'll be. Sit down."

"Who gave you the right to boss me around?" Brother Wade asked angrily. He shook her hand loose.

"Nobody. And I ain't never tried to do it before. Right now, I'm ordering you to stay," Sister Wade said.

Brother Wade mumbled under his breath and returned to his spot under the tree. He sat down, seemingly baffled.

"I'm going to ask Watema and Frank to tell us more," Tobias said, ignoring Brother Wade's outburst.

Brother Solomon stood closer to Watema. He whispered in her ear and she shook her head, "no."

"This is very humbling to reveal, but twenty-five years ago Watema and I had a fling. You already know Caleb is our son."

Most adults sighed deeply and stared at the ground. Sister Wade wiped tears from her eyes. She shook her head in disbelief.

"How could you, Frank Solomon? " Brother Wade shouted. "I raised your son while you were off gallivanting around at college. Why didn't you help?"

Oh, I hope nobody hears them fussin'.

"Because I didn't know," Frank answered. "I only learned about this for sure when I saw the pictures that Watema had put in a locket way back then. I found the pictures with Jenny's possessions the last time she ran away."

The last time is right. I won't do that again.

"It was on my mind all the time," admitted Watema, staring at the ground. "Ever time I looked in the mirror and saw these empty spaces, I thought about my missin' baby."

"Oh, no," White Rabbit exclaimed. "I wish I'd known that, I'd have treated you better."

"Mama, you really mean Caleb is my half-brother?" Junior asked, bewildered.

"Yes, son, he is," Watema answered. "That's why I went to boarding school to help take care of him. He's our flesh and blood."

"I wish Caleb could hear this," Tobias said. "Junior, go to the nurses' desk and ask if you can bring Caleb out here."

"There's no reason. He can't be moved," Brother Solomon said. "Caleb already knows who his parents are. We told him a few days ago."

"Frank, your family got big all of a sudden. Can you believe it?" Tobias asked. "Everybody who claims kin to Frank and Watema raise your hands."

Jenny felt left out as she gazed at the uplifted hands.

"If that don't beat the goose 'a gobblin'," Hallie said, looking at all her relatives on Junior's side of the family.

"Yeah, that's a big bunch of kin folks. Everybody kin to Paul and Sister Wade, go stand by them."

"We need to draw a line and let some of us straddle it. Several of us are kin to both families," Junior said.

"We're all here but Caleb," Sister Wade said, grabbing Maria's hand to pull her in with the group.

"You can leave out Caleb. He's not ours," Brother Wade said angrily.

"If that's how you feel, Paul. But I can tell you you're not going to have any peace until you straighten up things with Caleb," Tobias interjected.

"How would you know?"

"Some day I'll tell you about my real father, Hal Johnson. I had to forgive him before I was right with God," Tobias said.

"I know about Hal," Brother Wade said.

"Then there's my family," Tobias said. "That takes care of everyone, I believe."

"Me, too?" Jenny asked pointing to herself.

"Of course, you, too," White Rabbit said, reaching for Jenny's hand.

"Not me," Austin said. "Who's my family?"

Watema pulled Austin to her. "You belong to me and Caleb. You're ours."

Austin tumbled over his feet as he hurried to stand with her and Brother Solomon.

"Amen," said Brother Solomon.

Jenny felt that lump coming back in her throat. She and Austin were the only two without blood relatives. At least she felt comfortable staying with White Rabbit and Tobias until she moved closer to her brothers.

When the angry feelings calmed down some, two family members at a time visited with Caleb. When they weren't with Caleb, the others walked around the grounds at the hospital and visited among themselves. Often, Jenny saw folks holding their hands to their mouths, whispering.

They're shocked about Brother Solomon and Watema's big secret.

Everyone but Paul accepted the announcement graciously.

CHAPTER TWENTY-ONE

While Jenny rode in Doc Coleman's model-T with the two younger couples, Louisa turned to ask her more about the visit she postponed the day of Caleb's injury.

"What do you know about the woman you wanted me to meet?" Louisa asked.

"Not much," Jenny answered. "I stopped for a drink of water and found Granny Wesley passed out, laying in the floor. I wanted to see how she was doin'."

"What were you doing at Granny Wesley's?" Sammy asked.

"I got mad at Brother Solomon and decided to run away," Jenny admitted. "Back when I was actin' ignorant. Now I know how stupid I was behavin'."

"Let's hope so. But you didn't answer my question. What were you doing at Granny Wesley's?"

"I needed a drink and that's the only house I saw. Why?"

"I know Granny's grandson, Bailey. Did you see him?"

"You know Bailey?" Jenny asked in a high-pitched voice.

"He went to school when I did. He was an outstanding athlete back then. Remember him, Junior?"

"Yeah. He was good at football and other sports. Did Granny mention him?"

"No, but the cowboy who brought me back did. He said Bailey's a drunk now."

"No! That's hard to believe. He made good grades and seemed to have a bright future ahead," Sammy said. "I wonder, what happened to him?"

"The cowboy said his girlfriend died just before the wedding and he turned to alcohol."

"How sad. I'll try to go see him while I'm in this neck of the woods," Sam said.

"Can I go with you?" Jenny asked.

"Yes, you and Louisa can go along. Maria can, too. We'll do that tomorrow."

"I hope he's home from his drinkin' binge," Jenny said. She took comfort in knowing she would see Granny one more time.

* * *

Brother Solomon, Watema, and Austin had been the last family members to visit with Caleb. They were driving back to the boarding school to move their personal belongings—Frank's to the superintendent's house at Green Briar and Watema's to her home place.

"I'm taking a different route on the way back," Frank said as they rode along.

"I want to drive by the park in Valliant. I know members of the family who gave the land for the park."

"What family?"

"The Lucas family. I hear tell that it was part of the Indian allotment of Levicey Lucas. After her death, her husband gave the land to the people of Valliant."

"Yeah. I know that family, too."

Several miles later, Frank stopped the car at the park. The tree trunks had been newly whitewashed. "Doesn't everything look fresh and clean?" he asked.

"This would be a good place for a family get-together," Watema said.

A good place for a family to get together—like a wedding, Frank thought.

He gazed at the beautiful trees, the trunks of which were shimmering with a new coat of whitewash. He noticed a wide spreading tree that would be a good site for a special event to be held. *Like a marriage ceremony.*

"You and Austin go stand under that tall tree over there and let me see how you look," Frank said. He glanced around for Austin, but the boy had disappeared.

"Y'all go on by yourself. I'm playing," he called.

Watema walked to the tree. "Well, how do I look?"

"Like a bride," Frank said.

"Yeah, a bride twenty-five years too late," Watema answered. Her expression was one of disdain.

"This is the perfect place for a picnic. Let's go to a restaurant and I'll buy some hamburgers," suggested Frank.

"Do we have enough time?" Watema asked. "You've got to be out of your office and I need to pack my things. And Austin's and Caleb's, too."

"I believe we have the time," Frank insisted. "You want to go with me or stay here under the tree where it's cool?"

"I'll stay here and keep a eye on Austin," Watema answered.

Frank drove to a nearby restaurant to order the hamburgers. While he sat on a stool waiting, an older couple walked in. The man was dressed in a shiny blue serge suit. A droopy red rose was tucked into a buttonhole of his lapel. He tugged at his tie as if it were choking him. The woman wore a blue dress with lace at the collar and cuffs. Pinned on her shoulder was a red rose. They were laughing like a much younger couple. Discreetly, Frank watched as they sat in a nearby booth. They seemed to be so absorbed in each other; they were oblivious to everyone around them. Had they been to a wedding or what?

When the waitress came to take their order, Frank heard the woman say, "This will be our first meal as a married couple. We just came from the preacher's house where we got married."

"Congratulations!" the waitress said. "You're eating your first meal together at our restaurant."

Watema and I aren't nearly as old as that couple. I wonder . . ..

After a while, Frank returned to the park. He had decided once again to ask for Watema's hand in marriage.

He dropped the sack of hamburgers on a table and walked toward Watema. "Go stand under that tree again. Those green leaves make a pretty frame around your sweet face."

"Yeah. Don't they?" Watema commented, saucily.

"Austin, come stand with Watema," Frank said.

"What for?" Austin asked. "I'm playin'."

"Don't bother," Frank said. He walked to the tree and got down on one knee. "Watema Maytubby, I ask you to marry me. You and Caleb can move with me to Green Briar School."

"What about Austin?"

"And Austin, if it's lawful. But the marriage would be lawful; we know that."

"I'll think about it when I see how my new teeth look," Watema answered.

"In the meantime, let's seal it with a kiss," Frank said. He didn't give her time to decline.

Watema pretended to slap at Frank, but it was obvious she enjoyed his attention.

* * *

Everyone was so tired when the sedan pulled onto the grounds of the boarding school, Frank suggested since school was dismissed, Miss James take Watema to the high school girls' dorm. Austin could sleep in his room.

Late the next morning Frank, Watema, and Austin rode in a wagon to the cabin. It didn't take long for them to collect their belongings and Caleb's, too. Austin made sure they brought Caleb's knife, reeds, and the whistles and flutes he'd already carved.

Brother Solomon made arrangements for a truck to haul the belongings to Watema's homeplace. Before he, Austin, and Watema returned to her house, they needed to stop in Piney Ridge to have the dentist fit Watema's new teeth.

Watema couldn't hide her elation. With the teeth in place, Frank thought she looked more like the girl he once knew.

"How do I look, Austin?" Watema asked, gazing at Frank.

"Pretty," Austin answered.

"Beautiful," Frank mouthed.

They drove on to Watema's house, where Frank helped sort through the belongings that had been unloaded onto the porch. He watched Watema pause to smile at her reflection in the mirror every time she walked past it. She likes her appearance, Frank thought.

"Take Caleb's things in there," Watema said, nodding toward the room

with a cot. ."That was where Junior slept when he was at home. And you might as well put Austin's things there, too."

"Don't become too used to Austin living here," warned Frank. "He doesn't belong to any of us right now. We have to go through the legal process and find out about his mother. And his uncle."

After they finished unpacking, Frank decided to test his chances of marriage.

"Your new teeth were the main problem standing between us and the wedding. That's been settled. Let's go get married," Frank joked, grabbing her hand.

"There's lots of things standing between us and marriage," Watema said.

"Yes," Frank admitted. "A marriage license, a preacher, somebody to stand up with us at the wedding. A new dress for you, my belongings moved to the house at Green Briar," Frank counted off on his fingers. "Yes, you're right, there's lots of things to be done."

"I'd like for both my boys to be at the wedding. If I ever remarry, that is," Watema added, wistfully.

"I'm sure that can be worked out. We can take Caleb out of the hospital for a few hours," Frank suggested. He started toward the door. "I've got to go. I need to organize my house for the new bride to move in." He left Watema's feeling like a bridegroom.

Driving along, Frank wondered how the board would accept Watema as the wife of a superintendent. She was lacking in social graces, her language usage was not good, and she had a meager education, but she could learn. She was intelligent. She had survived the toughest of circumstances and God would provide.

Watema had requested the presence of her sons at the wedding. What special remembrance did he want from the day? He'd like for his friend Paul to be in the right relationship with God so he'd feel worthy of performing the ceremony, but was that to be? Paul's heart had grown cold as a stone since Louisa brought Maria home and announced before the congregation that Maria was her baby. He needed to be in communion with God before he enjoyed living again. Paul made life hard on all his relatives, especially Sister Wade and Louisa. Maybe he should visit Paul and ask him how he felt about performing the wedding.

Frank kept feeling that he was forgetting a really important part of the ceremony, but though he searched his mind, he couldn't recall what he had forgotten.

He hurried to the boarding school to finish getting his belongings packed. He had a good feeling about his new life. Of course, Caleb could present a problem, but Watema would take care of him.

Standing at the door, he noticed a car pull onto the school grounds and park. He watched Jenny and Sammy climbing out.

"Where are y'all headed?" Frank asked.

"We're on our way to visit Bailey Wesley. Want to go along with us?" Sammy asked. "I hear tell he's not doing too well."

"I don't have a lot of time, but I'll follow in the sedan. Okay?"

* * *

"I'm in a hurry to see Granny," Jenny said. Secretly, she wanted to meet Granny's rotten grandson, Bailey. Anybody who treated his poor granny the way he did, must be lower than a snake's belly. She wanted to give him a piece of her mind, but maybe not on the first visit.

"It'll be good to see Bailey," Sammy said. "We used to be close friends."

A while later, Jenny, Sammy, Louisa, and Maria stood outside the car waiting for Brother Solomon's sedan. Jenny walked to look at the wilted yellow roses. Still limp and dried-up. Maria followed her into the yard.

"You can play a game jumpin' on those rocks, Maria," Jenny said, pointing to the path made from stones. "Just be careful. The other day I saw ants."

Maria placed both feet on a rock and took a big jump. She counted as she leaped from rock to rock. Soon, she pointed to Brother Solomon's sedan pulling off the trail.

Jenny led the way onto the porch. She tapped on the broken-down door, hoping Granny would answer the first knock. Instead of Granny appearing at the door, a handsome Indian man appeared.

He can't be a drunk.

Looking past Jenny, Bailey smiled at Sammy and Frank. "Of all things.

I wouldn't have expected you to visit in a hundred years." He grabbed Sam's hand and shook it vigorously. Then he reached for Frank's hand. "Everybody come in. Even the little girl. Who does she belong to?"

"That's Maria, my daughter," Sammy said. He introduced Louisa and Jenny.

"You don't say. You have a daughter," Bailey turned and called, "Granny, come here, we've got company."

Soon everyone was seated either in chairs or on the floor, talking and laughing loudly. Bailey didn't look like he'd ever swallowed a drop of firewater. His wavy black hair framed a good-looking face. Jenny folded her hands together to keep them from trembling—like her heart was vibrating—but Bailey was so handsome, he stole his way into her heart. No wonder Sadie fell in love with him.

After a while, Sammy got to the purpose of his visit. "Bailey, you were always so intelligent in school, why haven't you gone on to college? From what we've been told, your life is messed up."

Bailey raised a faded curtain and pretended to look out the window. "Mama and Papa are both dead. It's mostly just Granny and me left. Oh, there's other kin folks in Valliant and Broken Bow, but we're here by ourselves. I can't go off and leave Granny."

"'Ceptin' when he goes on a binge," Granny said.

"That's what I'm worried about," Sammy said. "If you don't quit the drinking, you won't amount to a hill of beans."

"I can't help it," Bailey answered, defiantly. "I get to feelin' sorry for myself and first thing I know, I'm back drinkin', tryin' to forget my problems."

"I used to feel like that, too," Jenny heard herself saying. "I'd get to thinkin' about my parents bein' dead, and I'd feel sorry for myself. Then I'd run away or do something else to forget my problems. That's how I met Granny. I had run away from school, but I don't do that anymore."

"But I can't quit!" Bailey said angrily. "I have to shut off my memories someway, so I go on a cheap drunk."

"That's where trusting in the Lord comes in. He's the only way for us to stop the control sin has in our lives," Brother Solomon said.

"You're right," agreed Granny. "I've tried to tell him, but he won't listen."

Everyone gave his opinion as to how Bailey could overcome the problem of drinking. The conclusion of all was to lean on the Lord for help. The young man sat shaking his head in disbelief. "It won't work for me," he said.

Before leaving, Jenny promised to return with a copy of *In His Steps* for Bailey to read.

"It showed me that I needed to ask the question 'What would Jesus do?' before I made decisions. Maybe it can help you."

On the way back to the school, Jenny asked Sammy if he'd give her a minute to grab a copy of the book and they could take it to Bailey. He agreed.

* * *

The next day, Frank Solomon looked through the drawers of his desk in the chapel and found nothing of value he had left. He searched his closet and the drawers in his room and found them satisfactory. Yet a nagging feeling bothered him as he left Clear Creek heading to begin his new position as superintendent of Green Briar. What was he leaving behind that he'd remember later?

He'd need to make arrangements for Jenny to settle in the high school girls' dorm. He'd promised her she could visit with her brothers, too. He'd take care of that now. He wrote a letter to White Rabbit, requesting that she and Tobias put Jenny on a train to travel to see her brothers. Frank had other commitments to fulfill before his wedding day. The most important one was to see if Paul Wade would perform the wedding. He'd do that soon.

Several days later, Frank felt agitation building inside him as he drove toward Paul's house. How should he handle this situation? With much care, he knew. He hadn't decided on how to approach the subject to the former preacher when he parked the sedan at Paul's house.

Frank prayed for wisdom while he knocked at the door, but no one answered. He walked around the house and saw Paul's Model T. Surely, Paul was near. Because God had provided the courage for Frank to talk to Paul, Frank wasn't going to let the opportunity slip through his fingers. He wandered around looking at the remaining vegetables in the garden

and the blooming flowers. A few sprigs of grass grew among the plants. It wasn't like Sister Wade to let weeds and grass invade her garden spot. Could something be wrong? After knocking again and getting no response, he decided to walk up the street to see Doc Coleman while he waited for Paul to come home.

Doc Coleman looked over the rim of his round glasses when he heard the door creaking. He stood with outstretched hand to greet Brother Solomon.

"Well, Brother Solomon! I haven't seen you since Caleb had that run-in with Paul Wade," Doc said.

"Yes, it's been a while. Caleb is with his real mother now. Watema Maytubby is his mama."

"I'm not surprised. In my business, I see a lot of shuffling of babies. Most of the times, the mother is reluctant to give up her baby, but there are times her family demands it. So, is Caleb getting along well with Watema?"

"He was until his accident. He fell from a wagon and his feet were crushed. He had to have them amputated. I guess you hadn't heard. He's still in the Indian Hospital at Talihina."

"No, I didn't know. Brother Wade hasn't had anything good to say about Caleb since Caleb moved out."

"I came by to see Paul, but I can't find him. His Model T is parked in the yard, but no one answers the door," Frank said.

Doc shook his head thoughtfully. "Poor Paul Wade! He's really having his share of problems and he won't let anybody help him. From what I hear he never got over his anger toward Louisa, either. You may not know it, but that can cause illness. I've been treating him for ulcers."

"Is he in the hospital? I can't find him."

"Sister Wade is gone, I believe. So he's at home by himself. Why don't you just walk in?" Doc suggested. "He may be asleep."

"If I'm shot, it's your fault," Frank said and he laughed. He walked to the door to leave, but turned back to face Doc. "I guess you know that Sammy has finished college. He's debating about his future. And his wife, Louisa, is doing a good work helping girls who are in trouble," Frank added.

"That's good. There's lots of problems these days. Seems like they're

worse all the time. I saw Jenny ever so often when she came to visit White Rabbit."

"She's visiting with her brothers now. I asked White Rabbit to send her to her brothers' school before the new term starts."

"How's she doing? Seems I remember her going from extreme highs to real lows after her mother died. Has she got her problems under control?"

"I believe she's getting better. She studied a book that helped her to see her problems. It was required reading in Bible Class," Frank said. He rubbed his hands together and continued, "I've moved to Green Briar School. She'll be going to school there. I want to keep an eye on her, because she has no close relatives to see about her."

Should I tell Doc I'm getting married?

"And, by the way, if I can talk Watema into accepting my proposal, we're getting married."

A look of surprise covered Doc's face. He stroked his chin thoughtfully. "Are you taking responsibility for Caleb, too? It might be hard, since you're the superintendent of a boarding school."

Do I tell him the truth? Frank reached into his pocket and pulled out a handkerchief to mop the beads of perspiration forming on his brow.

Doc understands things like this.

"I'm aware that the problems may be great, and I'm facing the bare facts," he admitted. "Watema and I had a relationship about twenty-five years ago. As hard as it is to say this--Caleb is my son. Don't take me the wrong way; I'm not ashamed of Caleb. I'm ashamed of my behavior. God has forgiven me and I now have a chance to right the wrong."

There, I got it out!

Doc patted Frank's shoulder. "Bless you. I wish more men would take their responsibilities seriously. Only a lot earlier." He shook Frank's hand. "Should I wait to congratulate you?"

"Probably. Watema hasn't said 'Yes,' yet." He opened the door. "I need to see if I can find Paul. I want him to perform the ceremony."

Doc shook his head. "I doubt that he will."

"I'm asking him, at least once."

Frank hurried back to Paul's house. He walked out to the smokehouse, remembering the frightful experiences of the day that resulted in the changes in several lives. Probably, the most important change concerned Caleb.

And me and Watema and the biggest change is our wedding . . .

He walked back to the house. Again he knocked at the door but no one answered. He opened it a crack and peeked in, but saw no one. Pushing it further, he stepped inside the front room. He thought he'd entered the wrong house when he saw a haggard-looking Paul Wade sitting in his rocking chair, swaying back and forth. Paul looked several years older since Frank last saw him when they visited Caleb at the hospital.

"Paul, what's wrong?" Frank asked, kneeling beside his friend.

"She's gone," Paul said. He lifted a shaky hand to rub across his eyes. "She left."

"She—who's gone?" A person Paul cared about. But whom?

"Ila Mae, my wife."

"Not Sister Wade! Where's she gone? To visit one of your children?"

"I don't know. She left a note. Said she couldn't live with me unless I got control of my temper," Paul said.

"Have you searched for her? She might be in Durant with Louisa. There's all kinds of places she could be," Frank suggested.

"That's not the point. The point is—she dared to walk out on me and leave me stranded!" He put his head in his hands and sighed deeply. "She left me—."

Frank patted Paul's shoulder. What could he say? He knew Paul deserved the feelings of anger controlling Sister Wade. Practicing longsuffering and overlooking cruel remarks Paul hurled at Louisa and Caleb had taken their toll on the woman's life.

She reached the boiling point to where she couldn't take any more. No one in his right mind could blame her.

"What can I do? How can I help?" Frank asked.

"How would I know? I've set here for days on end waiting for her to come back and apologize to me, but she never came."

"You think she's looking at it the same way? Maybe, she's waiting for you to come apologize to her?"

"For what?"

"Face it, Paul. You've been angry with Louisa for years and with Caleb for a long time. When you kicked Caleb out, you could just as well have been kicking Sister Wade out. Taking care of him has been her life for twenty-four years."

Frank glanced at a faded place on the wall. Probably where Caleb's picture once hung. Sister Wade must have taken it with her when she left.

At least my son had a real mother to care for him. I must repay her somehow.

"Did you come here to condemn me? If you did, you've accomplished your purpose, so you can leave," Paul said, caustically.

"I didn't know about Sister Wade leaving. I came for a different reason. I wanted you to perform Watema and my wedding. I wondered if you felt close enough to the Lord to do that, but now I don't know."

"Don't get married. It brings pain and sorrow," Paul said, and he rubbed his hands through his tousled hair.

"Why don't you go wash up and let's go to a restaurant to eat a bite? You probably haven't had any food to eat lately."

Paul squirmed about in the rocker. He put his hands on the armrests and started to push himself up, then fell back. "No. I don't want to see anybody. It's too humiliating for people to know my wife left me."

"You need to get out of the house. Wash your face and comb your hair. I'll wait for you."

After a few moments, Paul dragged himself from the chair and got ready to go with Frank.

At the restaurant, Paul and Frank ordered plate lunches. While waiting, Frank glanced around at the other customers. His pulse quickened when he saw the newlyweds sitting at a nearby table.

How's their marriage going?

He walked to their table and smiled at them. "Excuse me, but I was here the day you came in as newlyweds to eat your first meal. It's nice to see you again," said Brother Solomon.

The bride bubbled enthusiastically. "Our marriage is just wonderful."

The husband nodded in agreement. "I thought I was too old to remarry, but it's good to have a companion to confide in. She's a good cook, too."

"He's so kind to me," the bride said, reaching for the farmer's work worn hand. "God was good to give me another chance at happiness."

"And for me, too," the man said.

Frank patted the husband's shoulder. "Congratulations. I hope you have a long life together. If the Lord is willing, I plan to marry soon. I believe I'll be as happy as you are."

"You can't be. We're the happiest couple in the world," the wife said.

"Well, I'll try to be."

Frank returned to his table. The plate lunches had been brought out, and Paul hunched over eating his meal as if trying to hide his identity. "Hurry up. I don't want to see anybody I know," he said. Dribbles of food lined the front of his shirt.

"No. I'm not going to hurry. I'm going to enjoy my meal. You need to lift up your head and look around. There's a couple over there that could set an example for you and Sister Wade. They're happy."

"Huh. Maybe for the first few days, but after that it's down hill all the way," Paul said. He swallowed a big gulp of milk and wiped his mouth with the back of his hand.

"I hate to see you so bitter," Frank said. "Did you know that bitterness eats at your insides and will destroy you; not the person it's aimed toward?"

"Who made you so bossy? I'm leaving without you if you don't hurry up," Paul said, pushing back from the table. He started to stand, but fell back into the chair, propping his head in his hands.

"Who are you trying to hide from?" Frank asked softly.

"It don't matter. Hurry up. Let's leave," Paul insisted. He tried to sneak a peak between his fingers at a new patron.

Frank saw the person Paul wanted to avoid. "Sam, what are you doing in town?" he asked, pulling out a chair to offer him.

Sam sat in the empty chair. Paul could do nothing but raise his head

and acknowledge Sammy, Louisa's husband's, presence. Sam sat staring at Paul for a few seconds then he got in Paul's face to rebuke him. "You really pulled a boner this time, Brother Wade. Treating Sister Wade like she was dirt. Do you know where she is? Or have you even tried to find her?"

Paul jumped from his chair, knocking it over. He started rushing between the tables disturbing the customers. Patrons stared at the man as he ran out the front door with Sammy behind him.

Frank stopped to pay for the meal. "Sorry for the disruption," he mumbled.

"If that man causes any more trouble, I'm calling the sheriff," the waitress said, staring out the window.

Frank watched Brother Wade grab Sammy's collar, twisting it. It seemed like Paul was cutting off Sammy's breath. If he didn't turn loose, Sammy would pass out.

"Go ahead. Call the sheriff," Frank said tersely. As he walked by the customers, he apologized. "I'm sorry if my friend disturbed your lunch. He's upset, as you can tell."

"Ain't that the truth," an elderly woman agreed.

"He needs a good marriage like ours," the new bride suggested.

"That's his trouble. His marriage is about to fall apart," Frank said. He rushed toward the front door. "Paul, the waitress just called the sheriff. Do you want to be arrested, just because of your pride?"

"My pride! You don't know what you're talking about," Paul turned loose of Sammy's collar, venting his wrath toward Frank. "This young buck thinks he can boss me around. He's got another think coming." He shook his shoulders and doubled his fists. "I'm about to give him what he deserves, taking Ila Mae into his house when she has no business leaving me. He should be horsewhipped, if the truth was told."

"Someone should be horsewhipped," Frank agreed. "You're afraid one of your old cronies will make fun of you, but you're the one who's drawing attention to yourself." Frank glanced up to see the sheriff's car barreling down the street. "Well, you're getting attention, all right. There's sheriff Lucky Lincoln with his handcuffs."

Lucky climbed from his car, with the confidence of a snarling bulldog.

The smirk on his face revealed his self-assertiveness.

"Fightin' on the street like a public drunk?" Lucky asked, tossing his keys in the air. "And a preacher at that!"

Paul Wade's nostrils flared and Frank expected to see smoke steaming from them. However, Paul didn't retort, he stood with fists doubled and an angry scowl covering his face.

"Sheriff, Brother Wade is having a rough time right now. I think tolerance is the best action to take," Frank suggested.

"He needs to keep his rough feelin's at home and not be flauntin' 'em before the town people. But since he wants the world to see, there, I'll give 'em somethin' to look at," Lucky said. He unfastened a pair of handcuffs dangling at his side and snapped them onto Paul Wade's hands.

Paul's pleading look cut deep into Frank's heart. He knew of no way to help. In a way, he felt it was his fault, because he'd been the one who insisted that Paul come to the restaurant to eat.

"Get in the car with me and let's go to the office," Lucky said, shoving Paul toward his vehicle.

"Yes, Sir," Paul said, rather humbly.

Lucky climbed into his car and roared the motor before he drove away with his prize trophy.

"Lucky should have blown a trumpet," Frank said. "He's making the most out of this episode." The two men stood on the sidewalk a few seconds. "What do we do? Let him sit in jail and think a while?" Frank asked.

Sammy straightened his ruffled shirt and then stared at the departing car. "I guess someone needs to defend him, even if he was about to choke me to death. It's not me that he's mad at. It's Sister Wade. He can't stand for her to not obey his every wish."

"Let's see what we can do. I already apologized to the waitress for causing a ruckus in the restaurant. I'll go on to Lucky's office," Frank said, walking toward his sedan.

"I'll stay here and eat. I'll meet you back at Brother Wade's house later," Sam said.

Is pride Paul's problem? He can't stand for his name to be associated with anything that causes him to look bad.

When Frank walked into the sheriff's office, Paul sat beside a desk, answering Lucky's questions. "Do you want to pay a fine and be freed or spend a few days in jail?"

"How much is the fine?"

"Ten bucks," Lucky said, and laughed. "You got that kind of money? Maybe paying through the nose will make you think before you start another fight on Main Street."

"What do you think, Frank? Should I bow and scrape to this public officer?"

"You don't have but two choices—go to jail or pay the fine. I'll lend you the money if you need it," Frank said. He suddenly realized he had a golden opportunity to ask about Austin. Perhaps Lucky could give him information about the boy.

"Where's your sister, Lucy, sheriff?" Frank asked.

"Why do you want to know?" Lucky asked, a quizzical look on his face.

"Just wondering."

"Paul, have you decided whether to stay or pay?" Frank asked.

"I'm sorry, Frank. I guess I should borrow the money and then talk to Sammy. He may be able to help me with Ila Mae."

Frank pulled the money from his wallet. "Be sure and give him a receipt, Sheriff. I want this to be done according to law." He handed the money to Lucky.

"Where'd you say Lucy is?" Frank repeated.

"Here and there, I guess," Lucky responded, unlocking the handcuffs.

"We've got her son. She never showed up at school to take him home," Frank continued.

Lucky looked up.

"What do we do with Austin?" Frank asked. "Is Lucy giving him away or do you want him?"

"Oh, no, I can't take him," Lucky responded. He juggled the handcuffs, then tossed them on the desk. "I've got important duties to perform."

"Well," Frank insisted, "we don't know what to do—put him on a bus like Lucy did—keep him in a teacher's home—turn in his mother for child abandonment or what?"

Maybe that will get his attention.

Lucky pulled out his carefully folded handkerchief and wiped his face. "Child abandonment?"

"Yes. Sending an underage child to school knowing full well he can't go to class. Did you know Lucy did that?"

Am I pushing this too far?

Lucky forced a cough. "Well," he said, clearing his throat, "I had 'a idea Austin was off somewhere. I hadn't seen him lately."

Just one more dig.

"Do you want us to put that tag around his neck and send him off the same way he came to us?"

"No. Don't do that. Do you know somebody at school that can take care of him? Maybe Lucy won't make it big in Hollywood and she'll have to come home."

"Hollywood?"

"Yeah. Gone there with her flapper act," Lucky answered, getting confused. "Here, Brother Wade, take the money back and leave."

Paul reached for the money. Frank pushed Paul's hand away. "No, Paul. Do not take the money. We're paying your fines fair and square."

He looked straight at Lucky. "Listen to me loud and clear. We can take care of Austin and maybe even give him up for adoption. But are you giving permission to keep him? Put that in writing, Sheriff."

Lucky shook his head. "Not the adoption part. I can't do that but I will give permission for somebody to take care of him maybe for years to come, 'cause I don't know about that sister of mine."

"Write that on paper and sign it," Frank said.

Lucky grabbed a blank sheet of paper and wet the pencil lead with the tip of his tongue, then he hesitated. "Tell me what to write."

"Something like, 'I hereby give permission for a person other than

family to take custody of my nephew Austin Lincoln until further notice.' Sign it and put the date on it."

"This'll take a few minutes. I want it done right," Lucky said and laboriously began to write. "How do you spell 'permission'?"

While Lucky wrote, Frank walked over to study the wanted posters that lined the walls.

"Paul, look here. See this man's picture? He's wanted for train robbery. And this one is wanted for beating up his wife."

"Okay, I get the message," Paul admitted.

At last, Lucky had written, dated, and signed the consent form. Frank folded it neatly and put it in his wallet. He extended his hand to seal the agreement. Lucky already seemed squeamish about the pact he'd signed. He kept looking over his shoulder as if he expected Lucy to walk in at any moment.

Soon, Frank and Paul left the befuddled sheriff, and climbed into Frank's sedan.

Frank felt that Lucky's signature scored a victory regarding Austin's protection. He had obtained a consent form to prove Austin was in the protective custody of himself and Watema or Caleb. Paul's problems seemed insignificant now.

Paul sighed and moaned all the way home. "What do I do now? I got arrested and almost thrown in jail. What happens next?" he asked.

"I think you and your son-in-law have a bit of talking to do," Frank suggested. "Do you want me to stay around and referee or can you admit you were in the wrong?

If you do what God would have you do, I'll repeat the question about performing my wedding."

"Stay with me, Frank. I feel so disgraced. When will it all end? First, Louisa tells the world about her baby—then Caleb tries to kill me. My wife leaves me and now I'm handcuffed in front of everybody in town. Do you know what it's like to be a jailbird?"

Frank chuckled. "You weren't actually in jail, but you were handcuffed, which is just a step away from being thrown in the brig. God can forgive you if you repent and ask Him."

"Why should I ask God for forgiveness when I didn't cause any of this? It's almost more than I can bear. I'm sure not forgiving that wife of mine. She knows better than to run out on me and leave me alone for everybody to see," Paul said.

It won't work.

CHAPTER TWENTY-TWO

Jenny hopped off the train after visiting with her bothers. She left with the assurance that the boys were content attending boarding school. They participated in all kinds of sports and even played musical instruments. She had nothing to worry about regarding the boys. They just needed to keep in touch with her.

She picked up her baggage and decided to walk around town for a while. Perhaps she'd run into someone driving toward White Rabbit's house, and she could catch a ride. She walked to the restaurant to buy a soda pop. She sat in a booth drinking small swallows, trying to make the soda last as long as possible. Rarely could she buy a bottled drink. She heard a woman in the booth in front of her clucking her tongue.

"I feel so sorry for that poor man. Fighting out on the sidewalk that way. Did you ever fight anybody out on the street, Fred?"

Jenny's ears perked up. What fight had she missed out on?

"No, Sweetie, I never was much of one to fight, especially for the public to see," a gentle voice answered. "We should pray for those men involved in the scuffle. I saw the sheriff handcuff the older man and put him in his car. I wonder if he's in jail."

Jenny took a big gulp of the soda. Maybe it was more important to find out about the fight than to make the drink last a long time. She'd ask the waitress about the ruckus.

"Some men got into a squabble out there. A nice looking young man and an older, kind of dignified, man. But when he started choking that young guy, he looked awful mean," the waitress said. She scratched her head with a pencil. "The sheriff handcuffed the older man and took him off to jail. It was exciting while it was goin' on. You missed out on the fun."

Fun? Depending on who's fightin'. I'll go see Sister Wade.

When Jenny approached Paul Wade's house, she recognized Brother Solomon's sedan parked at the front. *What's he doin' here?*

She hurried toward the house. Leaving her bag at the gate, she dashed to the house and had stepped onto the porch when she heard loud voices quarreling.

"I will not go begging Ila Mae . . ."

Who's Ila Mae?

" . . . to come home. She's the one who left. It is not acceptable for a man to go chasing after his rebellious wife."

Brother Wade! I'm not going in there with him. I'll wait out here.

"She's welcome to stay with Louisa and me for as long as she wishes, if that's the way you feel."

Sammy! So Sister Wade is at Louisa's house?

"I'm glad Maria is getting acquainted with her grandmother. If Sister Wade doesn't come back, she can take care of Maria while Louisa attends classes at college."

"It's sacrilegious! That's what it is! I don't believe that cock and bull story she told about Caleb. It was a good excuse, but I didn't fall for it like everybody else did," Brother Wade yelled. "I can't forgive her for disgracing me that way. Me! A preacher of the gospel!" A loud bang rattled the wall.

"Well, Brother Solomon, I suppose we need to leave. We aren't making any headway with my illustrious father-in-law," Sammy said. "I don't intend to stand around and listen to him tongue-lashing my wife like he's doing."

"I don't suppose you'll perform our wedding then?" Brother Solomon asked.

"No. Good evening, gentlemen," Brother Wade snapped. Loud footsteps headed toward the door. Jenny jumped off the porch and hid around the side of the house. She needed to sneak behind the bushes to the sedan so she could ride home with Brother Solomon.

While she crept from one bush to another, Jenny heard loud banging of doors slamming. She slipped to the far side of the sedan and climbed in before the men arrived.

"Look! Someone left his baggage here," Brother Solomon said, when he opened the gate. Jenny peeped over the seat to see him looking at the tag. "Jenny's! She's somewhere around. I'm sure glad she didn't hear Paul's ranting and raving."

"P-s-s-s-t!" Jenny whispered. "Bring my bag."

When Brother Solomon looked at her his eyebrows shot upwards, but he nodded and smiled. He grabbed the bag and put it in the backseat with Jenny. Hurriedly, the two men climbed into the sedan and Brother Solomon roared the motor. He shoved the foot feed and the car lurched ahead.

After they rounded the corner, Brother Solomon stopped the car at Doc Coleman's office. His head fell onto the steering wheel. "I don't know about Paul," he sighed.

"I know how you feel," Sammy said. "It's hard to see a man of God let bitterness ruin his life."

"It is ruining Paul's life," Brother Solomon agreed. He raised his head and turned to look at Jenny. "What goes with you, Jenny? Tell us something to think about instead of Paul Wade."

"I just got off the train from going to see my brothers and went to the restaurant to buy a soda pop. I heard about a fight and was goin' to Sister Wade's to see if she knew what was happenin'. I heard a lot of that noise," Jenny confessed. She expelled a long breath. "But I can't understand about Ila Mae. That's Sister Wade, ain't it? And she left Brother Wade?"

"She's staying with us in Durant," Sammy said. "She's really broken up over this. She's hurting as bad as Brother Wade. But he won't admit that he's in the wrong."

"We'll just have to pray for him," Brother Solomon said. He looked at Jenny. "Are you ready to go on home with me or do you want to stay with White Rabbit a while longer?"

"I guess I'll –" Jenny began.

"Excuse me just a minute. I need to visit my parents," Sammy interrupted. "If you'll drive me out there, I'd be much obliged. Jenny, you can decide what to do while we're on our way."

Jenny watched Sammy fidgeting in the seat, rubbing his face with both hands, like he wanted to say something important.

Finally, he lowered his hands. Turning to Brother Solomon, he said, "I'll perform your wedding ceremony if you want me to. I'm licensed to preach and registered to do weddings. I'm available if and when you decide to marry."

Brother Solomon reached over to clasp Sammy's hand. "Thanks, son. I appreciate your willingness. If my offer to Paul falls through, I'll see you about performing the ceremony."

CHAPTER TWENTY-THREE

"Can we buy twin dresses for the wedding?" Jenny asked. She watched Watema hold a dress with flounces to her body.

Watema laughed. "Just who's the bride at this wedding? Me or you?" she asked.

Jenny felt her face growing warm. "I thought it would be nice if we dressed alike, but I guess you're right. The bride does need to have her own dress. That dress you're looking at is pretty."

"Yes, I like the ruffles and the flounces. It ain't ever day a woman like me marries a handsome man like Frank. It's a miracle, really."

"Yeah. It's wonderful that you two got together after all these years. It's like a storybook wedding. I wonder if I'll ever marry."

"Of course you will."

"But how will I know if he's the right person?"

"You'll just know. Now, get your head out of the clouds and pick out a pretty dress for yourself," Watema said. "I'm sure Frank doesn't mind paying for it."

"And Austin needs a cute suit of clothes," Jenny said.

"What for? Probably he'll be climbing a tree during the ceremony," Watema said. She laughed. "But, he does need clothes for church, so let's buy him a new set. Frank don't need any new clothes. He's got his best suit to wear." She walked to the children's section to choose an outfit for Austin.

Jenny looked through a row of fancy dresses. "I want a dress I can wear to special programs at school," she said. "I don't know how the girls dress at Green Briar."

"Like girls at Clear Creek," Watema answered. "Any dresses they can find."

"I like this pink dress," Jenny said, pulling one from the rack. "I had to rip the bottom off my best one when I cut my foot. Pink's my favorite color. If this one fits me, can I buy it?"

"Sure. What size is it?"

"The right size," Jenny answered.

"We'll buy it then."

They walked to the counter and Watema dug into her new purse to pay for the clothing.

Jenny's insides tingled when she carried her new dress out of the store. She'd wear the new dress to places like church.

"I'm kind of worried about Frank. He's been dragging around a bit lately. I just wonder what's wrong with him. I hope he's not sorry we're gettin' married," Watema said, as they walked out of the store.

"It ain't that. He's worried about Brother Wade. He had his heart set on the man who raised his son to perform the wedding," Jenny said.

"Is that the problem?"

"Not just performing the wedding, but getting his life straightened out. Paul's letting his problem with Sister Wade ruin his health," Jenny said.

"I hope that's why Frank's draggin' around," Watema said. She and Jenny turned the corner and walked toward the sedan. Brother Solomon stood on the sidewalk waiting. Austin leaped on the sidewalk counting his jumps.

"Are we ready to go?" Brother Solomon asked, staring at his feet.

"Yeah. Watema and me both got new wedding dresses. And a new outfit for Austin to wear to the wedding," Jenny said, while she crawled in the backseat of the sedan.

"I see," Brother Solomon said quietly.

"Don't you want us to tell you about our dresses?" Watema asked.

"Let it be a surprise," Frank answered. "I don't want to know what either of you will wear to the wedding. Let my vision of you as a bride be totally new and different."

"You don't like the old me?"

"You know I do. I believe seeing you as a bride will be a picture to carry in my heart forever."

"Maybe somebody should bring a Kodak to the wedding," Jenny suggested.

Wonder who has one?

"That's a good idea, Jenny. Let's see if we can find one," Brother Solomon said.

"I've been thinking," Brother Solomon said. "How about us driving to White Rabbit's tonight? You girls can stay with them. Early in the morning, I've got to head out to Talihina and bring Caleb from the hospital. If we stay at White Rabbit's, we'll have a head start on everything. How about it?"

"If we can get packed," Watema agreed.

Two hours later, the sedan pulled into the yard at White Rabbit and Tobias' house. When Jenny saw another car parked there, she asked, "Who else owns a car and would be visiting White Rabbit?"

Jenny jumped from the sedan and ran up the steps. Opening the door, she threw up her arms. "A house full of company!"

"Yeah. We came early so we'd be rested for the wedding," Louisa said.

Maria ran toward the door and hollered, "Where's Austin?"

The two children found each other and danced gleefully on the porch while older folks staggered into the house. Stragglers stood on tiptoe at the door, peeking in to see the visitors. The small room overflowed and guests began spilling out the door into the yard.

"Come set under the pines," Tobias offered. After a round of handshaking, Tobias, Sammy, and Frank lounged under the trees and began to talk.

Sister Wade, Watema, and White Rabbit sat in chairs on the front porch, while Louisa and Jenny wandered across the yard, looking at flowers. The two children frolicked about, chasing Tobias' dogs.

"Your mama sure looks bad," Jenny commented, as she petted a dog. "She sure has fell off a lot."

"Yes, Mama had lost a lot of weight. She won't eat much because she's worried about Papa," Louisa confided. "Tobias told me Papa's skinny now. That's unusual."

"So both of them are sufferin'."

"Yes, and one of them is too stubborn to say he's wrong," Louisa said. She sighed deeply. "Mama's tolerated a lot because of Papa's mean attitude."

"Do you think he'll come to the wedding?"

"No. He's too headstrong. He thinks he's right about everything. Never in the wrong," Louisa said, shaking her head.

"Did you know Brother Solomon is going to Talihina to bring Caleb to the wedding? That's why we came tonight, so that he can leave early in the morning to have Caleb released from the hospital for a few hours."

Louisa sighed. "I hope that doesn't cause the pot to boil over."

"Yeah. It could. But Watema wants both her sons to be at the wedding," explained Jenny. She glanced at Brother Solomon who was looking at them as if he were listening to their conversation. He walked toward Louisa and Jenny. "Yes, Louisa, Watema wants her sons to be at the wedding. I know you don't care much for Caleb, but can you endure his presence for a few hours?" He looked into her face questioningly. "I know it hurts to see him."

"Not as much as it used to. After all, it's been five years. It's just that he ruined my relationship with Papa," Louisa said. "And that's ruining Mama and Papa's lives."

Brother Solomon put his arm around Louisa and gave her a tight squeeze. "We'll just have to do our best."

"Frank Solomon! Who are you hugging over there?" Watema called. "I'm the bride-to-be. I'm about to get jealous."

"You have nothing to worry about, Mrs. Solomon," Frank teased. He walked toward the porch. "Come go for a walk with me. We need to talk."

Frank and Watema walked up the dusty road. "You see all this crowd here. Wonder how we'll have room for everybody to sleep tonight?" Frank asked softly.

"Beats me. I need a place to get dressed tomorrow. I want to look nice. Now that I have my new teeth, I don't have any reason not to look my best," Watema said. Her wide smile emphasized the beauty of her new teeth.

"You will make a beautiful bride," Frank said. He spread wide his hands and looked at them. "Only one thing keeps the wedding from being perfect. It looks like my specific wish won't materialize. Unless there's an act of God, Paul won't perform the wedding, but Sammy will do just as well. He

told me he came up early to register in this county. We'll still be married, even if it's by a different preacher.

"Sorry, I'm too selfish. What about you, do you have any kind of special keepsake you want to wear or carry?" he asked.

Watema fiddled with her dress, pushing her finger through a buttonhole. "Yes," she admitted. "There's one thing I'd like, but I don't see no way of getting it."

"What's that? I'm going to bring Caleb early in the morning. Do you want a corsage?"

"Course not. I'll pick some roses from somebody's yard," Watema said. She looked into Frank's eyes and said, "I hate to say this, but do you remember the locket you gave me back when we first fell in love?"

Frank's heart jumped into his throat.

That's what I forgot! It's in the safe at Clear Creek. How do I get it?

"Yes. And I know exactly where it is. It's in a safe at school. I wonder . . . . I knew I was forgetting something when I moved. Just couldn't remember what it was." He turned to walk back to the yard. "I've got to go to town. I'll be back after a while."

Frank rushed toward his sedan. Pausing with his hand at the door, he asked, "Does anyone want to ride to town? I've got to go to the drugstore and use the phone. If you want to go, it's now or never."

"I'll ride with you, Frank. I think I have a plan that needs to be worked out," Tobias said. He hurried toward the car. "Sammy, you want to go with us?"

"I'll stay here and practice on the wedding sermon," Sammy said. He sighed and a look of concern covered his face.

Watema came running to the car. "I'll ride with y'all."

Riding along, Tobias explained why he had come along. "There's too many people to sleep in our house, even if some slept on the porch, so I'm going to try to find a place for everybody to stay tonight."

"Don't worry about it," Frank said. "I can go on to Talihina tonight and sleep there, if need be."

"No need. I believe I have a plan that will work. It involves the church," Tobias said.

"What about the church? We're getting married at the park in Valliant," Watema said.

"Yes, but I mean for tonight. If you and I go in and do some arranging, I think we can have a family get-together at the church. And some can volunteer to sleep there," Tobias said. He smiled. "How does that sound?"

"Fine," Frank said. "Do you want out at the church while I make the phone call?"

"That will be satisfactory," Tobias said. "Come with me, Watema. I need a woman's opinion about the get-together."

A few moments later, Frank bought a soda at the drugstore and went to the phone. He got through to the long distance operator. She rang the office at Clear Creek Boarding School.

"I need to speak to Miss James, anyway," he told himself. A few seconds later, the matron was on the line.

"Miss James, this is an emergency," Frank explained.

"Oh, no. Is Caleb worse?"

"No. This is a wedding emergency."

"Who's getting married?"

"Watema and I are getting married—"

"Watema Maytubby?" cried Miss James.

"That's right. I want you to come to the wedding. You can ride the train to Valliant and be a guest."

"Thanks, but . . ."

"I said this was an emergency. I want you to go to the safe and get the locket that I put there for safekeeping. Do you know which one I'm talking about?"

"Yes. The one I lost. I'm so glad to know it was recovered. Okay, get the locket and then what?"

"Bring it to the park in Valliant. Can you be here by two, tomorrow afternoon? I hate to ask this on such a late date, but it was an inexcusable mistake I made. Watema wants to wear the locket to the wedding."

"Yes, Brother Solomon. I promise I'll have the locket at the park by two tomorrow," Miss James replied.

Frank replaced the receiver. "Whee! That's taken care of. And am I grateful to the Lord." He picked up the soda bottle and took another swallow. Glancing around the drugstore, he noticed a showcase with interesting items for sale. Kodaks! He needed to buy one for picture taking at the wedding.

I'll buy one for Watema.

Even the idea of purchasing a Kodak for Watema didn't completely erase the disappointment about Paul building inside him. Paul Wade's anger and spiritual downfall shouldn't dry up his enthusiasm about the wedding. The responsibility for Paul's attitude fell on Paul, yet Frank longed to comfort the man who reared his son. Why couldn't Paul shoulder his responsibilities and realize that there is none perfect, no not one, not even Ila Mae?

While he stood staring inside the glass enclosure he felt a warm hand touch his shoulder.

"Remember me, Frank Solomon?" a cultured voice asked.

Looking up, he saw an attractive forty-something-looking woman standing beside him. The bright lipstick she wore reminded him of Lucy Lincoln, but she seemed more refined. She looked vaguely familiar. Where had he seen this person before?

"Your face is familiar, but I don't recall your name," Frank answered.

"Frank Solomon, don't you remember me? I'm Liz Turner from college days."

She gripped Frank's hand firmly and held it for too long.

"Yes, I remember you, Liz—homecoming queen the year I was king. How are you?" Frank pulled his hand away.

"I'm fabulous. And you?"

"Fine. Care to join me for a moment?"

"Of course. That's why I came over."

"I have a few minutes to spare," Frank said, walking toward a table. He pulled out his pocket watch to lay on the table. "Bring me up to date on your life."

207

Liz took too long talking about her two ex-husbands and her career as a singer. Frank kept glancing at his watch, hoping she'd take the hint, but she gave no indication of leaving.

Finally, he stood, ready to go. "Sorry, I need to pick up a couple of folks who are waiting for me. Nice to see you again, Liz."

"Aren't you going to give me a hug, Frank? You've done it before." She grabbed him in a tight embrace. Looking into his face she whispered, "Remember?"

"That was for the newspaper photographer. I'm engaged and getting married tomorrow. I'm going to pick up my fiancée right now. Nice to see you again," he said, pulling from her grasp. He wasn't eager to be seen in the arms of another woman the day before his wedding.

Hurriedly, he walked toward the clerk and told her which Kodak he wanted. Carrying his new Kodak and film, he stepped outside. Tobias and Watema stood waiting. Perhaps Watema hadn't seen Liz clinging like a cocklebur to him. Frank noticed Tobias staring at the sidewalk. He must have seen the embrace. Had Watema?

"Did you get the church ready for tonight?" Frank asked.

Turning to Watema, he held out the Kodak. "I bought a Kodak and film to take pictures at the wedding tomorrow."

Watema grabbed the package and drew back her arm. She looked like she was about to smash the Kodak. "I don't want no picture of you. I wanted you. Did you have to get one last big hug the night before your wedding? If I hadn't seen it, I wouldn't believe it," Watema said, sarcastically. She turned to Tobias. "Can you take me to the depot? Frank's not ready to get married—not to me, anyway. Looks like he still has more courtin' to do." She thrust the package in Frank's hand. "Here—take pictures of your lady friend."

Frank wanted to laugh, because Watema seemed to take the embrace seriously. He'd just play along with her. "When does the next train leave, Tobias?"

"Straighten up, you two. You're getting married tomorrow," Tobias said.

"Maybe, if Red River freezes over tonight," Watema answered.

"It seems pretty cold right now," Frank said, and pretended to shiver. He turned to see Liz coming through the door.

"Frank, introduce me to your friends," Liz said, grabbing Frank's arm. "Have you told them about the time we were homecoming king and queen back in college days?"

"Not really. It never came up. Liz, this is Tobias Grant. He's been a friend for quite some time. This is Watema, who will become my bride tomorrow."

"Don't believe him, Liz," Watema said. "He don't mean it. You still have a—"

"If you'll excuse us, we've got to leave," Frank interrupted, taking Watema's arm to accompany her to the sedan. She pulled loose.

"I can get in the car by myself, thank you," Watema said and ran toward the sedan.

"Nice to meet you, Liz," Tobias said and followed Watema to the sedan.

Frank hastened to the car and hopped in. "That leech! I couldn't get away from her."

"How hard did you try?" Watema asked. "You don't have to run away from her. Just take me to the depot and you can come back. Probably, she'll be waiting. Is this why you had to come to the drugstore? For a secret meeting before the wedding?"

"It's called a rendezvous," Frank whispered to Watema.

Watema pushed him away. "You and your big words. Were you aiming to use 'em on me if we got married?"

Just, I love you.

"Tobias, direct me to the depot. Watema seems determined to leave. Maybe it's best to postpone the wedding till somebody's temper cools off."

"Why doesn't Watema catch a bus? The drugstore is a bus stop."

"Fine with me," Watema said, opening the car door. "Unless that homecoming queen shows her painted face."

This is ridiculous.

Watema jumped from the sedan with the agility of a sixteen-year-old.

Frank watched as she sashayed into the drugstore. "What do we do

now?" he asked Tobias. He rested his head on the steering wheel. "The night before the wedding and we have our first fight."

"I guess you need to be sure it's true love. This fight will help solve the problem. I think I can drive your car, so pull around the block and get out. Then I'll go on to the house and tell everybody to come on to the church. Maybe you can make up with her while I'm gone. How does that sound?"

"Worth a try," Frank said, raising his head. He started the sedan and drove away.

In a few moments, he parked in front of the restaurant where Paul got into the fight with Samuel. He climbed out of the sedan, hoping Tobias could drive home safely. He'd hate to lose his future wife and his sedan the same night. He didn't need another soda pop, but stepped into the restaurant just to sit in a booth a few minutes and to reflect on what action to take.

Propping his chin on one hand, he closed his eyes, trying to decide how to approach Watema. He admitted to himself that he'd allowed his despondency over Paul Wade's spiritual decay to bother him too much. Seeing the way he'd hurt Watema brought life back into sharper focus. He wanted to marry Watema, regardless of her lack of qualifications to be a superintendent's wife. He would guide her through the learning process. He loved her. If he didn't, why hadn't he married another woman, like Liz?

He heard familiar voices in a booth. "You've brought so much happiness into my life, Sweetie. I am so grateful God put us together."

Frank felt a twinge of jealousy. The newlyweds sat nearby. Perhaps they could give him advice. He looked around to see where they sat. When he spotted them, he walked toward them. "May I join you for a moment?"

"Certainly," the farmer answered, scooting over. "Sit here."

"I've seen you two other times lately. You seem very happy. I'd like to ask you a question," Frank said, spreading his hands on the table.

"I probably can't answer it, but fire away," the man said, with a smile.

"My wedding date is tomorrow, but the bride just walked out on me. What do I do?"

The woman grabbed Frank's hand. She gave it a tight squeeze. "You poor dear. I never would have walked out on Fred. He's too precious."

"Does this woman know you really love her?" asked Fred.

"I hope so. I've told her I love her."

"Yeah, but have you proved it? Are you willing to stand up and fight for her?"

"If it became necessary, I'd fight for her. I'm not much of a fighter. I'd rather negotiate."

"Then you need to negotiate with her about whatever has come between you, if it's another person or something else," Fred's wife said.

"It's nothing. I ran into a woman I attended college with. My fiancée saw the woman give me an unexpected hug and she mistook it as a romantic gesture. She jumped to conclusions and called off the engagement. She didn't wait for an explanation; just called off the wedding. How do I convince her the embrace meant nothing? It was totally one-sided."

"I think you should fight for her," Fred said. "Go find her and tell her that you really love her."

"Stand up and fight for her," the wife said.

"Thanks, I hope the bus hasn't left yet. I wish y'all happiness," Frank said and left.

He hurried to the drug store to see the bus parked, taking on passengers. "I hope Watema hasn't boarded yet," Frank said, running the last few steps.

"Has an Indian woman wearing a red dress got on board yet?" he asked the driver.

"Most of the passengers are Indian and all the women wear red," the driver answered. "Describe her to me."

"She's in her forties and she's on the tall side, but slim. And very beautiful," Frank added.

"The woman standing in back of you fits that description," the driver said, nodding to someone behind Frank.

Frank turned around to see Watema staring straight ahead. The angry scowl on her face cut him to the core. Had he wounded her as much as she was hurting him? Frank took Watema by the arm to escort her inside the drug store.

"Watema, where is Liz? Have you seen her? I want to settle this problem right now."

Watema pointed toward a booth where Liz sat filing her nails. She looked toward Frank and smiled proudly. Her look reminded him of Sheriff Lucky Lincoln's expression when he arrested Paul. "Let's go talk to Liz," he said tersely.

"Liz, I'm a preacher now. This beautiful woman has agreed to become the wife of a preacher. Isn't that wonderful?"

"A preacher—?" Liz sputtered. "Like in church?"

"Or the superintendent of a boarding school," Frank said. "Why don't you wish her the best? We need to continue with the wedding plans."

"The best to you," Liz mumbled. "You have my condolences."

"Thanks, but the wedding's not settled on yet," Watema answered. "We've decided to call if off."

"She's joking, Liz," Frank said. "Learning to be a preacher's wife already." He led Watema out of the drugstore.

"What does con-do-lences mean?" Watema asked.

"Liz feels sorry for you because you're marrying a preacher," Frank said and squeezed her arm gently. "She'd never be able to live up to the calling of a minister's wife."

"Maybe I won't either," Watema argued. "I ain't started off very good so far."

"Yes, you will be a perfect wife. You've lived through tougher challenges. Lots of your experiences have helped prepare you to be a preacher's wife," Frank said.

Why didn't I realize that before?

"Lady, are you boarding the bus?" the driver called.

"No, thank you," Frank answered for her. "She's riding in my sedan from now on."

"You seem pretty sure of yourself," Watema fussed, pulling away.

"I'm sure of lots of things, so let's walk on over to church," Frank said, taking her arm. "We need to have a minute to catch our breath before everyone gets there."

"I need a while to calm down. That college lady is different from any Indian woman I ever saw," Watema admitted. "She's pretty, but I think she might go on the war path real easy."

"Like someone else I know?" Frank teased.

"You ain't seen me on the war path yet," Watema answered.

"Well, let's not have another fight just yet. You said you needed to calm down. Let's take our time and maybe we'll have time to cool off before we get to the church."

"Why did that beauty queen hug you right there before everybody in the drug store?"

"I certainly don't know. I'm guessing that was the reason—there was an audience to see her do it," Frank suggested. "Showing off, maybe."

"You could of knocked me over with a feather when I looked through the window and there you were in that woman's arms," Watema said, tightening her grip on Frank's arm. "I wanted to faint."

"You could have knocked me over, too. I certainly didn't expect it, but she did it just for show. And it accomplished its goal. The show caused us to have our first fight. It's over, isn't it?" Frank stopped for a moment to gaze into Watema's eyes. "We are getting married tomorrow, aren't we?" He pulled her toward him in a close embrace.

"Don't hug me out here on the sidewalk," Watema said, pushing him away. "Wait till we're by ourselves. Yeah, the wedding is back on."

"All is forgiven?"

"Yes. Just don't let me see it happening again."

"If I can get away fast enough," Frank said, and then he laughed. "I didn't see it coming."

"What'll we do at church tonight?"

"Just talk and have fun. It'll be nice to get together and listen to family stories. I want you to really listen, because I expect there'll be some serious talks since lots of decisions were made at the church when Sammy preached his first sermon. I made one that day."

"About what?"

"Telling someone about my relationship with you—"

"You didn't mention my name at church, did you?" Watema said, tightening her hold on Frank's arm.

"No. Don't you remember you told me your name was Alta? It wouldn't have mattered, anyway. I guess that was the start of getting back with you, even though I didn't know where to look. Now that pursuit is almost complete. Tomorrow we start a new life journey."

* * *

The small Indian Church reverberated with outbursts of laughter from Tobias' family as they told jokes about bygone days. They ate and laughed till almost bedtime.

Tobias stood before the group, to calm everyone. "Now, if anyone has any special memories, feel free to share them with Watema and Frank."

Frank knew that several folks had remembrances of the day Sammy preached on Vows and so many walked forward to make promises to God. He didn't know if they'd want to share them, but he recalled that was the day Louisa brought her newborn baby before the church and confessed that Maria was her child.

That's when Paul Wade lost his temper and never got over it. He's been angry that long.

I confessed that I wanted courage to come clean with a secret I'd been keeping for many years. That's why I'm here. I asked for forgiveness of my sins and now everyone knows Caleb is my son. And tomorrow I marry his mama, twenty-five years too late.

"I made a vow and tomorrow I marry a beautiful bride," Frank said. He took Watema's hand and led her to the front of the church. "You're all invited to the wedding at the park in Valliant tomorrow at two."

The younger men hooted, and the girls clapped. Watema turned her back to the crowd.

"It's okay, Watema. We're all happy for you," White Rabbit said.

Everyone stood and clapped for Frank and Watema. When folks quieted down, Tobias asked, "Does anybody have anything to say?" He looked around the church. After he waited a few minutes, he continued, "If not, I want to say a few words. When I was in the war, I made a vow that if I ever came home, I'd be a preacher. I confessed that vow and now I am preaching at this church, even though I would prefer that Paul Wade still

preached here. I could always serve at another church."

When Tobias finished his last words, the door burst open and a frail pathetic-looking Paul Wade staggered into the building. His belt was taken in several notches to hold up his trousers.

"Paul! What's wrong?" Tobias asked.

Sister Wade and Louisa rushed toward Brother Wade and seated him in a pew. They sat on either side of him, trying to comfort him. With trembling hands, he pushed them aside.

He is so weak I wonder how he managed to get here.

"I've been listening to all the laughing and fun you've been having. I stood on the outside looking in for a long time," Paul said, in a weak voice. "It's all because of my stubbornness." He looked around wildly. "Where's the baby girl? Where's Maria?" he asked. "Bring her to me."

Louisa jumped up and rushed to get Maria. "Here she is, Papa."

"I'm too weak to hold her, but stand beside me with her." Paul took her hand and said, " Maria, I'm your grandpa." Frank watched as Paul wiped tears from his eyes and blew his nose.

"My grandpa?" Maria asked in a loud voice. "What about Grandpa Grant?"

"I'm your other grandpa, child. A stubborn hard-hearted old man." Paul looked toward Frank. "Would you come up and read a verse for me? It's the one you read when you told us Caleb was your son. Read Galatians 6:1-2. I know it by heart, but I want the others to hear it. You can use my Bible." He pulled a ragged Bible from his pocket. Pages fluttered from it as the book was exchanged from hand to hand. "One of those pages that fell out should be part of Galatians. I've read it often enough." He fell back onto the pew, but clung to Maria's hand.

With trembling fingers, Frank flipped through the loose leaves. He turned to gaze into the faces of family members. Then slowly, he began to read.

"Brethren, if a man be overtaken in a fault, ye which are spiritual, restore such an one in the spirit of meekness; considering thyself, lest thou also be tempted.

"Bear ye one another's burdens, and so fulfill the law of Christ."

215

"Thanks," Paul said. He pulled himself up. "I confess that I have been overtaken in many faults. I'm sorry I've treated my wife, my daughter, granddaughter, and Caleb in such evil ways. I-apologize—" Paul's voice trembled and grew fainter—"to-everyone. I ask—." He grabbed for the pew to hold on, but missed it and fell to the floor. Sister Wade dropped down beside Paul. She leaned over to listen to his confession. ". . . for-give-ness—from God."

Sister Wade yelled, "Bring some water. He's fainted dead away."

Someone ran out the door to draw water. When he returned with a bucket of water, Louisa bathed Paul's face, but he lay still and silent.

"Go get Doc," yelled Frank.

Moments later, Doc Coleman hurried in with his black bag. He leaned over Paul's still body and listened with his stethoscope. Somberly, he shook his head. "I'm sorry, he's gone," he said. Frank leaned near to hear Doc mutter, "His anger killed him."

A few quiet sobs burst forth, but most family members swallowed back the tears. Sister Wade lifted her head and smiled sweetly. "He made things right with God. His last words were, 'I ask forgiveness from God.' That's all that matters."

* * *

Early the next morning, Frank started to leave for the hospital to get Caleb. A tug at his arm caused him to turn around. "Maria and I want to ride with you to the hospital," Louisa said.

"Are you sure?"

"Yes. There's still some unfinished business to take care of," Louisa said.

Later, Frank, Louisa, and Maria walked to the ward where Caleb stayed. Louisa asked Frank to excuse them for a moment, then they'd come out.

Frank heard some shuffling around in the area. He saw Louisa and Maria duck inside the curtained area. He couldn't make himself leave the ward.

"Caleb, I—" Louisa began.

"Let me speak first," interrupted Caleb. "I ask for forgiveness of mistreating you. Maria, I ask forgiveness of causing your mama so much pain. Will you forgive me, Louisa?" Caleb asked.

Frank heard sobbing coming from behind the curtain. "Oh Dear God, please help me. It's hard to do, but I forgive you, Caleb. And Maria doesn't know enough to understand. I guess someday I may tell her you're her father," Louisa said softly.

"Thanks, Louisa. That was all I wanted to hear. While I've been in the hospital, I've been thinkin' about the price you had to pay because of my sin," Caleb said. "Yeah, it was sin. I didn't own up to being Maria's dad. I let you suffer when Papa accused you of playin' around with other men. I just set back and played 'possum."

You should have confessed the error of your ways, Frank thought. *I can't say anything; I did the same thing. In a way it's like the whole human race; we've all stood by while Jesus died on the cross, paying the price for the sins of the entire world.*

"I'm glad to hear you admit that, Caleb," Lousia said. "Now let's try to put it behind us."

"Okay, then, I'm ready to go to my Mama and Papa's wedding." He laughed loudly. "I shouldn't have laughed, because I am sorry about Brother Wade's death, but I'm glad to have my real parents together."

Louisa rushed from behind the curtain and she and Maria fled to the hall.

After a while, Frank wheeled Caleb out of the hospital.

"It feels good to be outside, getting' ready to go to my Mama and Papa's weddin'."

* * *

A few minutes of two, Jenny watched as family members arrived at the park in Valliant. The tree trunks were gleaming from the whitewashing. She wondered why Brother Solomon paced back and forth and kept pulling his watch from his pocket, glancing at the time.

Surely Brother Solomon ain't getting nervous about his weddin'.

Jenny walked toward him, hoping to encourage him, but she stopped before she got to him. He had halted beside Caleb's wheelchair. Austin stood near Caleb. Jenny believed Austin wanted Caleb's full attention, but Frank said something that caused her heart to leap.

"Caleb, while I was at the hospital I read about an operation a person with clubfeet had. Want to hear about it?" Frank asked. "You might be able to do what that person did." He glanced toward the road.

"What?"

"That person had her feet amputated on purpose. You've already had that done because of the accident. Then she had artificial legs and feet made so she could walk around and look nice."

"I don't want no peg legs," Caleb said.

"These are artificial limbs that look like real legs and feet. The lady wore shoes and she walked around," Brother Solomon said. "I believe it's something you should think about."

Caleb smiled broadly. "Yeah. It sure is. I could even race with Buck."

"You might do that." Frank pulled out his watch.

That would be a miracle.

He glanced at his watch again. "When is Miss James coming? I can put off the wedding a few minutes if necessary."

Frank turned again to Caleb. "As soon as you are dismissed from the hospital, you'll come to live with your mama and me at Green Briar. And Austin will be living there, too."

"That's good, ain't it, Buck?" Caleb asked, looking at Austin.

"Yeah. You can whittle some more whistles and flutes and help me with my A B C's, can't you?"

"I sure can. I'll be glad when I come home."

"Right now, I'm trying to be patient while I wait for Miss James to arrive," Frank said.

Unexpectedly, Jim from Clear Creek, drove up and jumped from a car. He rushed toward Frank. He pulled an envelope from his pocket. "Here, Miss James sent this to you," he explained. "She couldn't make it. I brought Bailey with me instead."

Bailey's here, Jenny thought. She saw the good-looking man climbing from the car.

"Thank the Lord you came." Frank shook Jim's hand vigorously. "You and Bailey stay for the wedding, please."

"I wouldn't miss it," Jim answered.

Jenny watched as Frank rushed to find Hallie. "Would you give this to Watema? She needs it for the ceremony." Hallie grabbed the envelope and looked inside.

"I get this back after the wedding," Hallie said to Frank. She dashed to another area of the park.

Jenny looked up to see Bailey strolling into the park. She felt her insides start to jiggle like jelly. *He looks so handsome in his dark blue dress suit and pure white shirt.*

In a few moments, Sammy, pale and shaking, walked toward Bailey to shake his hand. "Glad you made it for the first wedding I'm performing. Why don't you stand over by that tree in front of me? While I'm giving the message I'll look at you. Okay?"

"Sure. You know it won't be easy on me, 'cause I was supposed to get married. I'll smile at you if I can," Bailey said.

Soon, Sammy stood before the group to join Frank Solomon and Watema Maytubby together in holy matrimony.

After Sammy pronounced the couple man and wife, Jenny tugged at Brother Solomon's arm. He leaned down and she whispered in his ear. He nodded in approval.

"Ladies and Gentlemen, the wedding is not over. Jenny is going to read a poem she wrote for the occasion. Go ahead, Jenny. Stand here so everyone can hear you."

Jenny unfolded the paper and stood up straight. She looked at Bailey. He smiled at her. "I wrote this last night after Brother Wade made peace with his family. It's called 'Making Peace'." She cleared her throat and glanced at the paper. In a clear loud voice, she read:

"Making Peace"

**"Last night our family felt ripped apart.
Because of hatred in one man's heart.
But that all ended, when he confessed.
God is greater than all the rest.
He asked for forgiveness from those he'd harmed.
Asked to see Maria, the girl who charmed . . ."**

Jenny heard someone sobbing. She looked up to see Sister Wade overcome with emotion. When the widow wiped her eyes and nodded, Jenny continued.

> **"The girl who charmed," Jenny repeated,**
> **"An ornery man, with her playful ways.**
> **Last night's bravery truly displays**
> **God forgives the most sinful of all,**
> **Who will on Him sincerely call.**
> **And now there's peace in all our hearts,**
> **We've got a new couple and fresh new starts.**
> **We've got peace like a river flowing so wide**
> **As we honor the groom and his beautiful bride.**
> **Welcome Brother and Mrs. Frank Solomon."**

Jenny felt flushed and looked at the ground. "Go ahead, Sammy, finish the ceremony. I just wanted to give a tribute to my new family," she whispered.

I hope reading that poem don't cause Bailey to dislike me 'cause I sure like him.

After Sammy closed the ceremony with prayer, Jenny peeked up at Bailey. He nodded to her and smiled. She turned to see Watema lifting the hem of her flouncing dress and waltzing toward Frank. "I got me a wonderful new husband," she said in a singsong voice.

"And I've got a beautiful new wife," Frank answered, taking Watema's arm.

"Austin and me got new parents, don't we?" Jenny added. She lifted the hem of her skirt and, grabbing Austin's arm, twirled him around. Secretly, she wanted to hold onto Bailey's arm, but she didn't dare.

"Someday I may have new feet and I can waltz, too," Caleb added, wistfully.

"Such a wonderful new family," Tobias said. "Praise the Lord."

Sister Wade walked toward Brother and Mrs. Solomon.

"I'm happy for both of you," Sister Wade said. "Your life together is just

startin' and my marriage just ended. But when Paul confessed that Maria was his granddaughter, that was worth everything. It took away most of the pain."

"And we'll keep Mama busy taking care of Maria," Louisa added, touching Sister Wade's shoulder.

"Sister Wade, with all the spunk you've got, you'll be back to normal in no time," Watema said. "The door's always open for you to come visit Caleb."

"Maybe you can stay with our family when Watema and I want to get off by ourselves for a day or two," Frank suggested. He smiled at Watema and squeezed her hand.

"I'll do that," Sister Wade promised.

"Frank, would you get somebody to take our pictures while I'm still wearing the locket?" Watema asked.

"Sure. Who wants to try to use the Kodak?" Frank asked.

"I'll do it," offered Bailey.

After the picture taking, Jenny watched as Watema unfastened the locket and removed it. "I'm glad I got to wear it to my wedding, but now it goes back to Hallie. It's hers. I gave it to Caleb when I left him on the steps of the church. He gave it to Louisa; she gave it to Hallie; it's hers. And she's my daughter-in-law, so it's still in the family."

Watema looked around. "Where is that girl anyway? Hallie, come here."

Hallie looked up from where she was playing with Maria and Austin. "Did you call me?"

"Yeah. Come take this family heirloom, while you've got the chance. Thanks for letting me wear it on the most important day of my life."

Hallie walked over to Watema. "I hate to take it back, but it really belongs to every woman in the family. So I guess I'll keep it for the time being. Some day, maybe there'll be another girl in the Grant family to wear it."

Jenny didn't hear any more of the conversation. She wanted to approach Bailey without letting on it was her idea. While she wondered about what she'd say, she felt a tap on her shoulder. Looking up, she saw Bailey's smiling face.

"We don't have no partners. Let's go over there and talk," he said, pointing toward a bench.

"Sure," Jenny answered. They sat watching members of the wedding party laughing and having a good time. When Jenny felt tears about to surface because of Bailey's problems, she took Bailey's hand and said, "I know this is hard on you. Sadie died, but you have to go on."

"Yeah. I know. But looking around I see most everybody here has been through some kind of trial. It's just part of life."

"Sadness and happiness are part of all our lives. I guess it depends on how you look at it."

Bailey squirmed uncomfortably. Finally he blurted out, "That book you brought over is really helping me. Even Granny says I'm actin' different."

Jenny wanted to jump up and down with gratitude. Instead, she said, "I'm glad about that. Reading it changed my outlook on life."

Her happiness was marred only with the thoughts that tomorrow the Wade family would gather for a funeral service. All during the wedding ceremony, she had watched Louisa and Sister Wade wiping away tears while they smiled. Jenny knew that Paul's final act changed the ending to his life. Spending his last ounce of energy to drag his tired wasted body inside the church so he could make reconciliation with his family and with his Redeemer was the most precious gift he could offer.

Austin interrupted Jenny's reverie. "Are y'all getting' married?" He demanded, pointing one finger at Jenny and another at Bailey.

"Austin! What are you talkin' about?" Jenny felt the heat of embarrassment flow through her body. How dare he?

"Well, you're over here actin' like you was—and I don't want you to go off and leave me till I start to school," Austin said.

"That's not far off," Bailey said. He winked at Jenny. "We'll think about it till school starts."

Thinking about my wedding ceremony is the most wonderful thought in the world.

About the Author

Dolores White Kiser grew up listening to stories her mother, Johnie Mae, told about life in Choctaw boarding schools. As an adult, Dolores drove her mother to visit these schools. She and her siblings relived the days when Johnie Mae rode the train to the schools. Johnie Mae told them that Christian principles were taught in the Presbyterian schools.

Mentally, Dolores rode the bus with her mother, reliving the days when she left for Oklahoma Presbyterian College with ten dollars in her pocket.

Now, Dolores tries to capture, through fictional stories, how life might have been lived in the early 1900's. She knows about life in a preacher/teacher household, so she chooses characters who are involved in the ministry and teaching to add more color.

For information about this or other publications by Dolores White Kiser, you may contact her via email at:

wobblywh@yahoo.com.